The Seasonal Hearth

The Seasonal Hearth

THE WOMAN AT HOME IN EARLY AMERICA

by Adelaide Hechtlinger
illustrated by Margaret Geiger

THE OVERLOOK PRESS
WOODSTOCK, NEW YORK

Published in 1986 by
The Overlook Press
Lewis Hollow Road
Woodstock, New York 12498

Library of Congress Cataloging In Publication Data

Hechtlinger, Adelaide.
The seasonal hearth.

1. Home economics—United States—History.
2. Women—United States—Social conditions— 18th
century. 3. Women—United States—Social conditions—
19th century. I. Title.
TX23.H4 1986 640'.973 86-12681
ISBN 0-87951-258-X

Contents

INTRODUCTION   17

WINTER

The Early American Housewife   19
Early Days in New England   20
Food in Early New England   21
New England, 1720–1775   22
Cooking in New England   23
Setting the Table: *A Letter from Ruth*   24
Serving the Food in New England   24
Lob! Lob!! Lob!!! Lobsters!!!!   25
Higginsons *New England Plantation*   26
Higginson on Fish   26
Cooking Utensils   26
For an Ointment to Cause Hair to Grow   27
Hasty Pudding   27
The First American Brooms   28
For Shortness of Breath   28
More about Cooking Utensils   29
Clam Pie   29
Portsmouth, New Hampshire, 1750   29
New England Home in the 1790's   30
American Cookbooks   31
Very Popular Cookbooks, 1766–1910   33
The Solitary Orphan   33
Indian Slapjack   34
The New Household Receipt Book   34
Miss Leslie's New Cookery, 1858   35
Egg Plants, Stuffed   35
Indian Cake or Bannock   36
How to Heat the Oven   36

The Stove   37
Of Eating   38
Winter   38
Hints and Maxims   39
Preservation of Winter Apples   40
For an Obstinate Cough   40
Odds and Ends   41
To Remedy the Creaking of a Door   41
Kitchen Furniture–1800   41
Victorian Kitchen   42
The Care of the Kitchen   43
Baking Bread   43
The General Store   43
Fashionable Routs   44
Cabbage Jelly   44
More about Kitchens   44
Almanacs   45
Convenient Kitchens Make Patient Housewives   45
The Dining Room   46
Food for the Urban Family—1800's   46
The Well-fed Family   47
Potato Pie   48
Fried Cabbage   48
Ransom Endorsement   48
A Good Recipe   48
To Keep Piano Keys Clean and White   49
New England Cook Book   50
Rum Pudding   50
Kitchen Furniture—1900   50
Kitchen Utensils—1900   51
Handiwork   52
New Year's Day Calls   53
The Foot Warmer   53
Fastnachts   54
The Weekly Bath: *Diary of An Early American Housewife*   54
Taking a Bath   54
Soap and the Skin   55
Sleigh Riding in New York   59

The Turkey   56
To Roast a Goose   56
Building the Fire: *A Letter from Ruth*   57
The Farmer's Choice   57
Soup   58
A Fish Tidbit   58
Travel on the Farm   59
Sleigh Riding: *Diary of An Early American Housewife*   57
Sleighing Parties   59
Mixed Spice   60
The Person   60
To Raise Hyacinths in Winter   61
Housecleaning   61
Heating the House   61
Potato Soup   62
Menus for the Winter Months   62
Holiday Menus   65

SPRING

Early Days in New Amsterdam   67
Visit to New York: *Diary of An Early American Housewife*   68
Dutch Furniture   69
Cleanliness   70
Advertisement, 1733   70
Milady's Dress   71
Madame Knight's Visit to New York: 1704   71
A Bride's Dowry   72
Table Furnishings   72
The Dutch Larder   73
Jamaica, Long Island   74
Waffle Frolic   75
New Amsterdam Housekeeping   75
Advertisement, 1730   77
More about New York: *Diary of An Early American
    Housewife*   77
Making Soap: A Letter from Ruth   78
Preparing Haddock   79

Food in Brooklyn   80
Washing Clothes   80
The Wash Tubs: *A Letter from Ruth*   80
Maple-sugaring Time: *Diary of An Early American Housewife*
     81
Maple-sugaring Time in New England   81
Scallop Fry   83
We Have Cows: *A Letter from Ruth*   83
Quilting: *Diary of An Early American Housewife*   84
Quilt-making in the Colonies   84
Advertisement, 1751   85
Random Note from a New York Newspaper   85
Spring in the Forest   86
Courtship and Marriage in New Amsterdam   86
Margaret Philipse   87
A Christening and a Dinner: *A Letter from Ruth*   88
Cheese Toast   89
New York in the Pre-Revolutionary Period, 1765-1775   89
Cooking   90
Sheep-shearing: *Diary of An Early American Housewife*   90
Sheep-shearing   90
A Trousseau   91
Fleece: *Diary of An Early American Housewife*   91
Preparation of the Fleece   92
A Baby Boy: *Diary of An Early American Housewife*   92
The Birth of a Baby   92
To Roast a Tongue   93
House-cleaning, 1785   93
Life in the Young Republic—the Early 1800's   95
Spring   97
Spinach Tarts   97
Love-making   98
The Lady's Answer   98
The Seamstress   98
Mother's Advice to Her Daughter   99
Fricandeau with Spinach   99
Beef Sanders   100
Love   100

Easter Cakes   100
Housecleaning, 1855   101
Life in the Young Republic—the Early 1800's   95
Spring   97
Spinach Tarts   97
Love-making   98
The Lady's Answer   98
The Seamstress   98
Mother's Advice to Her Daughter   99
Fricandeau with Spinach   99
Beef Sanders   100
Love   100
Easter Cakes   100
Housecleaning, 1855   101
Spring Housecleaning, 1884   101
For the Complexion   101
Heave Offering   102
Hopping John   102
Dutch Oven   102
A New Oven: *A Letter from Ruth*   103
Bundling   103
A Bride in New York, 1800   104
Odd Scraps for the Economical   105
Menus for Spring Eating   106
Menus for People of Limited Means   108
Menus for the Holidays   109

SUMMER

The Quakers   111
The Household and Food in Philadelphia   112
Gulia Penn   114
Trip to Philadelphia Markets   115
John Adams on Food in Philadelphia   115
The Holy Experiment   116
The Scotch-Irish   116
Scrapple   117
The Moravians   117

Pennsylvania Dutch   118
The Kloster of the Seventh-Day Baptists   119
Pennsylvania Dutch and Good Food   119
Ham with Green String Beans   120
Mouldasha   120
More about Pennsylvania Dutch Food   121
A Frontier Wedding   122
Farmer's Housewife   123
A Farmer's Dainty Dish   124
Farm Wives—Their Day   124
Apple Butter   125
The Housewife's Work Week   126
Fresh Air and Health   127
Kind of Wife   128
To Freshen Baked Goods   128
Nor Marriage Licenses   128
A Farmer's Breakfast   128
A Household ABC   129
The Old Eagle Coffee House   130
Maple Biscuit   131
Sauerkraut   132
Homemade Receipt Book   132
A Real Oven: *A Letter from Ruth*   132
The Arrival of the Germans   133
Godey's Lady's Book   133
Peterson's Magazine   134
Farming Villages, 1750   135
To Preserve Eggs   136
The Well-to-do Family   136
Perspiration   137
Graniteware   137
Food for Thought   137
Gadgets   138
Spiced Salt   138
New Kinds of Food: *A Letter from Ruth*   138
Apple Sauce Omelet   139
Biscuits   140
Cracknels   140

Schoolmaster 'Boarding Round'   140
Food, 1860–1900   141
Household Convenience: *A Letter from Ruth*   142
Food for the Vegetarian   143
Magazines   144
Juice Pie   144
Hunger is the Best Sauce   144
Breakfast   145
Dr. Fenner's Cook Book   146
Everyone Has Arrived   146
Grinding Corn: *A Letter from Ruth*   146
Corn on the Cob   147
To Dry Peaches   147
Herb Dyes of the 1700's   148
Tin Utensils   148
Early Herbs   149
Honey   150
Glass   150
Several Sauces for Roast Hens   150
To Stew Pears   151
To Pot Lobsters   151
Plum-Pottage   152
To Make a Catchup to Keep Seven Years   152
Mustard of Dijon   152
Corn Pudding   153
Home Remedies   153
Salads   154
Fashions in Philadelphia   154
Summertime in the Late 1800's   155
Baked Beets   155
Female Physicians   156
Mademoiselle Hazard   156
Fish a l'Orly   156
Clams   157
Houses, 1825–1860   157
Letter from Martha Washington to Her Sister   158
Roasting   159
A Salmon Pye   159

Miss Beecher's Domestic Receipt Book   159
To Pickle Mushrooms   160
Keeping Food Fresh   160
How to Bathe Plants   161
Flax: *A Letter from Ruth*   161
Gardening for Ladies   163
Charles Joseph Latrobe   163
Cheese-making: *Diary of An Early American Housewife*   164
Cheese-making   164
Iceboxes   165
Frying   166
Cookbooks and Cookstoves   166
Training Day: *A Letter from Ruth*   167
Housekeeping   168
Canning   169
Ice Cream Freezer   169
Dampness in the Closet   170
China: *Diary of An Early American Housewife*   170
Chinaware   170
A Good Bisque of Lobster   171
Experience Talks: Eggs   171
Home Medicine   171
What a Young Girl Does at Home: *A Letter from Ruth*   172
Frozen Coffee   173
The Woman Who Laughs   173
Dr. King's New Discovery   173
Kerosene Lamps   174
A Recipe for a Wife   174
Boiled Fowl with Oysters   174
To Clean Brushes   175
To Make the Teeth White   175
The Tongue   175
Fried Asparagus   176
Canned Bananas   176
Embroidery: *Diary of An Early American Housewife*   176
Embroidery   177
Baking Bread   177
Refrigerators   177

The Ice Wagon   178
Food: 1825–1860   178
Baking-Powder and Cocoa Cans   179
Monday: Washday   179
Tuesday: Ironing Day   180
Hints on the Preserving of Fruit   181
The Home in 1890   182
Menus for Summer Eating   183
Fourth of July Collation   185
Warm Weather Dinner   185
Items of Advice   185

AUTUMN

Early Days in Virginia   187
Setting the Table in the Early South   188
Food in the Early South   189
The South, 1765   189
Dining in the South   190
Food and Cooking in Charleston   191
Creole Cuisine   192
The Fall Season   194
The Autumn Food   194
Life of the Planter's Wife   194
Corn   195
Husking Corn: *Diary of An Early American Housewife*   196
A Corn Husking   196
To Keep Weevils Out of Wheat   197
Pies   197
The Farmer's Wife   198
How to Cook Water   198
About Virginia Women   199
Anne Foster's Party: *A Letter from Ruth*   199
Apples   200
The Cider Press   202
The Lard Kettle   202
Peddlers   202
Batter Bread   203

The Smokehouse   204
Duke of Cumberland's Pudding   204
Women's Health   205
A Simple Pilau   205
Cookbooks in Virginia   205
Chestnutting: *Diary of An Early American Housewife*   206
Chilblains   206
Cranberries   207
Pumpion Pye   207
Cure for a Common Cold   208
'Practical Housekeeping'   208
Southern Recipes   208
Lemon Bisketts   209
The Corn-sheller   209
The Corn Shock   209
Receipt to Stop Bleeding   210
Dinner at Mount Vernon   210
Habit   210
J.C. Ayer Co   211
Omelette Soup   211
Cooking Pumpkins: *A Letter from Ruth*   211
Cranberries and Their Uses   212
To Choose a Turkey   212
Apple Marmalade   213
Apple Cream   213
Weaving: *Diary of An Early American Housewife*   213
Weaving   213
What and How We Eat: *A Letter from Ruth*   214
Pork Apple Pie   215
Stripping Goose Feathers: *Diary of An Early American
    Housewife*   215
Goose-stripping   215
Goose, To Roast   216
Making Spoons or Dishes: *A Letter from Ruth*   217
Social Life on a Virginia Plantation   217
A Cheap and Quick Pudding   218
Creole Soup   218
Marriage   219

Making Candles: *A Letter from Ruth*   219
Washington's Breakfast   221
Brisket of Beef, Baked   221
Hog Killing: *Diary of An Early American Housewife*   221
Hog Killing   222
Corn and Beans   223
Ways of Cooking Indian Corn: *A Letter from Ruth*   224
Autumn Leaves   224
The Potato Harvest   225
Mince Meat   226
Mock Mince Meat   226
Creole Apples   227
Boned Turkey   227
Kitchen or Otherwise   227
A Shaker Thanksgiving   228
Pumpkin Pie?   229
For Thanksgiving   230
Thanksgiving in Early America   230
Thanksgiving Day, 1779   231
Thanksgiving Seventy Years Ago   234
The Roast Turkey   237
Twas the Week before Thanksgiving   239
The Turkey's Lament   243
The American Economical Housekeeper   244
Dr. Chase's Thanksgiving Dinner   246
Thanksgiving Menus, 1896, 1830   247
Thanksgiving Dinners   247
Candle-dipping Party: *Diary of An Early American Housewife*   248
Candle-dipping Party   248
Christmas in Early America   249
Christmas Season   250
Christmas in the South—Ante-Bellum Period   251
Christmas in Philadelphia, 1875   252
Christmas Dinners   253
Menus for Autumn Eating   254

INTRODUCTION

In the seventeenth and eighteenth centuries, American eating was limited by the manner of cooking and the food itself. Nothing was wasted; the grease skimmed from the top of the pot or dripping from the roast eventually was used to make soap or candles.

In the nineteenth century, cooking had changed. Gravies of all sorts were now used, and the ever-popular puddings became very complex. Responsible was the invention of the cooking stove, which radically altered the style of cooking and eating. Many different types of stoves were invented and perfected, and this plus several of the other inventions of the century such as the icebox changed the lot of the housewife. The various cleaning devices and cooking accessories now available also changed the manner of living for the first time in hundreds of years.

From the first starving years of the early settlements, the American housewife has managed quite well in feeding her family. She used ingenuity and determination to take the new foods she found here and turn them into tempting dishes ranging from baked beans to apple pie. The pioneer women cooked everything from Buffalo tongue to Beaver tail. They baked bread in front of fires or in makeshift stoves. They became experts at creating corn bread, pumpkin soup, and hasty puddings.

Those housewives who came from other countries besides England adapted their native dishes to the food found here. All of them were busy from morning to night just taking care of their own little households, food, clothing, and accessories for living. Their quiet determination in the home gave their menfolk the strength and courage to build in this new land. Perhaps the fact that the women stood so firmly behind their men gave the latter the confidence and impetus needed to rebel against the Mother country—England—and strike out on their own.

Although cooking is much more appealing in our day than in the days of our grandmothers and their grandmothers' era, I wonder what the Early American housewife would think if by some miracle she were able to visit with us for a short time today.

The range of recipes today is so wide that meals need never be routine, yet it is positively amazing to think of the meals that these earlier American housewives turned out with just the fireplace and, perhaps, if they were fortunate, a wall oven.

Our markets offer a wide variety of foods, especially of fruits and vegetables, which are easily and quickly shipped to us from all parts of the world. But we must remember that our forefathers were so happy to have food in the early days of their settling here that they complained very little, if at all, about the sameness of their fare.

Just stop to think about the various things we do today that were completely unknown even a hundred years ago. We can cook without a fire, on a piece of what seems to be furniture, with no obvious means of heat. We have microwave ovens that take just minutes to prepare a meal from "scratch." Our freezers keep our food fresh for months. We have frozen TV dinners for the person in a hurry, who wants a meal and has no time to cook. We also must not overlook our powdered eggs, milk, and other dehydrated foods, our instant liquid breakfasts, cake mixes, soup mixes, and dozens of other convenience foods.

Our Early American housewife did have what was called "portable soup," to which water was added to make a soup, as well as dried corn and dried beef which could be used on journeys. Her meat was fresh only when something was slaughtered, else the beef or pork had to be smoked or pickled. She did have lots of fresh fowl of all sorts and fresh fish, but again we must remember the sameness of her menus.

In this book I shall attempt to give a very brief history of the American housewife from 1607 to 1910. Each section of the country had its own customs and mannerisms and I have tried to give the reader a picture of what the role of the housewife was in a particular area.

I personally own many old cookbooks, home-remedy books, magazines, and almanacs which I have culled over to extract parts that I think will be of interest to the reader.

A.H.
Island Park, N.Y.
July 4, 1976

GRANDMA MOSES: *It Snows, Oh It Snows.*

THE EARLY AMERICAN HOUSEWIFE

Winter

JANUARY

FEBRUARY

MARCH

    Although there was some leisure for the men in the early days of America, even so much as a rainy day or one in the middle of the winter, which kept them indoors, it was the women who least of all knew the luxury of leisure. A common proverb ran, "Man works from sun to sun, but woman's work is never done." This was literally true. The Early American housewife was responsible for the care, clothing, and feeding of her family, whatever her social status. If she had servants, she had to direct them, see that they did their work properly, show them how to do certain things, look after them when they were ill, and maintain a watchful eye at all times.

    If she did not have servants, as was the case with most of the women in the early settlements, she had even less leisure. Not only did she have to bear and care for the children, but she also had to cook and wash for the whole family without the benefit of any labor-saving devices such as we have today. She not only had to make garments for the entire family, including the men, but she also had to spin the thread and weave the yarn into the cloth for these garments.

    She also had to knit socks and stockings. Her hands could never be idle, and she could not even afford the luxury of nodding quietly in the chimney corner. If she did, some duty was being neglected. She did not have time to worry about amusements, though she did manage at times to find pleasure in such communal activities as quilting parties. Pleasure in the colonial period, both for women and men, frequently had to be found in some essential activity.

    Colonial appetites were hearty, and there were no prepared mixes to satisfy them quickly and easily. Even sausages had to be made "from the ground up." She cooked over an open fire and so was constantly burning herself at the fire and with the hot pots. Since cooking space was limited, she often baked for several days in advance (remember, there was no bakery around the corner, or supermarket). She planted and tended her own herb garden, and if she was fortunate, the menfolk in the family took care of her kitchen garden, where she planted special foods needed for cooking. She did her own soap-making, candle-making, and preserving, too.

    It was not an easy life; no wonder the life expectancy was so short, considering that she gave birth and immediately went back to taking care of the rest of the family.

EARLY DAYS IN NEW ENGLAND

At Plymouth in 1620 there was first a temporary shelter or camp, then a common house. The settlers at first lived in "smoaky homes" dug into the hillsides, with roofs of bark and walls of sod. But it was not long before they built themselves simple frame houses. In the beginning, the village was surrounded by a stockade. Later, each house had its own, inside of which there was room for a "pretty garden plote."

The one-room structure of 1620 was built around a fireplace. It held only the bare necessities—it was many years before the colonies could think of physical comfort. At first the occupants had to do without windows, the only light being provided by the open fire, or a few tallow candles. Next, small latticed windows, with panes of oiled paper or linen, made their appearance. Some settlers brought glass with them, usually in the form of heavy, greenish, diamond-shaped panes.

The chimneys of the early structures were built on the ground, resting on a foundation set into the dirt. A Puritan family never knew when it might not be disturbed by a long-nosed fire warden peeking into the fireplace for "foul chimney hears," for the old chimneys often caught fire. Of the thirty-two buildings in Plymouth, seven burned down in one winter. In Boston during the first winter, there was a fire every week.

But it was not until the latter part of the century that the colonists began to build the houses customarily associated with seventeenth-century New England. There were the stark, rectangular garrison houses, with the second story jutting out a little over the first. There also were the pleasant, rambling frame houses, with windows of all different sizes, placed anywhere, hit or miss; floors of different heights; and walls of varying thickness. The shingled roofs often sloped from the top of the second story in front, to near the ground in back. Other houses had gambrel roofs with gables at the end.

The single room, found at first, was a small, low-ceilinged room that contained little more than a few benches; two or three four-legged stools; a settle by the fire; perhaps a plain deal table and a simple frame bedstead or jack bed in the corner.

The English four-poster bed was really a little house, designed to protect the occupant from drafts when the bed draperies were drawn. The same might be said of the Puritan settle. The high back and side pieces served as a protection against the wind that blew through the cracks between the timbers of those primitive homes.

Tables for eating purposes were improvised by laying rough boards across trestles. Blocks of wood about a foot square, hollowed in the middle, served as plates, a man and his wife, or a couple of children, often sharing the same one. These plates were called trenchers.

Because the same room was used for cooking, eating, living, and sleeping, the first real tables—known as "tuckaways"—were narrow, with wide leaves, so they could be tucked away in a corner, or trestle tables fitted with draw pins.

The most important part of the room was the kitchen with its big fireplace—known as "chimneys"—sometimes as much as eight or ten feet in width. Whole animals could be roasted in such a fireplace. A hard wood bar crossed the flue, and from it hung the pots and kettles for cooking, for making cheese, for boiling soap and dipping candles. Inside the fireplace was a bench to sit on during the cold winter evenings. The flickering firelight was reflected in the brightly shined copper and brass and pewter ware which hung along the walls. Ladles, skimmers, spoons, colanders, and candlesticks were made of brass and iron and pewter.

Fireplace of early Plymouth

The only light besides that of the open fire came from a few tallow candles, rushlights of reeds, or rushes, dipped in tallow, and long pieces of resinous pitch pine stuck between the hearth glads. Known as candlewood sets, these gave off a bright flare and a good deal of smoke.

"Betty lamps" were also used—small iron saucers filled with oil, with a handle at one end, and a nose or spout for the wick to lie in. These lamps dated back to the days of Pompeii and Athens.

FOOD IN EARLY NEW ENGLAND

The first winter was the hardest. In addition to being terrified by the roar of "lyons" and by wolves "who sat upon their tayles and grinned at them," the Pilgrims watched their scanty store of provisions shrink to almost nothing. By spring, half the members of the little colony were dead. The chance of survival of the others depended on the harvest, and when it came in, the rejoicing was great. For three days the settlers feasted on wild turkeys, geese, and eels and lobsters from the bay.

Flocks of wild pigeons darkened the sky, and lobsters were found in the bay that weighed from sixteen to twenty-five pounds and measured five to six feet from claw tip to claw tip.

Corn inevitably furnished the bulk of the settlers' fare, cooked Indian fashion, made into johnny cake, and hasty pudding—cornmeal mush and milk. It also provided bread in the form of "bannock"—cornmeal spread on a board and baked in front of the fires. Mixed with rye meal and baked in the brick oven along with the beans, it became the "Boston brown bread" of ever-popular fame.

In addition to corn, boiled meats and vegetables and stews predominated in the diet of the seventeenth-century New Englander. And the brick oven, in addition to beans, was used for the baking of peas, Indian puddings, pies, cakes, and sometimes meat and potatoes. Pumpkins with the seeds taken out through a hole in the stem were filled with milk and baked—and the empty shells were later used either to hold yarn and other housewifely items or as jack-o'-lanterns. Bean porridge was cooked in bulk and used over a period of time, hence the line in the old rhyme: "Bean porridge in the pot, nine days old." Cider came to be considered a necessity; a thoughtful husband would stipulate in his will that his widow was to be furnished with several—sometimes as many as eight—barrels a year.

Even in the Massachusetts Bay colony there were no stores for fifteen years; potatoes were not introduced for half a century; and though apple trees were planted, it was a long time before they bore fruit. Roger Clap of Dorchester wrote in his diary: "It was not accounted a strange thing in those days to drink water, and to eat Samp or Homine without Butter or Milk. Indeed it would have been a strange thing to see a piece of Roast Beef . . . though it was not long before there was a Roast Goat."

There was no lack of game and fish in these early days to help round out the diet.

NEW ENGLAND, 1720–1775

The houses became larger, often with four rooms to a floor for a two-story house, a stair hall or a large hall running through from front to back. These houses were of Georgian style. There was much woodwork on both the exterior and interior, although the houses retained their plain clapboard exteriors.

The furniture went from the simple and merely useful to the more elaborate and decorative. This was mostly true of the large towns and cities, however, for in the country plain homemade furniture continued to be the rule. During the long winter evenings, some of the men turned carpenter.

What people ate did not change essentially from one century to the other, but there was more variety. People ate beef, veal, mutton, lamb, pork, and chicken. There was butter, milk, and cheese. Gardens were green with vegetables, orchards luscious with fruit. There was much game and all kinds of fish.

The country folk and common fold had to content themselves with a fare of salted meat, fish, beans, and pudding. The "New England boiled dinner" of salted meat and cabbage, and perhaps one other vegetable, served as one dish, usually in a wooden trencher, was already in existence. During the winter, people ate pumpkins that had been baked in the ashes of the open fire.

An observer wrote of the Boston women in 1740: "They are not much esteemed now that will not treat high and gossip about. Tea has now become the darling of our women. Almost every little tradesman's wife must sit sipping tea for an hour or more in the morning, and maybe again in the afternoon, and nothing will please them to sip it out of but china ware, if they can get it. They talk of bestowing thirty or forty shillings upon a tea equipage, as they call it. There is the silver spoons, the silver tongs, and many other trinkets that I cannot name." Although tea was the common drink until the Revolution, coffee equaled it in popularity after that.

COOKING IN NEW ENGLAND

All cooking was done in and over the fire. The first pole on which the pots and kettles hung was made of wood and called the lug pole. Wood was considered a failure, however, when, after the pole had charred to a point of weakness, it let the meal down into the embers. So iron was then substituted and a Yankee invention brought about the "crane," thus called because it suspended from the side wall in such a manner that it could be swung out into the room. Various-length hooks were used to hold the pots, from those of six inches to some fifteen inches. A trammel was a hook which could be lengthened or shortened to accommodate the height of the fire and the size of the kettle. This was made of two pieces of iron, the end of one having a hook which set into the other which had notches. This arrangement was copied in wood and used for holding a candle, the whole suspended near the fireplace. In those first fireplaces, the pots and kettles stood on legs, raising them above the hot embers. If they swung on the crane, they had flat bottoms. Much later, kettles had an extension which set into the stove hole.

Preparing a meal in early Boston

SETTING THE TABLE

A letter written by one of the first settlers of Plymouth to a friend in Scrooby, England.

Dear Hannah:

I often ask myself what you of Scrooby would say could you see us at dinner. We have no table, and boards are very scarce and dear in price here in this village of ours, therefore father carefully saved the top of one of our packing boxes, while nearly all in the settlement did much the same, and these we call table boards.

When it is time to serve the meal, mother and I lay this board across two short logs; but we cover it with the linen brought from the old home, and none in the plantation, not even the governor himself, has better, as you well know.

I would we had more dishes; but they are costly, as even you at home know. Yet our table looks very inviting when it is spread for a feast, such as when guests come.

We have three trencher bowls, and another larger one in which all the food is placed. Then, in addition to the wooden cups we brought from home, there are many vessels of gourds that we have raised in the garden, and father has fashioned a mold for making spoons, so that now our pewter ware, when grown old with service, can be melted down into the spoons until we have a goodly abundance of them.

It is said, although I have not myself seen it, that a table implement called a fork is in the possession of Master Brewster, having been brought over from England. It is of iron, having two sharp points made to hold the food.

I cannot understand why any should need such a tool while they have their own cleanly fingers, and napkins of linen on which to wipe them. Perhaps father was right when he said that we who are come into this world for the single reason of worshipping God as we please, are too much bound up in the vanities of life, and father says he knows of no more vain thing than an iron tool with which to hold one's food.

I have seen at Master Bradford's home two bottles made of glass, and they are exceedingly beautiful; but so frail that I should scarce dare to wash them, for it would be a great disaster to break so valuable a vessel.

Ruth

SERVING THE FOOD IN NEW ENGLAND

Very simple folk sometimes put the cooking pot on the table and the whole family ate directly from it; but most people ladled the food onto the wooden trenchers and ate from them. A few families owned big pewter chargers on which they brought the food to the table.

Clean linen napkins were needed for every meal, because people ate with their fingers. If the nature of the food was such that fingers could not handle it, it was eaten with a spoon. If meat needed to be cut, you took your own knife out of its sheath and cut it. Spoons were made of wood, of horn, and of pewter. Silver spoons were unknown here until after 1650. Pewter is easily melted, so when spoons broke or wore out, they could be recast in a gunmetal mold.

Dining table of early Plymouth

Along with the trenchers and spoons, there were wooden noggins and tankards for milk, if the family owned a cow, and for beer whether there was a cow or not. There were pewter mugs for drinking, and some made of boiled leather, called "black jacks"—black for their color, jack from their material. Boiled leather was generally known as jacked leather; jack boots got their name the same way. Black jacks were sewn together with waxed linen thread and rimmed with pewter, copper, or silver.

When the meal ended, a basket called a voider was passed around the table and everything that had been used, including the napkins, was put into it to be taken away and washed.

Lob! Lob!! Lob!!! Lobsters!!!!
Who will buy my lobsters? Yesterday
These were down in Boston Bay.
Come, little maiden, buy one! Buy
And you may suck his claws all dry.

From A Quaint Old Picture Book

Higginson in his *New England Plantation* in 1630 realized how great the natural resources of the new country were when he said:

"Our Governor hath store of green pease growing in his garden as good as ever I eat in England. This country aboundeth naturally with store of roots of great variety and good to eat. Our turnips, parsnips and carrots are here both bigger and sweeter than is ordinarily to be found in England. Here are also store of pumpions, cowcumbers, and other things of that nature which I know not. Also, divers potherbs grow abundantly among the grass, as strawberries, penny-royal, winter savoury, sorrel, brooklime, liverwort, carvel and watercresses; also leeks and onions are ordinary and divers physical herbs. Here are also abundance of other sweet herbs whose names we know not. . . . Excellent vines are here up and down in the woods. Also mulberries, plums, raspberries, currants, chestnuts, filberts, walnuts, smallnuts, hurtleberries, and haws of whitethorn."

HIGGINSON ON FISH

"The abundance of sea-fish are almost beyond believing. . . . I saw great store of whales and grampuses, and such abundance of mackerels that it would astonish one to behold; likewise codfish, abundance on the coast and in their season plentifully taken. There is a fish called a bass, a most sweet and wholesome fish as ever I did eat; it is altogether as good as our fresh salmon, and besides bass we take plenty of scate and thornback, and abundance of lobsters. For my own part I was soon cloyed with them, and they were so great and fat and luscious. Also here is abundance of herring, turbot, sturgeon, cusks, haddock, mullets, eels, crabs, muscles, and oysters."

New England Plantation

COOKING UTENSILS

There was quite an array of cooking and roasting utensils for the big fireplace, first brought from the old countries and later made by the local blacksmiths.

The kettles were of many sizes and shapes, and pots vied with them in boasting of variety. Kettles have straight sides and no covers, while pots have bulging sides and covers. Brass and copper kettles were highly prized, coming as they did from across the water, while the lowly iron kettle was often used in trade with the Indians. The first iron kettle, rightly a pot, made in the new country was fashioned on a mold made by Joseph Jenks of Lynn in 1646.

Skillets were iron cooking utensils, standing on legs, with a protruding handle, and there were many sizes and often variety as to depth. The long handle of the fry pan measured three feet so that the housewife might stand away from the hot embers as she prepared dinner. Short-handled pans were called spiders, and aside from those, there were flat griddles which either hung on the crane by a hoop handle or stood on three legs. Gridirons were stands with gratings on legs. They were both round and square, and some even had a revolving head so that the food might be exposed to the fire on all sides. The long-legged stand was the trivet, and this was used to hold food to keep it warm after it had been prepared. Generally it had a handle for lifting it.

FOR AN OINTMENT TO CAUSE HAIR TO GROW

Take of boar's grease two ounces, ashes of burnt bees, ashes of southernwood, juice of white lily-root, oil of sweet almonds, of each one drachm; six drachms of pure musk; and according to art make an ointment of these; and the day before the full moon shave the place, anointing it every day with this ointment; it will cause hair to grow where you will have it. Oil of sweet almonds, or spirit of vinegar, is very good to rub the head with, if the hair grows thin.

The Complete Housewife, E. Smith, 1766

HASTY PUDDING

Puddings were a favorite New England food in the seventeenth and eighteenth centuries. They were easy for a housewife to make for a large gathering, the ingredients usually were at hand, they were an unpretentious way to satisfy a hankering for sweets, and they were economical. All these reasons made them ideal to Abigail Adams, who served puddings frequently. Least pretentious of any, and eaten in all homes, was hasty pudding, which is nothing more than boiled cornmeal mush served hot with maple sugar and butter. Here is a description of how to eat hasty pudding:

The hasty pudding being spread out equally on a plate, while hot, an excavation is made in the middle of it with a spoon, into which excavation a piece of butter as large as a nutmeg is put, and upon it a spoonful of brown sugar . . . The butter, being soon heated by the heat of the pudding, mixes with the sugar and forms a sauce, which, being confined in the excavation, occupies the middle of the plate. Thus for the array—now for the battle! Dip each spoonful in the sauce, before it is carried to the mouth, care being had in taking it up to begin on the outside, and near the brim of the plate, and to approach the center by gradual advances, in order not to demolish too soon the excavation which forms the reservoir of sauce.

THE FIRST AMERICAN BROOMS

During the winter, on the long, cold evenings when the family sat around the fireplace, the boys of the family made birch brooms for the household and earned spending money by making them for the country stores, from whence they were sent to the large cities, especially Boston, where there was a constant demand for them.

These earliest brooms made in America were simply slender birch saplings with the ends splintered. First, all the bark was removed from a sapling about six feet long and about two inches in diameter, then the wide end was splintered up about one foot, the hard core removed, and the splintered ends tied down tightly near the top with a length of hemp. About one foot, two inches above this tied section, more flat slivers were cut down from the opposite direction, leaving about a two-inch uncut ring between the two sets of splinters. The second bunch of splinters was folded over the first and bound securely. The rest of the sapling was shaped and smoothed to form a handle.

Tiny brooms similarly made were used for whisking eggs and whipping cream, slightly larger ones for cleaning pots and pans and for sweeping the ashes from the brick bake oven, and very large ones for heavy-duty sweeping, such as a barn floor. More bristly brooms were made by cutting and binding only the first section of slivers.

"Wing dusters," made from the wings of turkeys, geese, or chickens, were used as stove and hearth brushes. If the housekeeper was not careful, the cat managed to chew them up.

FOR SHORTNESS OF BREATH

Take two quarts of elder-berry juice when very ripe, put one quart in a pipkin to boil, and as it consumes, put in the rest by a little at a time; boil it to a balsam; it will take five or six hours in boiling. Take a little of it night and morning, or any time.

The Complete Housewife, E. Smith, 1766

MORE ABOUT COOKING UTENSILS

A busy utensil was the iron toaster for bread or cheese. The waffle iron was a pincher-shaped contrivance with a long handle.

Every fireplace had a Dutch oven, or fire pan. This was a shallow kettle with three legs, a cover, and a hoop handle. The cover had a rim which held the embers when the kettle was placed in the fire. This was a bake oven and was a result of the first principle of putting food directly in the embers to cook.

There were other tools and utensils at the fireside, such as the kettle-tilter, various spit turners, jack racks, and many forks, skimmers, and ladles for handling the meat cooking in the big pots.

CLAM PIE

1 pie shell, with crust to cover; 2 cups hard clams, chopped fine; ¼ cup clam liquor; 1 tablespoon butter, melted; ½ cup cracker crumbs; 1 egg, well beaten; 1 cup milk; salt and pepper.

Clean the clams and strain the liquor, saving ¼ cup of the liquor. Combine all of the ingredients, season with salt and pepper and pour into a deep pie shell. Cover with upper crust, seal all around and pierce top crust with fork. Bake in a moderate oven [350°F.] for about one hour. Serve very hot with mashed potatoes.

An Old Cape Cod Recipe

PORTSMOUTH, NEW HAMPSHIRE, 1750

James Birket visited Portsmouth, New Hampshire, in 1750, at which time it probably had a population of about 4,000. He described his visit thusly:

"The Town of Portsmouth is Scituated upon Piscataway river about 3 miles from the sea upon a Moderate rising ground, not only from the river, but also from the Adjacent country to the Parade or Center thereof; where 4 Principal streets meet in the nature of a + there are pretty Streight and regular through which you have a prospect of the country on every side; . . .

The houses that are of Modern Architecture are large and Exceeding neat this Sort is generally 3 Story high & well Sashed and Glazed with the best glass the rooms are well plastered and many Wainscoted or hung with painted paper from England the outside Clapboarded very neatly and are very warm. . . .

. . . The better sort of People here live very well and Genteel, They have no fixt market but the Country people come to town as it suits them with such of the Commoditys as they have for Sale by which the town is pretty well Supply'd with Beefe, Mutton, veal and other Butcher's Meat; they have plenty of large Hoggs and very fat bacon, they have also abundance of good fish of diferent Kinds, And abundance of Garden Culture as Beans, Peas, Carrots, Parnsips, Turnips, Radishes, Onions, Cabages, Colliflowers, Asparagus, English or whats commonly called Irish Potatoes also the Sweet Potatoe, Obtains almost all over North America, More so to southward, They have also Apples, Pears, Plumbs, Cherries, & Peaches in Abundance They have also Apricots & Nectrines from England, but do not Observe they had given any of them the Advantage of awall, there's likewise Goosberrys Currant Ditto Rasberries, Strawberries, Huckleberries Water & Muskmellions, Squashes and Sundry Other kinds of fruits roots &c &c There common drink is Cyder which they have in great Plenty, and New England rum And also a new rum from the West Indies, But People of fortune (especially the Marsh's) have very good rum and Madeira wine in their homes, Indeed the wine most commonly Drunk here is from the Canaries & Western Islands—called Oidonia, tis of a pale collor tastes harsh and is inclined to looke thick."

NEW ENGLAND HOME IN THE 1790'S

"The kitchen was large, fully twenty feet square, with a fireplace six feet wide and four feet deep. On one side it looked out upon the garden, the squashes and cucumbers climbing up and forming festoons over the door. The kitchen was in fact the most comfortable room in the house, cool in summer and perfumed with the breath of the garden and orchard; in the winter, with its roaring blaze of hickory, it was a cosy resort, defying the bitterest blasts of the season. . . . The cellar, extending under the whole house . . . was by no means the least important part of the house. In the autumn it contained barrels of beef and pork, barrels of cider, bins of potatoes, turnips, beets, carrots and cabbages. The garret, which was of huge dimensions, at the same time displayed a labyrinth of dried pumpkins, peaches, and apples, hung in festoons upon the rafters, amid bunches of summer savory, boneset, fennel and other herbs—the floor being occupied by heaps of wool, flax, tow and the like. . . ."

New England house and barn

AMERICAN COOKBOOKS

The first American cookbook was printed in Williamsburg, Virginia, in 1742. It was Eliza Smith's *The Compleat Housewife.* However, it was the most popular cookbook in England and there was nothing American about it. There were several printings after that.

The first cookbook published in Boston was Susannah Carter's *The Frugal Housewife* in 1772, and that, too, was British. Another English cookbook was *The New Art of Cookery* by Richard Briggs, printed in Philadelphia in 1792.

Since cookbooks were not actually in demand in young America, there was no cookbook written here until 1796. This was *American Cookery* and its author was Amelia Simmons, who called herself "An American Orphan." This cookbook introduced American dishes such as Indian pudding, Indian slapjack, and johnny cake. Since there were not enough American recipes to fill the book, she also included standard English recipes for meats, puddings, and vegetables.

After *American Cookery* came what can be called a rash of American cookbooks, such as *New England Cookery* in 1808 and an American version of an English cookbook in 1823 called *The Experienced American Housekeeper,* which contained just a few American recipes.

The first truly successful author of American cookbooks was Eliza Leslie, who started out in 1828 with a small volume called *Seventy-Five Receipts for Pastry, Cakes, and Sweetmeats*. From that she went on to *Domestic French Cookery, New Receipts for Cooking,* and finally, *Miss Leslie's New Cookery*. Although she had some English and French recipes, she included many that were purely American.

In 1824, the first of the regional cookbooks appeared with Mrs. Mary Randolph's *The Virginia Housewife,* to be followed by *The Carolina Housewife* in 1847 and *The Philadelphia Housewife* in 1855.

Meanwhile, many other cookbooks appeared and became popular. These served as springboards for the writers to project their views on thrift, morals, improved diet, and the evils of drunkenness. Mrs. Lydia Child in *The American Frugal Housewife* in 1835 extolled the value of thrift. Catherine Beecher, noted educator, was a supporter of the temperance movement and held out against tea, coffee, and certain types of food as well as alcohol.

Miss Beecher's Domestic Receipt Book made concessions when the author did fry some foods in lard and added wine to certain puddings, but on the whole she emphasized wholesome cooking and used many types of fruit. Catherine Beecher and her sister, Harriet Beecher Stowe, combined their talents and produced *The Housekeeper's Manual,* although Catherine had done a number of books prior to that on her own, and they also co-authored several other cookbooks.

Domestic Science became a part of the American school studies and Catherine Beecher was responsible for that. Also, special cooking schools were opened to teach the housewife the whys and wherefores of good and wise shopping and cooking.

Eventually there were many involved in the cooking schools, such as Maria Parloa in Boston who was then followed by Mary J. Lincoln and the most famous of all of the Boston cooking school heads, Fannie Merritt Farmer.

Sarah Rorer was a teacher of cooking in Philadelphia and was one of the first to publish a book with only vegetarian recipes.

Of all the cookbooks published prior to 1900, those by Fannie Merritt Farmer are still used today, as is *The Settlement Cook Book* by Mrs. Simon Kander, which was a schoolbook in the beginning in 1901 and today is one of the standbys in cookbooks.

VERY POPULAR COOKBOOKS, 1766 - 1910

The Complete Housewife, Eliza Smith, 1766

The Domestic Encyclopedia—Three Volumes, A.F.M. Willich, 1821

The Cook's Oracle, 1825

The Whole Art of Confectionary, 1831

The Cook's Own Book, 1832

The American Frugal Housewife, Mrs. Lydia Child, 1835

Directions for Cookery, Miss Eliza Leslie, 1837

The Good Housekeeper, Sarah Josepha Hale, 1839

The American Economical Housekeeper, Mrs. E.A. Howland, 1845

Mackenzie's Five Thousand Receipts, 1848

The Modern Housewife, Alexis Soyer, 1849

Receipt Book, Mrs. Putnam, 1849

American Lady's System of Cookery, Mrs. T.J. Crowen, 1850

Ladies Indispensable Assistant, 1851

The New Household Receipt Book, Sarah Josepha Hale, 1853

The Practical Housekeeper, Mrs. Ellet, 1857

Miss Beecher's Domestic Receipt Book, 1858

The Young Housekeeper's Friend, Mrs. Cornelius, 1859

The Virginia Housewife, Mrs. Mary Randolph, 1860

Dr. Chase's Recipes or Information for Everybody, A.W. Chase, M.D., 1866

American Woman's Home, Catherine E. Beecher and Harriet Beecher Stowe, 1869

Buckeye Cook Book, 1875

All Around the House, Mrs. H.W. Beecher, 1878

Housekeeping in Old Virginia, Marian Cabell Tyree, 1879

The Book of Household Management, Mrs. Isabella Beeton, 1880

Mary J. Lincoln's Boston Cook Book, 1883

Cookery for Beginners, Marion Harland, 1884

Breakfast, Luncheon and Tea, Marion Harland, 1887

Miss Parloa's Kitchen Companion, 1887

Boston Cook Book, Fannie Farmer, 1896

Mrs. Rorer's Cook Book, 1898

The Settlement Cook Book, Mrs. Simon Kander, 1901

Complete Cook Book, Marion Harland, 1903

Ladies' Home Cook Book, Julia MacNair Wright, 1903

What to Have for Dinner, Fannie Farmer, 1905

Queen of the Household, Mrs. M.W. Ellsworth, 1906

Mrs. Curtis's Cook Book, 1908

Aunt Babette's Cook Book, 1910

THE SOLITARY ORPHAN

It must ever remain a check upon the poor solitary orphan, that while those females that have parents, or brothers, or riches to defend their indiscretions, that the orphan must depend solely upon character. How immensely important therefore, that every action, every word, every thought, be regulated by the strictest purity, and that every movement meet the approbation of the good and wise.

American Cookery by Amelia Simmons, 1796

INDIAN SLAPJACK

One quart milk, one pint Indian meal, four eggs, four spoons of flour, little salt, beat together, baked on griddles, or fry in a dry pan, or baked in a pan which has been rubbed with suet, lard or butter.

American Cookery by Amelia Simmons, 1796

THE NEW HOUSEHOLD RECEIPT BOOK,
Sarah Josepha Hale, 1853

Sarah Josepha Hale was well-known as the editor of *Godey's Lady's Book,* but she also wrote several cookbooks which contained household hints.

In this one she said: "In the economy and well-being of a family, personal and individual improvement should be sedulously kept in view. It is not enough that the woman understands the art of cookery and of managing her house: she must also take care of herself; of children; of all who will be dependent on her for direction, for health, for happiness. . . ."

One of her topics for discussion was CORPULENCE: "Those who are afflicted with corpulence should not allow themselves above six hours' sleep in the twenty-four. They should take as much exercise as possible, and avoid cream, malt liquors and soups—at least until they have succeeded in reducing their bulk. Salt provisions are good, having a tendency to promote perspiration and carry off fat. Soda water is also beneficial. *Receipt*: Take Castile soap, in the form of pills or electuary, of from one to four drachms dissolved in a quarter of a pint of soft water, when going to bed. But let not our lovely girls abuse their constitutions by drinking vinegar for this purpose, for consumption has often been produced by that habit."

MISS LESLIE'S NEW COOKERY, 1858

By the time this, the last of Eliza Leslie's cookbooks, appeared, her original 75 recipes mentioned earlier had expanded to a thousand. Along with the recipes, she now included timely advice:

"No man (or woman either) ought to be incapable of distinguishing bad eatables from good ones. Yet, I have heard some few ladies boast of that incapacity as something meritorious, and declare that they considered the quality, the preparation, and even the taste of food, as things entirely beneath the attention of a rational being; their own minds being always occupied with objects of far greater importance.

"Let no man marry such a woman. If indifferent to her own food, he will find her still more indifferent to his. . . .

"Let all housekeepers remember that there is no possibility of producing nice dishes without a liberal allowance of good ingredients. . . .

"A sufficiency of wholesome and well-prepared food is absolutely necessary to the preservation of health and strength, both of body and mind. . . For those who possess the means of living well, it is false (and sometimes fatal) economy to live badly; particularly when there is a lavish expenditure in fine clothes, fine furniture, and other ostentations, only excusable when *not* purchased at the expense of health and comfort."

EGG PLANTS, STUFFED

Parboil them to take off their bitterness. Then slit each one down the side and extract the seeds. Have ready a stuffing made of grated bread-crumbs, butter, minced sweet herbs, salt, pepper, nutmeg, and beaten yolk of egg. Fill with it the cavity from whence you took the seeds, and bake the egg plants in a Dutch Oven. Serve them up with a made gravy poured into the dish.

Miss Leslie's New Cookery, 1858

Author's note: A nice tomato sauce would be delicious. Use your favorite bread stuffing.

INDIAN CAKE OR BANNOCK

Is sweet and cheap food. One quart of sifted meal, two great spoonfuls of molasses, two teaspoonfuls of salt, a bit of shortening half as big as a hen's egg, stirred together. Make it pretty moist with scalding water, put it in a well greased pan and bake it brown on both sides before a quick fire. A little stewed pumpkin scalded with milk improves the cake. Bannock split and dipped in butter makes very nice toast.

The Pocumtuc Housewife, 1805

HOW TO HEAT THE OVEN

Some people consider it economical to heat Ovens with fagots, brush and light stuff. Hard wood heats it quicker and hotter. Take four foot wood split fine, and pile it criss-cross so as to nearly fill the oven, and keep putting in. A Roaring fire for an hour or more is usually enough. The top and sides will at first be covered with black soot. See that it is all burned off. Rake the coals over the bottom of the Oven and let them lie a minute. Then sweep it out clean. If you can hold your hand inside while you count forty, it is about right for flour bread; to count twenty is right for Rye and Indian. If it is too hot, wet an old broom two or three times and turn it around near the top of the oven till it dries; this prevents pies and cakes from scorching on top. When you go into a new house, heat your oven two or three times to get it seasoned before you use it.

Bake the Brown bread first, then flour bread and Pies, then Cake or puddings, and last Custards. After everything else is out put in a pan of apples. Next morning they will be deliciously baked. A pot of Beans can be baking back side, out of the way of the Rest.

If bread runs short before baking day comes, light cakes can be baked in the bake Kettle or the tin Baker. Draw out a solid mass of coals, set the bake-kettle over it, put in your biscuit, put on the lid, and cover it with a thick layer of coals.

The Pocumtuc Housewife, 1805

Baking in fireplace oven

THE STOVE

Cooking stove of the 1800's

The convenience of the stove for cooking had more influence on its eventual popularity than all other factors combined. Food was said to be better cooked in a fireplace, but the operation was slow and much labor was required to prepare a meal. The first attempt at a closed fireplace was made by Cardinal Polignac of France in 1708. Holland invented the plain box-stove with a single door, a single hole in the top, and a small smoke pipe. Both styles saved valuable fuel but were not popular with the people.

Ben Franklin made many suggestions on the topic of stoves. In 1745, he invented an enclosed fireplace in which the current of flame and air passed through air boxes in the sides. Thus, most of the heat was saved and passed into the room. The stove had a damper and would have been airtight except that castings were not made to fit tightly.

In 1771, Franklin invented a stove for bituminous coal. It had a downward draft and consumed its own smoke. From 1785 to 1795, Count Rumford, an American, devised many improvements. He invented the cooking range and the ventilating ovens that were used in New York and Boston. These were first used from around 1798–1800.

Until 1835, the stoves were made at bog-iron and blast furnaces. The plates were cast directly from the iron in the smelting furnaces.

The first furnace to cast stoves from pig iron was built in New York by Jordan L. Mott. He had been making self-feeding coal stoves since 1827, and anthracite coal stoves since 1833. In 1835, Mott bought some of the immense refuse or tailings in the Schuylkill coalyards and screened them for nut and pea coal for his stoves. He sold this coal to the owners of his stoves. His success encouraged others to begin the manufacture of stoves, and plants were started in Albany and Providence.

Dr. Eliphalet Nott of the Union College began experimenting and developed the gas burner and other stoves. He was the president of the college, but he never reaped a reward for his many contributions to the stove industry.

With better transportation, cooking stoves were shipped and sold around the country. The early patterns were ten-plate oval stoves with the oven above the fire and a stove collar over it. The saddlebag design came next, with the oven in the center of the stove and the stovepipe and collar over it. By 1881, nearly a thousand patents had been issued on stoves.

In that same year, there were two hundred and twenty firms manufacturing all types of stoves. They were made with two, four, six, and eight holes for kettles. Some had fixed boilers and some had double ovens. Stove producers were indebted to the county fairs, which popularized and advertised the newest model of stove.

OF EATING

Accustom your palate to what is most usual; he that delights in rarities must often feed displeased, and lie at the pleasure of a dear market; common food nourishes best; delicacies please most; the sound stomach prefers neither; what is any man the worse for the last year's plain diet, or what now the better for last year's feasting?

An Astronomical Diary, or Almanack, for the Year of Christian Era, 1795,
Daniel Sewall, Portsmouth, N.H.

WINTER

Winter was the time to stay indoors and try to keep warm. Lots of baking was done in order to keep the kitchen warm.

Often the children of the family went to another town to attend school, since the local school was a one-room affair. In order to get a little more of an education, the children attended an academy in a neighboring village.

The housewife would cook the food and send it to or with the children so that it would be more reasonable to keep them in school. Also, the children preferred the food from home. Each weekend the family would be together, and the children would take the food for the following week with them late Sunday evening or very early Monday morning.

While the older children were away at school in the neighboring village, the younger children went to school locally, and the rural schoolteacher lived in one of the local households.

The winter was the time for the housewife to get her weaving, spinning, and other indoor chores done. Meanwhile, she was planning her spring activities; what herbs she would plant, and what plants and flowers she would put in the garden to pretty things up.

HINTS AND MAXIMS

If you chance to occupy the important position of a cook, remember that cleanliness is the first, second, and third requirement in point of importance, to be observed.

Keep your flour-box, sugar, salt, and spices always covered, that dust and insects may not get in.

Never put onion or cheese on the same dish with anything else, and never cut anything else with the knife you use for them. Keep a particular pitcher for beer or buttermilk, or you may chance to put milk or water into the remains.

Keep your tin and copper vessels as sweet and clean as glass or china. The saucepans are of far more consequence than tumblers or teacups. If glasses be dirty, those who drink from them are disgusted; but if saucepans be foul, they may chance to be poisoned. Many have died from this cause. The sort of rust which forms in copper vessels not kept clean is a deadly poison. If a housekeeper is careful, she will look into all her saucepans at least once a week, to see if they are well cleaned, or want tinning.

Let the dinner be served quite hot, and have the plates as hot as you can handle them. Cold plates spoil the finest joint of meat; and it is very easy to have plates hot. At breakfast and tea it will be your fault if the tea is not good. It is a very common fault in cooks, as soon as the teakettle boils, to set it on one side where the water cools a little, so that it is not *quite* boiling when poured on the tea.

The true economy of housekeeping is simply the art of gathering up all the fragments, so that nothing be lost. I mean fragments of *time*, as well as materials. Nothing should be thrown away so long as it is possible to make any use of it, however trifly that use may be; and whatever be the size of a family, every member should be employed either in earning or saving money.

Few know how to keep the flavor of sweet marjoram, the best of all herbs for broth and stuffing. It should be gathered in bud or blossom and dried in a tin kitchen at a moderate distance from the fire; when dry it should be rubbed, sifted, and corked up in a bottle.

Herbs should be kept from the air. Herb tea, to do any good, should be made very strong. Herbs must be gathered while in blossom. Those who have a little ground will do well to raise the most useful herbs; apothecaries make large profits on them.

Cut lemon and orange peel, when fresh, into a bottle kept full of brandy. This brandy gives a delicious flavor to pies, cakes, &c. Roseleaves may be preserved in brandy. Peach leaves steeped in it make an excellent seasoning for custards and puddings.

Potatoes boiled and mashed hot, are good in shortcakes and puddings; they save flour and shortening.

Let there be a place for every article, and when not in use let every article be in its place.

The Practical Housekeeper, Mrs. Ellet, 1857

PRESERVATION OF WINTER APPLES

Apples keep best in low temperatures, and may be well preserved in an ice-house. An English journal recommends the use of dry pit sand for preserving pears and apples. Glazed earthen jars are to be provided, and the sand to be thoroughly dried. A layer of sand an inch thick is then placed in the bottom of the jar; above this a layer of fruit, to be covered with a layer of sand an inch thick; then lay a second stratum of fruit, covering again with an inch of sand. An inch and a half of sand may be placed over the uppermost row of fruit. The jar is now to be closed, and placed in a dry situation, as cool as possible, but entirely free from frost. Some assert that apples may be kept in casks through the winter, in a chamber or garret, by being merely covered with linen cloths.

Farmer's Almanack, 1830, Robert B. Thomas

FOR AN OBSTINATE COUGH

Take a half pound of the best honey, and squeeze the juice of four lemons upon it; mix them well together, and add a small portion of sugar candy. A teaspoonful may be taken every time the cough is troublesome, and in a short time a cure will be effected.

The Housekeeper's Book, 1838

ODDS AND ENDS

There are certain odds and ends, where every housekeeper will gain much by having a regular time to attend to them. Let this time be the last Saturday forenoon in every month, or any other time more agreeable, let there be a regular fixed time once a month, in which the housekeeper will check rooms, closets, cellars, etc. to make certain that all is in order.

Miss Beecher's Domestic Receipt Book, 1846

TO REMEDY THE CREAKING OF A DOOR: Rub a piece of soap on its hinges, and it will be instantly silenced.

TO CLEAN PAPERED WALLS: Moisten with water a clean large cloth; gently wipe off the dust from the paper. Stale bread rubbed on will answer the purpose.

TO TAKE IRON STAINS OUT OF MARBLE: Mix equal quantities of spirit of vitriol and lemon-juice, shake it well, wet the spots, and in a few minutes rub with a soften linen till they are gone.

The American Practical Cookery Books, 1859

KITCHEN FURNITURE—1800

The kitchen floor should be covered with an oil cloth. Carpets, or bits of carpet, are not so good, because of the grease and filth that must accumulate in them, and the labor of sweeping, shaking, and cleansing them. Nothing is cleansed so easily as an oil cloth, and it is much better than a painted floor, because it can be removed to be painted.

If the cook is troubled with cold feet in winter, small bits of carpeting can be laid where she sits and stands the most. Otherwise they had better be kept out of the kitchen.

There should always be a clock in the kitchen, as indispensable to success in cooking, and regularity of meals.

Two tables, a large one for cooking, and a small one for meals, should be provided.

There should be tin boxes made with tight lapping covers, and of three sizes. In the largest put two kinds of sugar, and starch. In the medium size keep tea and coffee, table salt and ginger. In the smallest size keep cream of tartar, indigo, mustard, sweet herbs, and spices. In Junk bottles, keep a supply of vinegar, molasses and catsup.

Miss Beecher's Domestic Receipt Book, 1846

VICTORIAN KITCHEN

The Victorian kitchen was a bright, warm, and cozy room with a pleasant window or two, plants on the window sill, and an easy chair with a work basket nearby for sewing, mending, and darning materials. The curtains were either white muslin or a gay print.

The walls were painted or calcimined, while the floor usually had a linoleum on it since this was easier to care for than a plain wooden floor.

The kitchen sink was of iron, soapstone, wood, granite, or crockery, depending upon the means and preferences of the housekeeper. The stove burned hard or soft coal, wood, or cobs; it cooked the food, heated the water, boiled the laundry. In the winter the stove heated the room to a cozy warmth, while it made the same room uncomfortably hot in the summer.

The kitchen table was wood, plain or painted. Sometimes a piece of linoleum matching that on the floor was shaped into a durable table covering. Small rag rugs by the stove and sink made a comfortable spot for the cook or dishwasher to stand on. These rugs were either bought from a door-to-door salesman or made by the woman of the house.

Most kitchens had a pantry next to it. This was a small room provided with a table or table-shelf that could be raised or lowered as necessary and shelves and drawers for storing supplies. The shelves were either open or concealed behind doors that were solid wood or had curtained glass panels. The flour barrel and sugar bucket were also stored in the pantry.

On one side of the pantry there were hooks on the walls for aprons and towels. The broom, mop, carpet beater, pails, dust pans, feather duster, and other cleaning equipment were also kept here, as were oil and wicks for the oil lamps and a handy small stepladder.

Kitchen sink of the 1880's

THE CARE OF THE KITCHEN

If parents wish their daughters to grow up with good domestic habits, they should have, as one means of securing this result, a neat and cheerful kitchen. . . .

A sink should be scalded out every day, and occasionally with hot lye. On nails, over the sink, should be hung three good dishcloths, hemmed, and furnished with loops; one for dishes not greasy, one for greasy dishes, and one for washing greasy pots and kettles. These should be put in the wash every week. The lady who insists upon this will not be annoyed by having her dishes washed with dark, musty and greasy rags, as is too frequently the case.

American Woman's Home, Beecher and Stowe, 1869

Scrubbing the floor

BAKING BREAD

It used to be said that Sunday was go-to-meeting day, Monday was washday, Tuesday was ironing day, Wednesday was mending day, Thursday was get-together day, Friday was cleaning day, and Saturday was baking day. This schedule was followed religiously by most of the housewives after the Civil War.

Baking a week's supply of bread was a regular chore on Saturday for every housewife or some other female in the household. It did not stop with bread or rolls. Our housewife also baked a pie or two and at least one cake and maybe some doughnuts.

THE GENERAL STORE

The smaller towns could not support separate grocery, meat, fruit, hardware, and notions stores, so they had their general stores. These handled food, housewares, hardware, farm supplies—almost anything you might think of. If the general store was out of a particular size or brand that you wanted, you either took a substitute, waited for a new shipment to come in, or got back in your wagon or buggy and drove to the next town to get what you wanted.

Usually the general store was also the post office and general meeting place for the area. There were cracker barrels to sit around on inclement days and checkerboards where one could while away the hours with a friend or with the owner. Or one could gossip about crops or about the antics of the local residents.

FASHIONABLE ROUTS

"How strange it is," said a lady, "that fashionable parties should be called routs! Why routs formerly signified the death of an army and when the soldiers were all put to flight or to the sword they were said to be routed." "This title has some propriety too," said a clergyman. "For all these meetings whole families are frequently ROUTED OUT OF HOUSE AND HOME."

The New England Almanac, 1836, Anson Allen

CABBAGE JELLY

A tasty little dish, and by some persons esteemed more wholesome than cabbage simply boiled. Boil cabbage in the usual way, and squeeze in a colander till perfectly dry. Then chop small; add a little butter, pepper, and salt. Press the whole very closely into an earthenware mould, and bake one hour, either in a side oven or in front of the fire; when done, turn it out.

Godey's Lady's Book and Magazine, 1861

MORE ABOUT KITCHENS

"A man knows—or thinks he does—just what he needs in his study or library. . . . But a woman who practically understands what it is to do the work, or daily arrange for others to do, naturally realizes more truly than a man can do, that, in building a kitchen, whenever beauty and utility are not compatible, utility must be the major, and beauty the minor, consideration.

"To be sure, we see no reason why a particular apartment cannot be made tasteful and attractive, yet perfectly convenient. . . .

"Much time is wasted, and not half the efficient labor performed, for lack of

Churning butter

more attention to the architectural design of many of our kitchens. Some are so small that one cannot but feel 'cribbed, cabined and confined,' just to step inside of them. In others, one is bewildered and lost in the great "SAHARAS" which are called kitchens—a wilderness, where everything is lost, and nothing can be found; . . .

". . . . a long table, fitted so closely to the sink that no water can drip between is much needed. It is better to have it permanently fastened to the wall, and made as wide as the sink—a kind of long, wide shelf or table on which to clean vegetables, dress meat, poultry, game, etc., and, by being thus made of easy access to hot and cold water, it saves time and many steps. . . ."

All Around the House, H.W. Beecher, 1878

ALMANACS

The origins of the modern almanac go well back into the eighteenth century, when the annual publication of each volume was a significant event in the life of colonial America. Almost every household had need of the information contained in its pages in order to plan the planting of crops, care for the ill, educate the young, and take care of dozens of household chores. The pages also served as handy places, for those who could write, to jot down personal information, recipes, cures, and agricultural data.

In many a colonial household where the Bible and Psalmbook formed the sole standing library, the almanac was the only other book that crossed the threshold.

In the latter part of the nineteenth century, almanacs were issued by various companies to advertise their products. They often contained the basic material found in the old almanacs and in addition contained recipes, games, songs, etc., for the edification of the entire family.

CONVENIENT KITCHENS
MAKE PATIENT HOUSEWIVES

Three large windows are desirable, and for a spacious kitchen, four will make work more comfortable.

A range, or cooking-stove, should never be placed opposite a door or window if it can be avoided; for sunlight or wind, striking across them, will deaden either coal or wood fires, and thus prevent the oven from baking evenly.

Some kind of ventilator is important over the range or stove, by which steam and all disagreeable odors can be carried off without pervading the whole house.

It is more convenient to have the sink on the left side of the range; but, whichever side it is placed, it should be as near the window as possible, to secure plenty of light.

All Around the House, H.W. Beecher, 1878

THE DINING ROOM

Let your breakfasts be of wholesome and substantial food. The system needs nourishment in the morning after the long, unbroken fast of the night. The practice of taking only a cup of tea or coffee, or chocolate with hot biscuits, and possibly pie or doughnuts, gives a very poor foundation for the morning's labor, which is and should be the hard labor of the day. The morning meal should be taken as soon as possible after rising.

The midday and evening meal may vary with the occupations and habits of the family; but a regular hour for eating should be observed, whether the more substantial meal come at noon or night; and if at night sufficient time should be allowed for digestion to be completed before sleeping. A supper of cold bread and cake or pie is neither appetizing nor satisfying for those who have been hard at work throughout the day.

Boston Cook Book, Mary J. Lincoln, 1883

FOOD FOR THE URBAN FAMILY—1800'S

Fresh foods had to be purchased in quantity when they became available and then immediately processed so as to remain fresh. Often the entire family was pressed into kitchen duty.

Fruits and vegetables arrived in the kitchen in sacks or baskets from local gardens and farms.

Out-of-season foods would arrive in the kitchen in smaller quantities, if at all, only as they could be purchased in the general store. These foods usually included oranges, grapes, raisins, pineapples, bananas.

Flour, cornmeal, and other grains were bought by the barrel or the fifty-pound sack and then transferred to kitchen canisters as needed.

Sugar came in large cones or loaves, sometimes two or three feet high, weighing anywhere from twelve to fifty-five pounds. The housewife hung them from the ceiling by cords and put a netting over the cone to discourage flies. To prepare the sugar for use, the housewife knocked a chunk from the cone with a hammer or cut off a piece with "sugar cutters" and pounded it into granules.

Salt arrived in the kitchen in large blocks, and of course peppercorns, nutmeg, cloves, and cinnamon had to be ground as needed.

Ale and cider came in large stoppered jugs. These were the most popular drinks prior to the Civil War, when the men were introduced to coffee as regular fare and it soon became the national beverage.

The housewife bought the coffee beans green, so she roasted them first in a special home coffee roaster and then ground the coffee in a coffee mill when needed.

Chickens, turkeys, and ducks came to the kitchen trussed up but alive and had to be processed by the housewife before being used. The same was true of fish, which may not have been alive but which had to be scaled, shelled, and prepared at sink or counter.

The only way a family could be certain of having meat on the table was to buy it in quantity when available and "put down" a supply in the cellar after smoking and pickling the parts. They also made their own sausages.

In many homes dairy products also involved the entire family since, to be assured of a regular supply, families usually kept a cow or two that had to be fed, milked, the cream separated, butter churned, and cheese made.

With all that the housewife had to do just to keep her family fed, it was no wonder that she had little leisure time.

The dumbwaiter—1870's

"The well-fed family, especially when that family is not 'eating up its margins,' is usually the cheery, comfortable, amiable family, and any physician can speedily expound the close connection between good morals and good digestion."

POTATO PIE

Scald one quart of milk, grate in four large potatoes while the milk is hot; when cold add four eggs well beaten, and four ounces of butter; spice and sweeten to taste; lay in paste. Bake half an hour.

Mrs. Winslow's Domestic Receipt Book, 1871
Brown's Bronchial Troches for Coughs and Colds

FRIED CABBAGE

Chop cold boiled cabbage fine and drain very dry, add two well beaten eggs, three tablespoonfuls of cream, one of melted butter, salt and pepper. Heat all in a buttered frying pan, stir until smoking hot. Then let it stand long enough to brown slightly on the bottom. Turn upside down on a platter and serve.

Ransom's Family Receipt Book, D. Ransom & Son, Buffalo, N.Y.

Bloomville, O., Jan. 31, 1900
D. Ransom Son & Co.
On the 1st of April next, I will have sold Ransom's Hive Syrup and Tolu for 23 years. Of a family of five boys, the youngest of whom graduates this summer, every one has been carried through Croup on this medicine. Have found Physicians here honest enough to send such cases to Drug Stores for this remedy.

F. A. Chatfield
Ransom's Family Receipt Book, D. Ransom & Son, Buffalo, N.Y.

A GOOD RECIPE

Here is a receipt which I once read, and always remember it because of its goodness. I sent it that others may try it.

Take a gill of forbearance
A pinch of submission
Twelve ounces of patience
A handful of grace
Mix well with the milk of the best human kindness.

Household, January 1876

TO KEEP PIANO KEYS CLEAN AND WHITE

Dampen a piece of muslin with alcohol, and with it rub the keys. If this does not remove the stains, use a piece of cotton flannel wet with cologne water. The keys can also be bleached white by laying over the keys cotton flannel cloths that have been saturated with a solution of oxalic acid.

Marion Harland's Complete Cook Book, 1903

A musical evening

In no department of industry has the last century brought greater changes than in the department of housekeeping. Then, the housekeeper was at the head of, and the principal worker in a manufacturing plant in which was made nearly everything used by the family. . . .

Today all this is changed. While food has still to undergo some measure of preparation within the household, and while there are still a sufficiency of duties for the housekeeper, the work has been greatly simplified and made easier by the invention of many labor-saving devices, appliances, and processes.

The New England Cook Book, 1905

RUM PUDDING

Take 19 eggs (yolks and whites beaten separately), 1 pint of sweet cream, ½ pound sugar, ½ pint rum and 1½ ounces gelatine; stir the yolks of the eggs and sugar to a cream, add the cream and rum, put this in a tin pail and set in a vessel of hot water; keep stirring with an egg beater until just about to boil; then quickly remove from the fire; have gelatine soaked in a little cold water, add it to the cream and mix well; when cold add the beaten whites of the eggs, pour into a mould and set on ice; in serving turn out and send fruit sauce to table with it.

Desserts and Salads, 1907

KITCHEN FURNITURE—1900

The kitchen of 1900 was a huge and often severely plain room with a large table used as a family gathering place. The table also served as a work area for preparing the daily meals, a handy place for after-school snacks, a desk for doing homework, and a place to gather for family discussions.

A washstand stood close by the back door. On it were a pitcher or pail of water, a washbasin, and a hand towel to be used by anyone who came into the house from outside chores.

The kitchen stove was wood-burning, and next to it was a built-in water reservoir. It was the responsibility of the boys in the family to keep the woodbin and water reservoir filled at all times.

There was a pie safe with perforated tin doors that held all the baked goods that had been prepared on the previous bake-day.

In city homes and homes that had an icehouse, there was an icebox for keeping milk, butter, and other perishable foods. Usually the farm kitchen had no icebox but there was a well house or spring house to serve the purpose.

Kitchen cabinets were free-standing and had flour and coffee bins built in above the work counter along with built-in sifters and grinders. The space beneath the counter contained storage bins for potatoes and other dry storage vegetables.

KITCHEN UTENSILS—1900

Since the kitchen was large and used constantly, there usually was a small rocking chair and sewing drawer in it so that mending might be done while the baking was in progress. Butter-churning was also done in the kitchen, so this equipment was kept handy there.

Storage vessels ranging from small butter crocks through milk jars of assorted sizes to huge pickle and kraut crocks were of pottery or stoneware, while mixing bowls of all sizes were of woodenware or stoneware. Dishpans, coffee pots, pie pans, and other baking pans were usually of graniteware. In fact, most of the cookware was of graniteware, except for the cast-iron beanpots and frying pans.

Butter molds and various types of mashers and mallets were made of wood, with the most important item in the kitchen being a set of stirring spoons of all sizes. No self-respecting housewife used a metal spoon, since it was said that metal spoiled the taste of the food and could contaminate it.

There was a glass-front cabinet filled with "company" china, glassware, and silver, used only for special occasions. The everyday table was set with the cheaper ironstone dishes and a form of metal alloy tableware.

The kitchen was well stocked with labor- and time-saving gadgets—for this was the age of gadgetry. Graters and grinders ranged from the tiny metal nutmeg grater to the heavy iron sausage grinder. Potato ricers and graters did double duty, helping to prepare horseradish and relishes as well as finely ground infant and invalid foods.

The iron sausage grinder was clamped to a table top and kept in constant use during the butchering season.

Apple peelers and cherry seeders also clamped to the table top, and not a kitchen was without these utensils. Also needed were iron ice tongs and stove lid lifters, and a long iron poker for the kitchen stove.

Some of these may seem like useless gadgets to us today, but they certainly were of the utmost importance to the housewife in 1900. Perhaps some of the utensils used today will appear obsolete in seventy-five years.

HANDIWORK

The long winter months were an opportune time for the women of the family to concentrate on their handiwork. Little girls were taught to knit as soon as their hands could hold the needles. Sometimes girls four years of age could knit stockings. Boys had to knit their own suspenders. All the stockings and mittens for the family, and coarse socks and mittens for sale, were made in large numbers. Much fine knitting was done, with many intricate and elaborate stitches. Those known as the "herringbone" and "fox and geese" were great favorites.

An elaborate and much-admired form of knitting was the bead bag and purse which were made with great variety and ingenuity. Beautiful bags were knitted to match wedding gowns. Knitted purses were given as gifts to husband and lover.

Netting was another decorative work. Netted fringes for edging the coverlets, curtains, tests, and valences were made of cotton thread or twine, while silk or cotton netting was used to trim sacks and petticoats.

Small fishing nets were also netted, but of twine.

Prior to the Revolution there was a boarding school kept in Philadelphia by a Mrs. Sarah Wilson, who advertised thusly:

"Young ladies may be educated in genteel manner, and pains taken to teach them in regard to their behavior, on reasonable terms. They may be taught all sorts fine needlework, viz., working on catgut or flowering muslin, sattin stitch, quince stitch, tent stitch, cross-stitch, open work, tambour, embroidering curtains or chairs, writing and cyphering. Likewise waxwork in all its several branches, never as yet particularly taught here; also how to take profiles in wax, to make wax flowers and fruits and pinbaskets."

NEW YEAR'S DAY CALLS

The custom of paying New Year's calls originated in New York, where the Dutch held open house on New Year's Day and served cherry bounce, olykoeks steeped in rum, cookies, and honey cakes. Gradually the custom spread throughout the country, and General Washington on the first New Year's Day after his inauguration held an open house and continued to do so while he was President.

However, eventually it became so popular that those who intended to receive company listed in the newspapers the hours they would be receiving. It soon got out of hand as strangers went from house to house for a glass of punch and a bit of a meal. The public announcements were dropped, and open house was just for invited friends.

THE FOOT WARMER

The foot warmer in its various forms was an indispensable item of family equipment since it was used to keep warm in church and in sleighs and carriages in winter. Some took the form of metal boxes and cylinders into which live coals could

One-horse shay

be placed; others were heated stones with handles and wrapped in blankets, and some consisted merely of woolen bags into which the feet could be inserted.

However, the most popular was a long-handled, covered pan containing hot coals, which was inserted between the sheets of a bed on cold nights. Thus cold feet were eliminated for at least a few minutes upon retiring in an unheated bedroom.

FASTNACHTS

These Pennsylvania Dutch doughnuts were served traditionally on Fastnacht Day (Shrove Tuesday), a last sweet before the Lenten season began.

THE WEEKLY BATH: *Diary of An Early American Housewife*

February 10, 1772—Although it was one of the coldest days of this winter, I would not let the children go without their personal ablutions this week. Personal cleanliness is a duty and with the coming of Sabbath must be carried out.

Original Saturday night bath

TAKING A BATH

From the beginning of the New Englander's Sabbath, at sunset on Saturday evening, the housewife must have found that portion of sacred time anything but a rest period. The Saturday evening meal was hastened so that the dishes might be washed on secular time. However, personal washings were held to be of religious importance, since personal cleanliness was considered a religious duty.

The conscientious scrubbing of each member of the family began with the youngest and concluded with the oldest member of the household.

There were no special rooms for bathing. Hot water could only be procured by heating in great iron pots over the open fire, and the tubs used for baths were, in general, the same that were used for the washing of clothes. However, there were some tubs made for bathing purposes only. These were of cedar and large enough for a tall man to lie in at full length. As there were no particular rooms for bathing, the tubs were usually left in the damp cellars through the week, that they might not become dry enough to leak.

If a fire was not kept in the best room throughout the week, one would be lighted there every Saturday during the cold weather and maintained until late on Sunday night. This left the fires in the kitchens free for the servants, and those in the living rooms, for the family. If there were no servants, often the kitchen would be the improvised bathroom for the entire family.

If the best room was used, the carpets, if any, were protected and the tubs were set, each one shielded from view on all sides, save that nearest the fire, by heavy woolen coverlets or blankets hung over clotheshorses. With the fireplaces being generally large, as many as three or four or even more such curtained cabinets might be made in front of each fire. As much cold water as was desired was poured into the tub and was then brought to the required temperature by the addition of boiling water from the great iron or brass kettles.

Carrying out the water that had been used by each bather and emptying the tubs at a little distance from the house was hard work, and usually the strongest servants and members of the family were assigned this task.

Nothing but a case of severe illness was allowed to excuse any inmate of a self-respecting household from taking the weekly Saturday night bath.

SOAP AND THE SKIN

Since the soap was of home manufacture and very harsh in quality, as little of it as possible was used on the body. Those who were careful of their complexions rarely used any soap about their faces, but instead softened the water by using a very little lye made from the ashes of hard woods. Rose-water made by the housewife and various unguents also made by her were then applied to heal the smart. In warm weather, buttermilk was considered excellent for the complexion, and in severe winter weather, cider brandy was used by some, while an ointment of mutton tallow and lard was used by others.

SLEIGH RIDING IN NEW YORK

"Their diversion in winter is riding in sleighs about three miles out of town, where they have houses of entertainment at a place called the Bowery; and some go to friends' houses, who handsomely treat them. I believe we mett fifty or sixty sleighs one day; they fly with great swiftness, and some are so furious that they turn out for none except a loaded cart."

Madame Knight's Visit To New York, 1704

THE TURKEY

The origin of the name "turkey" has been variously explained but one of the most reasonable explanations is that it comes from the Indian name *turkee,* for the bird.

Benjamin Franklin once wrote his daughter, Sarah, that he wished the Bald Eagle was not the bird of our land but that "the turkey is a much more respectable bird, and withal a true original Native of America."

TO ROAST A GOOSE

Take a little sage, and a small onion chopped small, some pepper and salt, and a bit of butter; mix these together, and put it into the belly of the goose. Then spit it, singe it with a bit of white paper, dredge it with a little flour, and baste it with butter. When it is done, which may be known by the legs being tender, take it up, and pour through it two glasses of red wine, and serve it up in the same dish, and apple-sauce in a bason.

The Complete Housewife, E. Smith, 1766.

BUILDING THE FIRE: *A Letter from Ruth*

Carrying the fire scoop

Dear Hannah:

The greatest trouble we have, or did have during our first winter here, was in building the fire, for the wood, having just been cut in the forest, is green, and the fire very like to desert it unless we keep a close watch. Neither mother nor I can strike a spark with flint and steel as ably as can many women in the village; therefore, when as happened four or five times, we lost our fire, one of us take a strip of green bark or a shovel, and borrowed from whosoever of our neighbors had the brightest blaze, enough of the coals to set our own hearth warm again.

Some of the housewives more skilled in the use of firearms than my mother or myself, kindle a blaze by flashing a little powder in the pan of a gun, allowing the flame to strike upon tinder, and thus be carried to shavings of dry wood. It is a speedy way of getting fire but one needs to be well used to the method, else the fingers or the face will get more of the heat than does the tinder. Father cautions us against such practice, declaring that he will not allow his weapons to remain unloaded simply for kitchen use when at any moment the need may arise for a ready bullet.

Ruth

THE FARMER'S CHOICE

Our ancestors lived on bread and broth,
And woo'd their healthy wives in home-spun cloth;
Our mothers, nurtur'd to the nodding reel,
Gave all their daughters lessons on the wheel.
Though spinning did not much reduce the waist,
It made their food much sweeter to the taste:
They plied with honest zeal the mop and broom,
And drove the shuttle through the noisy loom.
They never once complained as we do now—
"We have no girls to cook, or milk the cow;"
Each mother taught her red-cheeked son and daughter
To bake and brew, and draw a pail of water:
No damsel shunn'd the wash-tub, broom, or pail,
To keep unsoil'd a long grown finger-nail.
They sought no gaudy dress, no wasp-like form,

But ate to live, and work'd to keep them warm;
No idle youth—no tight lac'd mincing fair,
Became a living corpse for want of air!
No fidgits, faintings, fits or frightful blues;
No painful corns from wearing Chinese shoes.

Troy Almanac for 1839, Robert Wasson

SOUP

Nothing can be easier than to make a good soup if one only knows how and has the will to do it; and if one will, it is easy to know how. Considerations of economy and healthfulness make it the duty of every housekeeper to thoroughly inform herself on the few essential points in soup-making. When these are learned it will be as simple as any other duty. . . .

Soups are made with meat, fish, and vegetables, with water or milk; seasoned or flavored with any or every kind of vegetable, sweet herbs, spices, curry powder, catchups, aromatic sauces, and with some kind of fruit. They are served thin and clear, thickened with vegetables or cereals, and with or without meat.

Buckeye Cook Book, 1875

A FISH TIDBIT

Take what is left of boiled or baked fresh fish, remove the bones and skin, and warm it in hot milk enough to moisten. Turn it out on a platter. Poach three or four eggs, lay them on the fish. Mix one tablespoon of chopped parsley, a few grains of cayenne, a little salt, with two tablespoons of butter melted. Pour this evenly over the eggs, and serve at once and very hot.

The American Kitchen Magazine, 1892

TRAVEL ON THE FARM

Throughout the months when there was no snow on the ground, the horse was used to pull some sort of vehicle on wheels. But in the winter, a sleigh was used since it was much easier for a horse or a team to pull a vehicle on runners. The sleigh was used instead of the buggy and carriage, and the sled replaced the farm wagon. For rides in the sleigh, the farm family was usually equipped with a lap robe, earmuffs, wool mittens, and heavy scarfs, not to mention high boots and a foot warmer.

SLEIGH RIDING: *Diary of An Early American Housewife*

February 26, 1772—Priscilla told me that she went on a sleigh riding party while she was in Boston. It reminded me of the time that I was visiting my uncle Silas Green in Boston when I was a young girl. Joshua was also visiting some of his cousins in Boston and one day a party of young people gathered to go on a sleigh party. It was a wonderful day.

SLEIGHING PARTIES

Sleighing parties came comparatively later to the New England colonies than they did elsewhere. Sleighing had been a great thing in New York in 1704 when Madame Knight of Boston had visited that city.

Several years later, sleighing parties were begun in Boston and a young British officer, Alexander Macraby, wrote to his brother: "You can never have had a party in a sligh or slidge. I had a very clever one a few days ago. Seven slighs with two ladies and two men in each proceeded by fiddlers on horseback set out together upon a snow of about a foot deep on the roads to a public house, a few miles from town where we danced, sung, romped, and ate and drank and kicked away care from morning till night, and finished our frolic in two or three side boxes at the play. You can have no idea of the state of the pulse seated with a pretty woman mid-deep in straw, your body armed with furs and flannels, clear air, bright sunshine, spotless sky, horses galloping, every feeling turned to joy and jollity."

However, not everyone approved of sleighing parties, as we learn from a letter written by Hannah Thompson to John Mifflin in 1786: "This Slaying match Mr. Houston of Houston St gave his Daughters, Dear Papa, Dear Papa, do go us a slaying—he at last consented, told them to get ready and dress themselves warm, which they accordingly did and came running. We are ready papa. He ordered the Servants to have some burnt wine against they came back. He desir'd them to step upstairs with him before they went. As soon as they got in an Attick chamber, he threw up all the windows and seated them in two old Arm Chairs and began to whip and Chirrup with all the Spirit of a Slaying Party. And after he kept them long enough to be sufficiently cold he took them down and call'd for the Mulled Wine and they were very glad to set close to the Fire and leave Slaying for those who were too warm."

MIXED SPICE FOR RICH CAKES AND PLUM PUDDINGS

½ teaspoonful each of cloves and allspice
1 teaspoonful each of mace and grated nutmeg
3 teaspoonfuls of cinnamon

THE PERSON

Cleanliness, absolute purity of person is the first requisite in the appearance of a gentleman or lady. Not only should the face and hands be kept clean, but the whole skin should be subjected to frequent ablutions. Better wear coarse clothes with a clean skin, than silk stockings drawn over dirty feet. Let the whole skin be kept pure and sweet, the teeth and nails and hair, clean; and the last two of medium length, and naturally cut. Nothing deforms a man more than bad hair-cutting, and unnatural deformity in wearing it. Abstain from all eccentricities. Take a medium between nature and fashion, which is perhaps the best rule in regard to dress and appearance that can be given.

Ladies Indispensable Assistant, 1851

TO RAISE HYACINTHS IN WINTER

When they are put into the glasses or earth, set them into a dark closet until they sprout. If they are in glasses, do not let the water touch the bulb, by an inch. When the roots have shot down to the water, fill the glass, put in a piece of charcoal, and set them in the sun.

The Young Housekeeper's Friend, 1859

HOUSECLEANING

The latter part of the 1800's was a period in which inventors tackled all the basic housecleaning problems. The housewife was still doing most of the work by hand. She untacked the carpets, hung them out on the line, and beat them with a wicker carpet beater. Dragging along a bucket of soapy water, she got down on her knees and applied the scrubbing brush to the floor. Then she got down again and applied wax.

Carpet sweepers appeared quite early in the 1900's. The simplest models just rolled a stiff rotary brush over the carpet. Later on they contained agitators or polished metal bars that would turn the brush and help loosen the dirt in the rug. Then came a form of vacuum cleaner in which the housewife created the vacuum by means of a hand pump.

HEATING THE HOUSE

From the earliest time, most houses relied upon the open fireplace to heat the room. If they were fortunate, the bedrooms had fireplaces, else our Early Americans slept in an ice-cold room. The fireplaces were cozy and cheerful, but they used an enormous amount of wood, and most of the heat went up the chimney.

The Dutch and Swedish immigrants brought to America six-plate stoves which brought the fire out into the room to radiate heat in all directions instead of just from the front. In 1744, Benjamin Franklin developed what became known as the Franklin stove and that was the beginning of America's great stove-manufacturing industry.

POTATO SOUP

Potato soup is suitable for a cold day. Make it in the following manner: get as many beef or ham bones as you can, and smash them into fragments. Add a little bit of lean ham to give flavor. Boil the bone and ham for two hours and a half at least. The bone of a roast beef is excellent. Strain off the liquor carefully, empty the bones and debris of the ham, restore the liquor to the pot, and place again on the fire. Having selected, wash and pare some nice potatoes, cut them into small pieces and boil them in the stock till they melt away. An onion or two may also be boiled among the bones to help the flavor. I do not like thick potato soup, and I usually strain it through a hair sieve, after doing so placing it again on the fire, seasoning it with pepper and salt to taste. A stick of celery boiled with the bones is an improvement. Make only the quantity required for the day, as potato soup is best when it is newly made.

Compendium of Cookery and Reliable Recipes, 1890

MENUS FOR THE WINTER MONTHS

JANUARY

MONDAY. *Breakfast*— Milk toast, rolls, broiled steak, fried apples. *Dinner*— Roast duck, apple sauce, beef stew, mashed turnips, baked sweet potatoes, celery, plum pudding with sauce, fruit cake, oranges. *Supper*— Light biscuit, cold meat, whipped cream with preserves, sliced beef.

TUESDAY. *Breakfast*— Waffles, broiled fish, fried raw potatoes. *Dinner*— Tomato soup, salmi of duck, roasted potatoes, cabbage salad, canned pease, celery sauce, pumpkin pie. *Supper*— Toasted muffins, cold tongue, tea rusk, baked apples.

WEDNESDAY. *Breakfast*— Griddle cakes, pig's feet souse, baked potatoes. *Dinner*— Boiled bacon with cabbage, potatoes, turnips, carrots, onion sauce, chicken pie, bread pudding with sauce. *Supper*— Biscuit, cold bacon shaved, bread and milk, sponge cake and jelly.

THURSDAY. *Breakfast*—Hot rolls, corned beef hash, potato cakes. *Dinner*—Escaloped turkey, baked potatoes, pickled beets, cottage pudding, cake. *Supper*—Cold rolls, frizzled dried beef, hot buns, fried apples.

FRIDAY. *Breakfast*—Graham gems, broiled mutton, fried potatoes. *Dinner*—Turkey soup, roast beef with potatoes, stewed tomatoes, celery, rice pudding, mince pie. *Supper*—Cold buns, sliced beef, Indian pudding (corn mush) and milk, sponge cake, sauce.

SATURDAY. *Breakfast*—Steamed toast, fried mush and maple syrup, fried liver and bacon. *Dinner*—Meat pie with chili sauce, mashed turnips, stewed corn, apple dumplings with sauce. *Supper*—Tea rolls, sardines with sliced lemon, rusk, jelly.

SUNDAY. *Breakfast*—Buckwheat cakes, croquette of sausage meat, breakfast hominy. *Dinner*—Roast turkey, mashed potatoes, lima beans, cranberry sauce, celery, mince pie, ambrosia cake. *Supper*—Cold biscuit, sliced turkey, cranberry jelly, eggless cake, apple sauce.

FEBRUARY

MONDAY. *Breakfast*—Corn pone, ham and eggs, potatoes *a la Lyonnaise*. *Dinner*—Whole boiled potatoes and carrots, baked heart, stewed tomatoes, ginger puddings, fruit sauce. *Supper*—Toasted pone, cold heart sliced, plain bread, quince preserves with whipped cream.

TUESDAY. *Breakfast*—Buckwheat cakes, broiled sausage, chipped potatoes, toast. *Dinner*—Celery soup, roast mutton, mashed potatoes, baked macaroni, celery, currant jelly, chocolate blanc mange, peach pie. *Supper*—Cold mutton sliced, currant jelly, buttered toast, rusk, stewed apples.

WEDNESDAY. *Breakfast*—Graham bread, broiled bacon, fried potatoes. *Dinner*—Boiled corned beef with horse-radish sauce, boiled potatoes and turnips, slaw, hot apple pie with whipped cream, oranges and cake. *Supper*—Toasted Graham bread, cold corned beef sliced, grape jelly, hot buns, cake.

THURSDAY. *Breakfast*—Broiled fish, corn batter cakes, potato rissoles. *Dinner*—Roast beef with potatoes, tomatoes, canned beans, celery sauce, tapioca cream, cake. *Supper*—Cold roast beef, drop biscuit, floating island, tea cakes.

FRIDAY. *Breakfast*—Broiled oysters on toast, tomato sauce, flannel cakes with honey or maple syrup. *Dinner*—White soup, baked or boiled fish if fresh, or fricassee, if canned, mashed potatoes, fried parsnips, cabbage salad *a la mayonnaise,* apple dumplings with sauce. *Supper*—Dried beef shaved and warmed up in butter, hot corn mush with milk, canned fruit and light cakes.

SATURDAY. *Breakfast*—Broiled mutton chops, toast, rolls, scrambled eggs. *Dinner*—Beef soup, boiled potatoes, boiled ham, cabbage, parsnips, mixed pickles, cottage pudding with sauce, pie. *Supper*—Light biscuit, cold ham shaved, apple croutes, plain rice with sugar and cream.

SUNDAY. *Breakfast*—Sally Lunn, ham balls, fried raw potatoes. *Dinner*—Oyster soup, roast duck, baked potatoes, mashed turnips, cranberry sauce, celery, mince pie, oranges, iced cakes. *Supper*—Cold Sally Lunn, cold duck, dried apple sauce, cakes.

MARCH

MONDAY. *Breakfast*—Griddle cakes, chicken croquettes, potatoes, escaloped eggs. *Dinner*—Soup, boiled beef's tongue dressed with sauce piquante, stewed potatoes, boiled onions, pudding. *Supper*—Cold biscuit, shaved tongue, orange sauce, cake.

TUESDAY. *Breakfast*—Buttered toast, pork chops broiled, stewed potatoes. *Dinner*—Tomato soup, pigeon pie, creamed potatoes, canned corn or beans, pickles, steamed pudding with sauce, almonds, raisins. *Supper*—Graham biscuit, cold meat, apple fritters with sugar, sponge cake.

WEDNESDAY. *Breakfast*—Griddle cakes, broiled mutton chops, potatoes. *Dinner*—Beef soup, broiled steak, boiled potatoes, salsify, oyster salad, sweet pickles, transparent pudding, cream puffs, oranges. *Supper*—Plain bread, sardines with lemon, light coffee cake or sweet buns and jam.

THURSDAY. *Breakfast*—Graham bread, broiled fish, potatoes. *Dinner*—Corned beef boiled with turnips or parsnips, canned corn, boiled onions, horse-radish sauce, cocoanut pie. *Supper*—Toasted Graham bread, cold beef shaved, warm rusk and jelly.

FRIDAY. *Breakfast*—Corn batter cakes, broiled bacon, boiled eggs, or omelette souffle. *Dinner*—Veal broth, baked or boiled fish or steaks of halibut, mashed potatoes, stewed carrots, onion sauce, eggless ice cream, apples and nuts. *Supper*—Pates of fish, plain bread, toasted rusk, sweet omelette and sauce.

SATURDAY. *Breakfast*—Bread puffs, fried liver, boiled eggs, potatoes. *Dinner*—Bean soup, escaloped oysters, tomatoes, pickled beets, kiss pudding with sauce, pie. *Supper*—French rolls, cold tongue, bread fritters, cake and canned fruit.

SUNDAY. *Breakfast*—Baked beans with pork and Boston brown bread, omelette. *Dinner*—Roast turkey, potatoes, canned corn, plum jelly, Charlotte russe, sponge cake and jelly. *Supper*—Cold turkey, cranberry jelly, canned fruit, jam and cake.

Queen of the Household, 1906

HOLIDAY MENUS

LINCOLN'S BIRTHDAY DINNER

Cherry stone clams, cream of squash soup, croutons, celery, olives, oyster pie, brown bread sandwiches, baked ham, candied sweet potatoes, corn pudding, Virginia apples, spiced grapes, soda biscuits, molasses pie, Stilton cheese with salt biscuits, coffee.

VALENTINE DINNER

Lobster cocktails, cream of tomato soup in cups, roasted squab chickens, potato hearts, peas with pimiento, savory beet salad, raspberry sherbet, cocoanut frosted cake, coffee.

WASHINGTON'S BIRTHDAY SUPPER

Chicken bouillon, whipped cream, cold roast turkey, scalloped oysters, vegetable salad, pickles, jelly, soda biscuits, cherry pie with vanilla ice cream, coffee.

ST. PATRICK'S DAY SUPPER

Lobster salad in green pepper cases, bread and butter sandwiches, peppermint ice cream, coffee.

Modern Priscilla Cook Book, 1909

GRANDMA MOSES: *Hoosick Valley (from the window)*.

EARLY DAYS IN NEW AMSTERDAM

The very first comers among the Dutch settlers must, like the New England pioneers and all others, have lived in huts of rough, or at best, squared logs; but instead of being treated with biting neglect as the colonies from England were, the Dutch received every possible aid and comfort from the government of their motherland, and stores and supplies of all sorts were sent out to them as rapidly as possible and with a liberal hand, so that they were supplied with the comforts of those days sooner than their neighbors.

Even had the English so desired, they could not have given to their colonies as many comforts as could the Dutch, for the latter were far in advance in all the peaceful and domestic arts. In addition to the help which they received from the homeland, the Dutch were fortunate in being most advantageously placed for acting as "middle-men" between Holland and native American tribes, and thus they rapidly accumulated property; hence their dwellings speedily became seats of comfort, or even of luxury, as these terms were then used.

The early houses in New Amsterdam were usually a story and a half high, with the gable end fronting the street. On the first floor were low-ceilinged rooms, the most important being the kitchen and parlor. The half-story had bedrooms, and a large attic above them. The parlor was frequently furnished with a bed and used also as a guest room. The walls and furniture were kept scrupulously clean, and the floor was adorned with figures made in the sand that covered it. The attic and cellar were also important parts of the home. The attic was used as a place for drying clothes in the winter. In it there was also a kind of smokehouse, in which were hung hams, bacon, and other kinds of meat after it had been cured. The cellar was used as a storeroom for potatoes, turnips, apples, parsnips, beets, firkins of butter, barrels of salt pork, tubs of hams, and many other food supplies.

Before the front door there was a little porch called a "stoop," a word which comes from the Dutch *stoep*. From these stoops came the idea for porches and verandas. On warm evenings it was the custom for everyone to sit on the stoop, and the street had a lively appearance with all the vivacious front-door parties laughing and singing, and visiting one another.

Spring

APRIL

MAY

JUNE

There were no sidewalks, nor was there a street-cleaning department in the town administration. But every Friday the year round, the streets had to be cleaned by the householders and the refuse thrown into the river. Each resident cleaned only that part of the street which lay in front of his house.

The street lighting was done by the citizens. One householder in every seven hung out a lantern before his residence, and six of his nearest neighbors shared with him the expense of keeping the light burning.

VISIT TO NEW YORK: *Diary of An Early American Housewife*

April 10, 1772—We have just returned from a visit to New York City where we visited with some friends of ours, the Beekmans. They live in a house that had been built about one hundred years ago and it combines both Dutch and English ideas.

When the house was built land was very cheap, even more so than today, and the house was built on a large scale. In the center of the house there rose a great chimney-stack of stone, having four immense fireplaces, each striding across the corner of a wide, low-ceiled, broad-windowed room about twenty-two feet square. On either side, beyond the four rooms thus grouped around the chimney-stack, were two others of about equal dimensions, each having its own fireplace, for two more chimneys rose, one in each gable-end of the house.

The exterior walls of the upper stories were covered by overlapping cedar shingles, clipped at the corners to produce an octagonal effect. In front and at the gable-ends the second stories projected a little beyond the lower. At the rear there was but one story, the long roof sloping from the peak by a slightly inward-curving sweep till it terminated over the low, comfortable-looking stoep, upon which opened the rear windows and doors of the first floor.

All the first-floor rooms were handsomely wainscoted, and these, as well as the heavy ceiling beams, were cased and painted white. Each fireplace was surrounded by borders of tiles, all illustrating scriptural or naval scenes.

Walls of the best rooms were hung with a very substantial sort of paper, pictured with sprawling landscapes in which windmills, square-rigged boats, and very chunky cows figured prominently. According to the customs of the local people, the bedrooms were always washed with lime.

On the second floor there were six rooms across the front extending to the center of the house. The rest was left unceiled—a big open garret with square windows at each end and dormers along the sides of the roof, which sloped from the peak to the floor. In this great garret flax-hatcheling, wool-carding, and weaving went on almost without cessation, save in the very coldest weather, when the looms were abandoned.

The diamond-paned and leaded window-sashes had originally been brought from Holland when the house was first built and are very clear even today.

Of course, I must mention the door, which is different than ours. I was told that this is a typical Dutch door. The door is in two sections. The upper, in fair weather, was left open to admit light and air; the lower was kept closed to prevent stray pigs and other animals from coming into the house.

DUTCH FURNITURE

The furniture of the Dutch reflected their solid home- and comfort-loving temperaments. There were large, heavy beds, huge chests, and substantial chairs of dark wood which were sometimes elaborately carved and ornamented. There were dressers for the proud display of well-polished silver, pewter, glass, and china, most of which was never taken off the shelf.

A favorite type of bed in the early days was a closet-like bunk built into the wall, with two doors which were kept closed when the bed was not in use. Inside was a large feather bed, with a smaller one above it, and in between these two layers, like the filling in a sandwich, lay the sleeper himself. The Dutch were hospitable, and the family sitting room often boasted an auxiliary bunk for guests. There might also be a pile of skins and rugs close to the fire, known as a "Kermis bed," because at festival time the house overflowed with visitors.

Probably the most important article of furniture in the early Dutch home was the great cupboard or universal hold-all known as the "Kas." Their moldings and cornices were not infrequently heavily carved, and some had elaborate marquetry depicting familiar scenes. Others were painted. Often there were secret drawers tucked away behind the regular drawers and shelves, and the lock might be concealed by a carved piece of wood which could be swung aside. So large was the key that it "seemed more fitted to unlock a fortress than a marriage-chest." But then, these valued cupboards, stocked with household linen patiently gathered together by the women of the family over the long years, constituted an important part of the dowry.

Trader or farmer, the Dutchman's ideal was to convert the fruits of his industry into a quantity of handsome objects that bore eloquent, if mute, witness to his success and to his social standing. The shelves of the dresser were crammed with handsome pewter, fine glass, Delftware and china, and silver beakers, candlesticks, and spoons polished to the dazzling point. Typical also was the wooden spoon rack, or *lepelbortie,* with narrow shelves containing holes into which the spoons were inserted.

When the family gathered around the kitchen table, the plainest of wooden ware and pewter was used, the china making its appearance only for some special occasion, such as a tea party. Tea was a luxury, to be taken in sips from a tiny cup, alternating with nibbles at a piece of sugar loaf laid beside each plate.

CLEANLINESS

In addition to having a dresser of beautiful things which were rarely taken out, the Dutchman had a "best room" into which persons were rarely invited. But let no one imagine that the dust was allowed to accumulate there; with typical Dutch thoroughness, it was given a good cleaning once a week.

One thing is certain: in an uncleanly age, the Dutch were the cleanest people in the world. Outside of clothes brushes and hair brushes, inventories mention scrubbing brushes, dish brushes, floor brushes, rake brushes, whitening brushes, painting brushes, hearth hair brushes with brass and wooden handles, chamber brooms, hearth brooms, "Bermudian brooms with sticks," not to mention washing tubs, pails, rain water casks, sticks to hang clothes on, smoothing irons, and wicker baskets. One family owned fifty-six brushes and twenty-four pounds of soap.

ADVERTISEMENT: 1733

This is to give Notice, That Richard Noble, living in Wall Street, next Door to Abraham Van Horn's, Esq; in the City of New York, makes White-Wash Brushes, and mends all Sorts of other Brushes, at reasonable Rate: He also gives ready Money for good Hog-Bristles, at the following Rate, viz. For clean'd comb'd, and five Inches in Length, one Shilling per Pound, and for uncomb'd, six Pence.

MILADY'S DRESS

The patroon's lady or any other well-to-do woman of the colony might wear a satin or velvet gown trimmed with gold braid, a pointed bodice with full slashed sleeves showing white undersleeve, and a lace collar or stiff ruff. She also wore a long linen over-dress, open down the front to show the dress beneath. It was tied at the elbows with bands of ribbon. Later it evolved into a loose knee-length jacket, trimmed with fur.

Women of lesser degree than the patroon's wife wore as many petticoats as she, and over them a full skirt gathered at the waist. They wore little waistcoats with tight, elbow-length sleeves, and a demure folded white kerchief over their shoulders. Their fine lace, linen, or cambric caps were worn over a metal headband, trimmed with metal ornaments sometimes consisting of spirals or rosettes.

The young bride wore all the petticoats she had—they were part of her dowry and indicated the wealth of her family. Her bridal gown—that precious memento which was carefully stowed away after the wedding and handed down from mother to daughter—was of silver set with precious stones, provided her family could afford it. Otherwise it was made of cardboard, covered with gold and silver silk.

Apron and cap were indispensable to the Dutch woman's wardrobe. One New Amsterdam dame had one purple apron and four blue ones, and twenty-three cambric and linen caps.

The usual costume of peasant women and house servants consisted of short woolen petticoats with loose red or blue jackets of coarse linen, long white aprons of coarse homespun, white kerchiefs about the shoulders, and close-fitting white caps.

MADAME KNIGHT'S VISIT TO NEW YORK: 1704

"The English go very fashionable in their dress. But the Dutch, especially the middling sort, differ from our women, in their habitt go loose, wear French muches which are like a Capp and headband in one, leavin their ears bare, which are sett out with jewells of a large size and many in number; and their fingers hopp'd with rings, some with large stones in them of many Coullers, as were their pendants in their ears, which you should see very old women wear as well as Young."

A BRIDE'S DOWRY

No bride went to her new home without a large dowry. The family began to lay aside linens as soon as the child was born, and it was considered essential that a young woman be amply endowed with these worldly goods. At first thought it would seem that this custom developed from financial and social reasons. But when one reads deeper into the history of those first years, one finds that the large linen dowry was a personal necessity. Washing was done only twice a year, preceding summer and winter, and the necessity of enough linens to last the season was most essential. Later, washing was performed three and finally four times a year. With no conveniences, with the crudest of implements, and with heavy homespun linens and blankets, one can well see why these household goods went through the process of being cleaned so infrequently.

TABLE FURNISHINGS

The Dutch had appointments for the table similar to those of the people of New England, but much more silver was used since the Dutch of that period were more affluent than the pilgrims. However, pewter was universally possessed in the New Netherlands. Brass candlesticks were in great demand. Judging from the prevalence and the amount of pewter, brass, and copper listed in the old documents, the homes of the Dutch residents must have been filled with brightly shining metal articles for domestic use.

During this century, Delft potteries reached the height of their activities, and collecting this type of porcelain became a craze with the Dutch. The inventories of New Amsterdam prove that the colonists shared this luxurious taste with their relatives back in Holland. The Dutch were using more china quite a while before the New Englanders.

THE DUTCH LARDER

The Dutch were very fortunate. Their land was rich and fertile. The rye was tall, as was the barley and wheat. In fact, all the crops grew well. The Dutch readily took to the native corn, since they were fond of all cereal food.

Indian corn became a staple with the Dutch, too. Samp and samp porridge were soon their favorite dishes. Samp is Indian corn pounded to a coarsely ground powder in a mortar. Samp porridge usually boiled for a week at a time. Pork or beef and various root vegetables were added to the samp porridge, and it was then cooked slowly for at least three days. At the end of that time, it could be taken out of the pot in one chunk. Suppawn was another favorite made of thick cornmeal and milk porridge.

The river was full of fish. Lobsters, five to six feet in length, were in the bay. Crabs were large, and there also were foot-long oysters. The shad caught in the Hudson River was dried and salted. This was the result of shad being so plentiful and so cheap.

Plenty of game was to be had; passenger pigeons, wild turkeys, and venison could be bought for pennies. There also was an ample supply of partridges, wild ducks, white swans, grey geese, and pelicans.

The Dutch ate much cheese which they grated, stating that it enhanced the flavor of the food. They also had butter on their bread, which the English did not. The housewife could buy her bread in public bakeries.

There were plenty of vegetables, such as chibbals, peas, artichokes, carrots, lettuce, beets, parsnips, and radishes; pumpkins and squashes were not as widely used as in New England. There also were a variety of melons. The Dutch, in fact, are believed to be the fathers of cole slaw, shredded cabbage with vinegar and oil.

Domestic swine gave the Dutch many varied and appetizing foods, such as headcheese, while there were similar dishes made of lean meat stewed in tripe. All sorts of sausages were made from the swine.

The Dutch also used an open fire for cooking. The smoke rose into a projecting canopy that was a little lower than the ceiling but led directly into the chimney. With the Dutch penchant for concealing things, it is not surprising to learn that the canopy was covered with a ruffled, linen valence which was changed every Sunday. The utensils were the same long-handled iron ones used all over, but the Dutch also had special long-handled utensils to bake their beloved waffles and other "Baker's Meats."

The "Baker's Meats" were all sorts of cakes and breads. The bakers had to use just weights and good materials. They were ordered to bake twice a week and to charge certain prices, such as 14 stuyvers for a double coarse loaf of eight pounds, with smaller loaves at proportionate prices. Bakers were not permitted to sell sweet cakes unless they had coarse bread for sale. There were "pye-women" as well as bakers.

The Dutch were partial to various types of doughnuts and crullers fried in deep fat. Their *olijkoeck* was a doughnut of apples, citron, and raisins. Tea cakes were called "izer-cookies," since they were baked in long-handled irons called "izers" or wafer irons which had the initials of the owner impressed in the metal and thus on the cakes. These wafer irons were usually wedding presents with the initials of the bride and groom intertwined. There also were many other cakes made of chopped pork with spices, almonds, currants, raisins, and flavored with brandy.

There were many apple trees, and cider soon rivaled domestic use of the beer of the Fatherland. It was used during the winter, and in summer made a good drink diluted and sweetened and flavored with nutmeg. There also was an abundance of peaches, plums, and cherries.

Cans of buttermilk or good beer, brewed by the patroon, washed down a breakfast of suppawn and rye bread and grated cheese and sausage or headcheese. The Dutch did not use as much rum as the English, but at any transaction, private or public, there was a drink. If either party to a contract did not sign the contract, he had to furnish half a barrel of beer or a gallon of rum to assuage the pangs of disappointment.

Much beer, wine, and brandy was drunk daily. Workmen building a house were supplied with liquor to keep them contented, and the cost of the liquor was often figured into the cost of the house. When a Dutchman married, he laid in a "pipe" of Madeira. This wine was broached at his wedding feast, and for the christening of his first son. What was left of the 126-gallon pipe was finally finished by his friends at his funeral.

JAMAICA, LONG ISLAND

"Such an abundant of strawberries is in June that the fields and woods are dyed red; which the country people perceiving, instantly arm themselves with bottles of wine, cream and sugar, and instead of a coat of Mail every one take a Female upon his Horse behind him, and so rushing violently into the fields, never leave till they have disrobed them of their red colors and turned them into the old habit."

A Briefe Description of New York, Daniel Denton, 1670

WAFFLE FROLIC

"We had the wafel-frolic at Miss Walton's talked of before your departure. The feast as usual was preceded by cards, and the company so numerous that they filled two tables; after a few games, a magnificent supper appeared in grand order and decorum, but for my own part, I was not a little grieved that so luxurious a feast should come under the name of a wafel-frolic, because if this be the case I must expect but a few wafel-frolics for the future; the frolic was closed with *ten sunburnt virgins lately come from Columbus's Newfoundland,* besides a play of my own invention which I have not room enough to describe at present. However, kissing constitutes a great part of its entertainment."

Description of Wafel-Frolic, William Livingston, 1744

NEW AMSTERDAM HOUSEKEEPING

Soon after daybreak the family arose, sometimes even before the bells of the city rang, for early rising was the custom. The first to get up, as a rule, was the head of the house, who would go downstairs in his dressing gown and slippers, with nightcap on, open the door and shutters, look at the weather, and call the servant. While she lighted the fire and got things ready for breakfast, the rest of the family would get up. The maid set the table, shook up the pillows in the chairs, heated the foot warmer for the mistress, and placed the Bible before the master's chair. The family now came downstairs, washed, combed, and dressed, and took their places at the table. The servant also took her place at the end of the board. Then the father stood up and led the family in prayer, after which breakfast was eaten. After the meal and at the end of the reading of a chapter from the Bible which was done during the meal, all stood up, sang the hymn, and the father said grace.

Bread, butter, and cheese always appeared upon the table, but many families included pastries of venison and meat. Fried fish was a favorite dish at breakfast.

Burghers (who lived in the towns) seldom ate two relishes at once. Butter and cheese on a "piece" of bread was considered a wicked extravagance. With the bread, milk was drunk, and sometimes a small beer. Coffee did not make its appearance until the end of the seventeenth century.

After breakfast, everybody went her or his way—the husband to his office or his business, the boys to their offices, shops, or schools; but the girls usually helped their mother and the servant with the housework. The husband and wife attended to their special duties and hardly met except at meals or at night. Before going to market, the mistress saw that the kitchen was put in order, cooking utensils scoured, brasses polished, and floors scoured.

The mistress worked along with the servant, and after the house was in order, she in a simple dress and with a headcloth folded over her head would go to market, accompanied by the servant with the basket.

Although the Dutch housewife was a very clever cook and superintendent of the kitchen, for great occasions she called in the help of the baker, who was also a confectioner.

Toward noon the tablecloth was spread on the table. Prayers were again said at the meal. A large pewter dish with boiled food was served. Seldom were more than two or three dishes served at the noonday meal. The first cooked dish was generally "potage," made of brown and green peas, mashed with butter, ginger, and celery, or some bean dish; the second course was fish, and the third, meat or chicken.

A couple of hours after the noonday meal, the family gathered again to eat the "piece" of bread cut by the father of the house, with either cold or warm beer or water. Later, cake, fruit, and tea were added to this, as well as coffee or chocolate when available.

At the stroke of nine the maid came to spread the table. The supper was very simple, and consisted in most houses of bread, butter, and cheese; but some people had *gekookte pot* (a cooked meal), consisting of three courses. Grace was said before and after the meal. At ten o'clock, all would retire.

ADVERTISEMENT

To be sold, a good New House, with a Kitchin, and Store-House, and a good Stable, and a Lot of Ground Containing in the Front and Rear about 83 Foot in Length, about 125 Foot lying within 50 Yards of New-York Ferry, Landing on the high Road on Long Island very convenient to keep a Shop.

Whoever Inclines to Purchase the same may apply to Daniel Boutecou now living on the Premises, and agree on Reasonable Terms.

New York Gazette, June 26, 1730

MORE ABOUT NEW YORK:
Diary of An Early American Housewife

April 11, 1772—I shall now continue to write about our trip to New York City.

While we were with the Beekmans, they took us to visit their Aunt Aletta who lived in the country about 5 miles outside of the city. Since it was not easy to go into the city and visit the markets as the Beekmans did, Aunt Aletta supervised everything needed for household consumption. She and her daughters supervised the cleaning of the house and other labors around. They did not personally scrub the uncarpeted floors or tend the fires, or hatchel the flax, or card the wool, or weave the cloth, or make the soap, or chop the sausage meat, or dip the candles, or wash the linen, but they knew exactly what had to be done.

Aunt Aletta kept flocks of hens, geese, and ducks. There were no public bakeries out in the country, so she made her own bread, which was delicious to eat, especially warm.

She used leaven, which is a lump of the latest baking buried in flour and kept in a cool, dry place until needed for the next baking. Numberless were the accidents which might happen to this. A degree too cold or a trifle too damp, and the leaven would not rise, so the bread was heavy; or a degree too hot, and the leaven would ferment, and so the bread was sour. If the sponge stood too short or too long a time, or its temperature was not just right, again there was trouble. If the big brick oven was under-heated, the well-made loaves would over-rise and sour before they were sufficiently baked, or they might be removed too quickly from the oven, and the half-baked dough would fall into flat and solid masses. If the oven was over-heated, the loaves would again be heavy, for the crust would form before the bread had had time to take its last rising in the oven as it should.

Aunt Aletta superintended every step of the way, and when the bread was baked, they were full, round loaves of a brown so light as to be almost golden. I would like to bake bread so good.

MAKING SOAP: *A Letter from Ruth*

Dear Hannah:

It seems strange that some industrious person, who is not overly fine in feelings or in habits, does not take it upon himself to make soap for sale. Verily it would be better that a family like ours buy a quart of soap whenever it is needed, than for the whole house to be turned topsy-turvy because of the dirty work.

I wonder if there are in this country any girls so fortunate as not to have been obliged to learn how to make soap. I know of none in Boston, although it may be possible that in Salem, where are some lately come over from England, live those who still know the luxury of hard soap, such as can be bought in London.

For those fortunate ones I will set down how my mother and I make a barrel of soap, for once we are forced to get about the task, we contrive to make up as large a quantity as possible.

First, as you well know, we save all the grease which cannot be used in cooking, and is not needed for candles, until we have four and twenty pounds of such stuff as the fat of meat, scraps of suet, and drippings of wild turkey or wild geese, which last is not pleasant to use in food, and not fit for candles.

Well, when we have saved four and twenty pounds of this kind of grease, and set aside six bushels of ashes from what is known as hard wood, such as oak, maple, or birch, we "set the leach."

I suppose every family in Boston has a leach-barrel, which is a stout cask, perhaps one that has held pickled pork or pickled beef, and has in it at the very bottom a hole where is set a wooden spigot.

This barrel is placed upon some sort of platform built to raise it sufficiently high from the ground, so that a small tub or bucket may be put under the spigot. Then it is filled with ashes, and water poured into the top, which, of course, trickles down until it runs, or, as some say, is leached, out through the spigot, into the bucket, or whatsoever you have put there to receive it.

While running slowly through the ashes, it becomes what is called lye, and upon the making of this lye depends the quality of the soap.

Now, of course, as the water is poured upon the contents of the barrel, the ashes settle down; as fast as this comes to pass, yet more ashes are added and more water thrown in, until one has leached the entire six bushels, when the lye should be strong enough, as mother's receipt for soap-making has it, to "bear up an egg, or a potato, so that you can see a portion of it on the surface as big as a ninepence."

If the lye is not of sufficient strength to stand this test, it must be ladled out and poured over the ashes again, until finally, as will surely be the case, it has become strong enough.

The next turn in the work is to build a fire out of doors somewhere, because to make your soap in the house would be a most disagreeable undertaking. One needs a great pot, which should hold as much as one-third of a barrel, and into this is poured half of the grease and half of the lye, to be kept boiling until it has become soap.

Now just when that point has been reached I cannot say, because of not having a sufficient experience; but mother is a master hand at this dirty labor, and always has great success with it.

Of course, when one kettle-full has been boiled down, the remainder of the lye and the remainder of the grease is put in, and worked in the same manner as before.

It is possible, and we shall do so when time can be spent in making luxuries, to get soap from the tallow of bayberry plants. I have already said that we stew out a kind of vegetable tallow from bayberries with which to make candles, and this same grease, when boiled with lye as if you were making a soft soap, can be cooked so stiff that when poured into molds, it will form little hard cakes that are particularly convenient for the cleansing of one's hands.

There can be no question but that bayberry soap will whiten and soften the skin better than doe's soft soap; but the labor of making it is so disagreeable that I had rather my hands were tough and rough, than purchase a delicate skin at such an expense.

Making lye for soap

Ruth

AN OLD CAPE COD RECIPE
FOR PREPARING HADDOCK

You cut the innards out, 'an you cut the head off and that's all. You don't never bone 'em nor split 'em.

FOOD IN BROOKLYN

"Then was thrown upon the fire, to be roasted, a pail full of Gowanes oysters which are the best in the country. They are fully as good as those of England, better than those we eat in Falmouth. I had to try some of them raw. They are large and full, some of them no less than a foot long. Others are young and small. In consequence of the great quantities of them everybody keeps the shells for the burning of lime. They pickle the oysters in small casks and send them to Barbados. We have for supper a roasted haunch of venison which he had bought for three guilders and half of a sea want, that is fifteen stivers of Dutch money (fifteen cents), and which weighed thirty pounds. The meat was exceedingly tender and good and also quite fat. It had a slight aromatic flavor. We were also served with wild turkey, which was also fat and of good flavor, and a wild goose, but that was rather dry. We saw here lying in a heap a whole hill of watermelons which were as large as pumpkins."

Diaries of Labadist Missionaries, 1679

WASHING CLOTHES

The first method of washing clothes was at a nearby brook, with a stone for the washboard and a wooden club for a beater. However, in the colonies there was a wash tub in the dooryard, water heated in kettles over fires often built outdoors, and wooden washboards on which to rub.

THE WASH TUBS: *A Letter from Ruth*

Dear Hannah:
It was during this third winter that the cooper spent three days in our home, making for mother two tubs which are fair to look upon, and of such size that we are no longer troubled on washdays by being forced to throw away the soapy water in order to rinse the clothes which have already been cleansed. You may think this strange to hear me speak thus of the waste of soapy water, because you in Scrooby have of soap an abundance, while here in this new land we are put to great stress through lack of it.

It would not be so ill if all the housewives would make a generous quantity, but there are some among us who are not so industrious as others, and dislike the labor of making soap. They fail to provide sufficient for themselves, but depend upon borrowing, thus spending the stores of those who have looked ahead for the needs of the future.

Ruth

MAPLE-SUGARING TIME:
Diary of An Early American Housewife

April 16, 1772—Josh and the boys are making sugar. They are spending the next five days in the maple woods back of our house and hope to get enough sugar to last us for the year. Perhaps there will be enough sugar to sell in Boston. If the weather holds as nicely as it is at this time, we might have some of our neighbors join the men in finishing the process of making the sugar. We have not had a party for some time now. It will be good to see the neighbors again now that the winter is ending. This winter was not good; there was too much snow to get around visiting.

MAPLE-SUGARING TIME IN NEW ENGLAND

The end of the long, cold, harsh winter was hailed with the maple-sugaring, especially in Vermont, New Hampshire, and New York. The art of making maple sugar was learned by the settlers from the Indians.

In the 1700's, many inland families used no sugar but that which they made themselves from the sap of the maple. Every farmer in the districts where these trees flourished wished to have his "sugar orchard and sugaring-off." This was as much a part of the agricultural year as plowing or haymaking. On the coast, cane sugar was imported from the West Indies, but this was, of course, more expensive to the farmer than that which he could extract from his own trees.

In the northern colonies, harvesting of the sugar was begun in February or March. The maple trees were generally a few miles from the homestead, and among the trees was a cabin and a sugar house. The entire family or else the father and the sons often lived in the cabin while the sugaring went on. The best weather for sugaring was frosty nights, a westerly wind, and clear thawing days. Thawing days started the sap flowing.

The first spouts were made of sumach or elder with the pith turned out. A notch was cut in the trunk of the tree at a convenient height from the ground, usually four or five feet, and the running sap was guided by setting in the notch a semicircular basswood spout cut and set with a special tool called a tapping-gauge. In earlier days the trees were "boxed," that is, a great gash was cut across the side and scooped out and down to gather the sap. This often proved fatal to the trees and was abandoned. A trough about three feet long was placed under the end of the spout. These troughs were made deep enough to hold about ten quarts.

In later years a hole was bored in the tree with an auger, and sap buckets were used instead of troughs. The sap bucket had one protruding stave in which there was a hole so that the bucket might hang on the spout, also called the spile. The children would keep watch of the running sap, and when the buckets were full, they poured the sap into the carrying buckets.

The carrying buckets had two protruding staves, each with a hole through which a stick was run to serve as a handle. To carry these buckets, one used a shoulder yoke. Oxen were used to pull the sleds on which the buckets were placed if the sugar house was a distance from the trees and if there was still a deep snow on the ground.

Dry wood had to be gathered for the fires. It was hard work to keep them constantly supplied, so wood was often cut a year in advance. Under the huge kettles the fires were kept burning day and night for three days. Someone had to constantly watch the kettles, so shifts of watchers were formed. Although little stirring was needed, the sap was closely watched and the fires not allowed to go out. A scoop was used to stir the sugar when necessary.

The syrup was then skimmed, strained through woolen cloths, boiled again, and strained again. Each time that the process was repeated, the syrup became clearer. The number of times that it was strained depended upon the clarity of the syrup wanted.

The first run of the sap made the purest and whitest sugar, so this was made into cake form for selling by putting partitions between the large forms and placing elaborate patterns on the cakes of sugar to be sold. The sugar used by the family was usually left in large cakes to be stored in the attic or shed chamber.

The second run was darker and used only for soft sugar. After being boiled down and strained, this was poured into covered tubs near the bottom of which was a hole with a wooden stopper or plug. As the sugar hardened, a sugar molasses, called maple molasses, was drawn off and used as sweetening in cooking. The soft sugar was also kept in the attic or shed, tightly covered and the plug tight so that no ants or other tiny insects could get into the tub.

Many families lived on the proceeds of the sugar sales, since a fifty-year-old tree yielded about five pounds of sugar a year.

The sugar-making season was always greeted with delight by the boys of the household, who found in this work in the woods a wonderful outlet for the love of wild life. If the camp was near enough to the farmhouse to have visitors, the last afternoon and evening in camp was turned into a country frolic. Great sledloads of girls came out to taste the new sugar, to drop it into the snow to candy, and to have an evening of fun. The farmers also took turns inviting their neighbors to a "sugaring-off." It was said that the sugar season of New England did more to encourage marriage than almost any other industrial phenomenon in nature.

Making maple sugar

SCALLOP FRY

8 pieces bacon; 36 bay scallops; 2 eggs; 2 tablespoons water; ½ cup bread crumbs; salt; pepper; 4 sprigs of parsley; 1 lemon, sliced.

Fry bacon, drain on paper towels and cut into 1-inch squares. Reserve bacon fat in fry pan. Cut a slit in each scallop and insert 1 or 2 pieces of bacon in each slit. Beat eggs slightly with water. Roll scallops in bread crumbs, then dip into egg mixture, then again in crumbs. Heat bacon fat. Fry scallops in hot fat and season with salt and pepper to taste. Serve with parsley and lemon slices.

From An Old Long Island Favorite

WE HAVE COWS: *A Letter from Ruth*

Dear Hannah:

Can you imagine how I feasted when for the first time in four years I had milk to drink, and butter and cheese to eat?

You must not believe that we drank milk freely, as do you at Scrooby, for there are many people in Plymouth, all of whom had been hungering for it even as had I. Father claimed that each must have a certain share, therefore it is a great feast day with us when we have a large spoonful on our pudding, or to drink.

A beautiful churn was made for mother; but many a long month passed before we would get cream enough to make butter, so eager were our people for the milk. Now, however, when there are seventeen cows in this town of ours, we not only have butter on extra occasions; but twice each year mother makes a cheese.

Ruth

QUILTING: *Diary of An Early American Housewife*

April 28, 1772—Invited to a quilting party at Martha Worthington's. This will be the first time I have been away from the farm since the blizzard last month. I have many pieces to be exchanged for other cotton goods. However, I have been doing some samplers and Susan, although only 7, has made two this winter.

QUILT-MAKING IN THE COLONIES

Quilt-making during this time period was most important. The quilt was in the beginning a strictly utilitarian article, born of the necessity of providing warm cover for beds, and hangings for doors and windows that were not sufficiently set to keep out the cold of a New England winter.

Warm clothing and coverings were needed when going out on a cold winter's day, and the New England woman made quilted clothing, such as hoods, capes, and waistcoats for men, as well as quilted "petti-skirts" or underskirts.

The feminine love of color, the longing for decoration, as well as pride in the skill of needlecraft found an outlet in quilt-piecing. All the fragments and bits of stuff which were necessarily cut out in the shaping of garments helped to make the patchwork a satisfaction to the woman.

Nearly all the quilts made in America prior to 1750 were pieced quilts, and most of the quilts in New England were of woolen garments and pieces. Many of the quilts of that period were square, as the beds were wider than those of the present day.

Many were made of four blocks measuring thirty-five inches square to which was added an eighteen-inch border, making the finished quilt 108 inches square.

Although fabrics had been hard to obtain at first, with the expansion of trade calicoes, silks, and velvets were available from the Indies, England, and France. These cloths were extremely expensive, and after cutting enough material for clothing, the scraps were used to make quilts and their ornamentation.

Quilting not only provided warm coverings for beds in poorly heated homes but also filled a social need. Neighbors could be invited to a "quilting bee," and such affairs were gala events. They usually ended with supper and dancing—the men arriving when the quilting was finished.

ADVERTISEMENT

Elizabeth Boyd gives notice that she will as usual graft Pieces in knit Jackets and Breeches not to be discern'd, also to graft and foot Stockings, and Gentlemens Gloves, mittens or Muttatees made of old Stockings, or runs them in the Heels. She likewise makes Childrens Stockings out of Old Ones.

New York Gazette, April 1, 1751

RANDOM NOTE FROM A NEW YORK NEWSPAPER

Moses Slaughter, Stay Maker from London, has brought with him a Parcel of extraordinary good and Fashionable Stays of his own making, of several Sizes and Prices. The Work of them he will warrant to be good, and for Shape, inferiour to none that are made.

He lodges at present at the house of William Bradford, next Door but one to the Treasurer's near the Fly Market, where he is ready to suit those that want, with extraordinary good Stays. Or he is ready to wait upon any Lady's or Gentlewomen that please to send for him to their Houses. If any desire to be informed of the Work he has done, let them enquire of Mrs. Elliston in the Broad-Street, or of Mrs. Nichols in the Broadway, who have had his work.

SPRING IN THE FOREST

Spring in the forest provided the colonists with an assortment of wild berries, such as huckleberries, whortleberries, cranberries, gooseberries, raspberries, blackberries, boxberries, gingerberries, checkerberries, blueberries, and strawberries. The freshly picked fruits were eaten much as they are today, with cream and sugar, or baked into pies. One particularly popular fresh berry dish was a baked pudding of fresh cranberries, flour, and molasses. The cranberry was unknown in Europe before the settlement of the colonies, and early settlers named the plants bearberries, because eastern bears so frequently ate the fruit.

The settlers found that the fresh food season was short, and so most berries were sugared or otherwise preserved for future use. Berries were dried, pounded into a hard paste, and then cut into squares which were chewed like candy. The fruits were boiled with syrup or sugar to produce marmalades and jellies.

Wild elderberries, mulberries, and grapes were used for wines, and other alcoholic drinks were produced from pears, peaches, currants, and shrub roots. Wild plums were preserved to be used in the Christmas puddings.

COURTSHIP AND MARRIAGE IN NEW AMSTERDAM

Two festivals were particularly honored among the Dutch—the christening and the wedding. Parents began to provide for the future from the very birth of the child, and betrothals sometimes took place while the babies were lying in the cradle. Gold coins and medals were accumulated for dowry, silver and jewels were collected, and coffers and chests filled with linen; and as she grew up, the maiden spun and collected her linen, and made a lace collar and cuffs, her bridal gift to her future husband.

This custom of infant betrothal was naturally most prevalent among the upper classes, where wealthy alliances were of importance for political or business reasons; but in the family of the average burgher, considerable latitude of choice was allowed, and as long as the prospective bride, or groom, was not absolutely objectionable to the parents on either side, the course of true love ran fairly smoothly.

The binding nature of the betrothal in the eyes of the law is evident from many entries in the records. The offense of breaking the engagement after the publication of the banns was a very serious one. Parental consent was necessary for the publication of the banns, and to render the marriage legal.

Once married, it was impossible for husband or wife to have the bonds of matrimony broken except on the ground of unfaithfulness. Even a separation was difficult to obtain except for persistent cruelty. If one did divorce, the offending party could not remarry without permission from the authorities.

It was the custom among the wealthier classes, after formal consent had been given, to invite all relations and friends to the betrothal, where the contract was signed in the presence of a notary.

The days preceding the wedding were spent in festivity and general merrymaking. The homes of both bride and groom were beautifully decorated during the period between the betrothal and wedding ceremonies, and nearly every day a dinner was given in honor of the couple by relatives and friends. These "banns dinners" were returned by the bride and groom's "antenuptial dinner." The bride also received in state. She sat on a sort of throne while friends and relations came with congratulations and wedding gifts.

The procession to the wedding ceremony and the elaborate dinner that followed were held only by the wealthier Dutch. Poorer people were often married in numbers on the appointed day, and went on foot, sometimes preceded by the strewers, who continually strewed flowers and greens from a basket. So accompanied by a crowd of people they would walk to the church and back again.

MARGARET PHILIPSE

A merchant princess from whom many New Yorkers are descended was Margaret Hardenbrook, who married, in 1658, Rudolphus De Vries, an extensive trader of New Amsterdam, and after his death became the wife of Frederick Philipse. During her widowhood, Mrs. De Vries undertook the management of her husband's estate, which is said to have been a practice not uncommon in New Amsterdam, and was early known as a woman trader going to Holland repeatedly in her own ship as supercargo, and buying and trading in her own name. After her second marriage, Mrs. Philipse continued to manage her estate; through her thrift and enterprise, as well as his own industry, Mr. Philipse soon came to be the richest man in the colony, trading extensively with the Five Nations at Albany, and sending ships to both the East and West Indies. From this marriage was descended Mary Philipse, whose chief claim to distinction now rests upon the tradition that she was an early love of Colonel George Washington.

A CHRISTENING AND A DINNER: *A Letter from Ruth*

Dear Hannah:

The other day, we girls had a most delightful time, for there was a baby baptized in the house where are held the meetings, and one of the gentlefolks who came here with Master Higginson was to give a dinner because of his young son's having lived to be christened.

To both these festivals, Sarah and I were bidden. The christening was attended to first, as a matter of course, and, because of his so lately arrived from England, Master Winthrop was called upon to speak to the people, which he did at great length. Although the baby, in stiff dress and mittens of linen, with his cap of cotton wadded thickly with wool, must have been very uncomfortable because of the heat, he made but little outcry during all this ceremony, or even when Master Higginson prayed a very long time.

We were not above two hours in the meetinghouse, and then went to the home of Mistress White, getting there just as she came down from the loft with her young son in her arms.

Mother was quite shocked because of the baby's having nothing in his hands, and, while she is not given to placing undue weight in beliefs which savor of heathenism, declares that she never knew any good to come of taking a child up or down in the house without having first placed silver or gold between his fingers.

Of course it is not so venturesome to bring a child downstairs empty-handed; but to take him back for the first time without something of value in his little fist, is the same as saying that he will never rise in the world to the fathering of wealth.

The dinner was much enjoyed by both Sarah and me, even though the baby, who seemed to be frightened because of seeing so many strange faces, cried a goodly part of the time.

We had wild turkey roasted, and it was as pleasing a morsel as ever I put in my mouth. Then there was a huge pie of deer meat, with baked and fried fish in abundance, and lobsters so large that there was not a trencher bowl on the board big enough to hold a whole one. We had whitpot, yokhegg, suquash, and many other Indian dishes, the making of which I shall tell you about soon.

Ruth

CHEESE TOAST

Take a slice of good, rich, old cheese, cut it up into small pieces, put it into a tin or iron stew-pot, and to one cup of milk add 3 eggs; beat eggs and milk together and pour on to the cheese; set it on the stove, and when it begins to simmer stir briskly until it forms a thick curdle, then pour over the toast and carry to table.

Boston Cultivator, May 17, 1873

NEW YORK IN THE PRE-REVOLUTIONARY PERIOD, 1765-1775

The city of New York at this period was, in politics, in culture, and in social display, the capital. The Governor resided here and the General Assembly met here. The British Commander-in-Chief and the only garrison in the colonies for some years after the close of the French War added the peculiar influences which gather about military quarters.

For the high gentry, the English officials, and those of the colony in particular who had country estates in the neighborhood of New York, racing was the chief delight.

Cockfighting was a more aristocratic pastime. Good fighting cocks were advertised in the New York papers, as were cock-gaffs of silver and steel, and the sign of the Fighting-Cocks hung next door to the Exchange Coffee House.

Fox-hunting was a favorite pastime in the colony. There were foxes on this island, but the less broken grounds of Long Island afforded better running, and by permission each year three days' sport was had on the Flatland plains, the hunters meeting at daybreak during the autumn racing season.

Good living was the rule, not the exception, in this colony. Nowhere on this continent, nor perhaps on any other, was there such a profusion of native and imported products to delight the inner man as in the New York province. The dinner hour was from one to three and tea at nightfall was what today would be called "high tea." A supper invariably followed at a tavern or coffee house.

In the costume of the period the ladies wore stiff-laced bodices, skirts with deep panniers, hooped petticoats of considerable width, high-heeled colored shoes, and, later, slippers of dainty satin or white dressed kid. They carried fans of the latest pattern. Materials were rich and heavy brocades in bunches of gold and silver of the large English pattern. By day they were simple as Cinderella at the chimney-corner.

COOKING

Despite elaborate chimney systems for numerous types of ovens, baking never became the most common method of cooking. Hashes, ragouts, and the traditional boiled dinner that could be slowly stewed were undoubtedly the most widely accepted dishes, primarily because of their relative ease of preparation.

Cooking was simply another chore for the early housewife, who had scores of other daily tasks to complete while dinner was in the making. Combinations of chopped meat and vegetables could simmer unattended in the pot for several hours, during which time she attended to her other jobs.

Slow boiling was also ideal for cooking porridges, which were often mixed after supper and allowed to cook at low temperatures throughout the night. Many wild meats, which tended to be tough, also needed a long period of cooking or stewing to make them edible.

SHEEP-SHEARING: *Diary of An Early American Housewife*

June 2, 1772—The sheep are being washed today so that they can be sheared next week.

SHEEP-SHEARING

The sheep were usually washed on a fine morning in June. The sheep-shearing, which followed a few days after the washing, had its interests, too, especially for the younger members of the family. The sheep were driven home and placed in a stable; the barn floor was nicely swept. Then the poor animal, trembling with fright, was brought out and made to assume an awkward sitting posture, where, with its back toward and between the knees of the shearer, it was ready to be sheared. The shearer then parted the wool under the neck and his nimble shears worked their way close to the skin and beneath the matted wool which soon began to fall around the shoulders of the sheep. After the neck was done, the sheep was laid on its side, and soon the fleece was removed in one piece. The sheep was now so small that it did not seem to be the same animal of minutes before.

The Bride—1880's

A TROUSSEAU

Great simplicity characterized many colonial weddings, but, yielding to the sweet and wholesome instinct that has always led parents to rejoice and make merry over their children's settling for life, the colonists gradually surrounded their weddings with more ceremony and gaiety. In families where large fortunes were acquired, a handsome trousseau was usually prepared for the bride. Before the marriage of his daughter to Nathaniel Sparhawk, Sir William Pepperell wrote to England for an outfit which included:

"Silk to make a woman a full suit of clothes, the ground to be white padusoy and flowered with all sorts of coulers suitable for a young woman—another of white water *Taby* and *Gold Lace* for trimming of it; twelve yards of Green Padusoy; thirteen yards of Lace, for a woman's head dress, 2 inches wide, as can be bought for 13 s. per yard; a handsome Fan, with a leather mounting, as good as can be bought for about 20 shillings; 2 pair silk shoes, and cloggs a size bigger than ye shoe."

FLEECE: *Diary of An Early American Housewife*

June 10, 1772—The sheep have all been sheared and now it is necessary that Mother and I work on the fleece so that we might have some material ready for our heavy clothing.

Spinning

PREPARATION OF THE FLEECE

Fleece had to be opened with care and have all pitched and tarred locks, daglocks, brand, and felting cut out. These cuttings were not wasted, but were spun into coarse yarn. The white locks were carefully tossed and separated and tied into net bags with tallies to be dyed.

After the dyeing, the next process was carding into small fleecy rolls, which were now ready for spinning.

All these processes were tedious and required much skill on the part of the workers. It was a task that was not looked forward to but had to be done in order to have warm clothing for the cold New England winters.

A BABY BOY: *Diary of An Early American Housewife*

June 15, 1772—A baby boy was born to Dorothy Mullins this morning. It is a nice big boy and let us pray that he makes it to manhood. Dorothy has not been very lucky with her sons. She gave birth to six of them and only this new one is alive; the others died very young before they were two years of age. However, she does have her three lovely girls who are a great help to her.

THE BIRTH OF A BABY

Babies were born at home, in a room commonly called "the borning room" since births were so frequent. The delivery became something of a social event, with all the participants female unless the infant proved to be a boy. Midwives were always called, but, nonetheless, the neighboring women would gather to help and to hover over the mother while they kept the males at a distance.

Once the child was born, the new mother could relax for a while since there was so much help. Friends dropped in with small presents for the mother, usually pincushions. Whether or not the child was christened, his first gift of value was a christening blanket of fine cloth, often quilted and sometimes embroidered. The cradle was usually a hand-me-down unless it was the first child and the father had just fashioned one for his first-born.

There were many manuals on ways of raising children, but most of them were long on moral advice and short on practical suggestions. Farm children, once they got past the first two critical years when weaning, teething, scarlet fever and diptheria took a fearful toll, were generally healthy.

By the time the child was weaned, about two years of age, he usually sat at the family table and ate what the adults ate. The fare usually consisted of meat twice a day, vegetables of all sorts, as well as fruit and berries, pastry in abundance, homemade bread, pies and puddings. Babies drank milk, but once they were old enough to be seated at the table with the adults, they, too, had either apple cider, beer, or tea.

Rocking baby

TO ROAST A TONGUE

Take a Tongue well powdered boyl it put it stuck well with Cloves then Roast it and for the Sauce take Clarrett Crumbs of bread Sinomon & sugar boyl it then put it into the dish under the Tongue Serve it up.

Isabella Ashfield, *Her Book*, April 1, 1724

HOUSE-CLEANING *by Francis Hopkinson* (1785)

When a young couple are about to enter on the matrimonial state, a never failing article in the marriage treaty is, that the lady shall have and enjoy the free and unmolested exercise of the rights of white-washing, with all its ceremonials, privileges, and appurtenances. You will wonder what this privilege of white-washing is. I will endeavour to give you an idea of the ceremony, as I have seen it performed.

There is no season of the year in which the lady may not, if she pleases, claim her privilege; but the latter end of May is generally fixed upon for the purpose. The attentive husband may judge by certain prognostics, when the storm is nigh at hand.

If the lady grows uncommonly fretful, finds fault with the servants, is discontented with the children, and complains much of the nastiness of everything about her: these are symptoms which ought not to be neglected, yet they sometimes go off without any further effect. But if, when the husband rises in the morning, he should observe in the yard, a wheelbarrow, with a quantity of lime in it, or should see certain buckets filled with a solution of lime in water, there is no time for hesitation. He immediately locks up the apartment or closet where his papers, and private property are kept, and putting the key in his pocket, betakes himself to flight. A husband, however beloved, becomes a perfect nuisance during this season of feminine rage. His authority is superseded, his commission suspended, and the very scullion who cleans the brasses in the kitchen becomes of more importance than him. He has nothing for it but to abdicate, for a time, and run from an evil which he can neither prevent nor modify.

The husband gone, the ceremony begins. The walls are stripped of their furniture—paintings, prints, and looking-glasses lie in huddled heaps about the floors: the curtains are torn from their testers, the beds crammed into windows, chairs and tables, bedsteads and cradles crowd the yard; and the garden fence bends beneath the weight of carpets, blankets, cloth cloaks, old coats, under-petticoats, and ragged breeches.

The ceremony completed, and the house thoroughly evacuated, the next operation is to smear the walls and ceilings with brushes, dipped in a solution of lime called white-wash; to pour buckets of water over every floor, and scratch all the partitions and wainscoats with hard brushes, charged with soft soap and stone-cutter's sand.

The windows by no means escape the general deluge. A servant scrambles out upon the penthouse, at the risk of her neck, and with a mug in her hand, and a bucket within reach, dashes innumerable gallons of water against the glass panes, to the great annoyance of passengers in the street.

I have been told that an action at law was once brought against one of these water nymphs, by a person who had a new suit of clothes spoiled by this operation: but after long argument it was determined, that no damages could be awarded; inasmuch as the defendant was in the exercise of a legal right, and not answerable for the consequences. And so the poor gentleman was doubly non-suited; for he lost both his suit of clothes and his suit at law.

These smearings and scratchings, these washings and dashings, being duly performed, the next ceremonial is to cleanse and replace the distracted furniture. You may have seen a house-raising, or a ship-launch—recollect, if you can, the hurry, bustle, confusion, and noise of such a scene, and you will have some idea of this cleansing match. The misfortunate is, that the sole object is to make things clean. It matters not how many useful, ornamental, or valuable articles suffer mutilation or death under the operation. A mahogany chair and a carved frame undergo the same discipline: they are to be made clean at all events; but their preservation is not worthy of attention. For instance: a fine large engraving is laid flat upon the floor; a number of smaller prints are piled upon it, until the superincumbent weight cracks the lower glass—but this is of no importance. A valuable picture is placed leaning against the sharp corner of a table; others are made to lean against that, till the pressure of the whole forces the corner of the table through the canvas of the first. The frame and glass of a fine print are to be cleaned; the spirit and oil used on this occasion are suffered to leak through and deface the engraving—no matter! If the glass is clean and the frame shines it is sufficient—the rest is not worthy of consideration. An able arithmetician hath made a calculation, founded on long experience, and proved that the losses and destruction incident to two white-washings are equal to one removal and three removals equal to one fire.

This cleansing frolic over, matters begin to resume their pristine appearance; the storm abates, and all would be well again: but it is impossible that so great a convulsion in so small a community should pass over without producing some consequences. For two or three weeks after the operation, the family are usually afflicted with sore eyes, sore throats, or severe colds, occasioned by exhalations from wet floors and damp walls.

LIFE IN THE YOUNG REPUBLIC—THE EARLY 1800'S

CLOTHING: About 1795 a change took place in the fashionable dress of women. Instead of the rich, heavy brocades and damasks, soft, clinging muslin, gauze, or similar materials were used. Skirts were narrower and shorter, reaching only to the ankles. The bodice was very short and had a low neck. Sometimes a gauze or muslin handkerchief was draped over the shoulders. These gowns were either sleeveless or had short puff sleeves, sometimes with long sleeves attached to the puffs.

When it was warm outdoors, women wore long scarves reaching to the feet, and long cloaks when it was cold. Slippers, for indoors and out, were light and had no heels.

The hair was dressed in loose curls, either hanging about the shoulders or caught up with ribbons or combs. Sometimes it was lightly powdered. Hats were very large and were tied under the chin; turbans were popular. Older women wore caps.

FOOD: Food was distinguished by its abundance rather than by its quality. Corn, most often in the form of corn bread, or "rye and Injun," which was the bread made of mixed corn and rye, was still the chief staple of the American diet. Except among the well-to-do, salt pork was the staple meat; in many parts of the country it was served three times a day. In those days there was no way of preserving meat except by salting or smoking. Hogs were plentiful and cost nothing to care for, since they could be allowed to run loose and pick up their own food. A hog slaughtered by the farmer could be salted and eaten by the family before it spoiled.

There was always an abundance of potatoes, squash, turnips and beans, but some of the vegetables familiar today, such as cauliflower, rhubarb, and eggplant, were unknown. The tomato was grown for ornamental purposes only, as it was thought to be poisonous. It was called the "love apple." Fruit was abundant but inferior in quality to that of today. Pears, peaches, plums, and cherries were dried for winter consumption; apples were made into cider. Strawberries and raspberries grew wild. Exotic fruits like oranges and bananas were found only on the tables of the wealthy.

In New England, especially among the common people, the three daily meals were very much alike. At each of them pea and bean porridge, salt pork, cornmeal with milk, and perhaps dried or salted fish appeared practically every day in the year. Of course, the menu of the New England merchant or banker showed a greater variety of tasty dishes.

The Southern gentleman, with numerous slaves to grow, cook and serve his food, paid more attention to what appeared on his table, which groaned under a burden of various kinds of soups; turkey, ham, chicken, bacon, beef, mutton; sweet potatoes prepared two or three different ways; hot bread and hot biscuits, muffins and corn bread; jellies, relishes, and pastries; wines and liquors.

North or South, there were still few stoves; food was usually prepared in the open fireplace.

SPRING

Every season of the year had its own tasks and triumphs for our American housewife. The only thing that changed the weekly routine of work—in fact life itself—was the coming of a new season.

Spring was a period in which life came back into the trees, the snow was melting away, animals were being born, such as the spring lambs and sheep. This was the time of the year when the housewife dug up the horseradish root, picked the dandelion greens, brewed spring tonic, and opened the windows and started the annual spring housecleaning after a winter of being shut indoors. Seeds were put into a cold frame. Visiting started up again with friends coming over, while the village seamstress would pull in to stay a week or so and help get all the children fixed up. This was also the calling time of the peddler, the scissors grinder, and the tramp. But above all, the two big occasions were (1) the making of maple sugar, and (2) arrival of the seed catalog.

The making of the maple sugar was a big event which, as described earlier, almost always ended with a sugaring-off party and maple syrup being poured over dishes of snow.

After 1800, spring also heralded the arrival of the Shakers, a religious sect. The Shakers made trips through the farm country peddling seeds and their well-built hickory and maple splint-bottom chairs. Shaker seed was considered the best in America, and its salesmen went from place to place selling it.

However, in the late 1800's, the seed catalog for mail order buying began to replace the Shakers'.

SPINACH TARTS

Scald some spinach in boiling water, and then drain it quite dry; chop it, and stew it in some butter and cream, with a very little salt, some sugar, some bits of citron, and a very little orange-flower water. Put it into a very fine puff paste, and let it be baked in a moderate hot oven.

The Whole Art of Confectionary, 1831

FARMER'S ALMANAC, 1840

LOVE-MAKING

Most worthy of admiration,
After a long consideration
And serious meditation,
Of the great reputation
You have in this region;
I have a strong inclination
To become your relation.
I am now making preparation
To remove my habitation
To a more convenient situation,
To pay you adoration,
By more frequent visitation.
If this kind of oblation
Be but worthy of observation,
It will be an obligation
Beyond all moderation.
Believe me in every station
From generation to generation.

Yours, &c.

THE LADY'S ANSWER

I received your adoration,
With much delineration,
And some consternation,
At the seeming infatuation
That seized your imagination,
When you made such a declaration,
On so slender a foundation;
But on examination,
Supposed it done from ostentation.
To display an education
Or rather multiplication
Or words of the same termination,
Though with great variation
And different signification,
Which, without disputation,
May deserve commendation;
And I think imitation
A sufficient gratification.

Yours, &c., Jane

THE SEAMSTRESS

Before the Civil War and even shortly after, most clothing was made either by a housewife, a grandmother, a spinster daughter, or an individual called a needle-woman, modiste, semptress, or seamstress. Known today as a dressmaker, she either went to the customer's home with her needles, pins, threads, thimbles, scissors, beeswax, and tape measure and did her work in a spare bedroom or parlor, or else she had a small shop to which customers brought their materials and had their fittings.

MOTHER'S ADVICE TO HER DAUGHTER ON THE DAY OF HER MARRIAGE

Now Polly, as you are about to leave us, a few words seem appropriate to the occasion. Although I regret the separation, yet I am pleased that your prospects are good. You must not think that all before you are Elysian fields. Toil, care, and troubles are the companions of frail human nature. Old connexions will be dissolved by distance, by time, and death. New ones are formed. Everything pertaining to this life is on the change.

A well cultivated mind, united with a pleasant, easy disposition, is the greatest accomplishment in a lady. I have endeavored, from the first to the present moment, to bring you up in such a manner as to form you for future usefulness in society. Woman was never made merely to see and be seen; but to fill an important space in the great chain in nature, planned and formed by the Almighty Parent of the universe. You have been educated in the habits of industry, frugality, economy, and neatness, and in these you have not disappointed me.

It is for the man to provide, and for the wife to take care and see that everything within her circle of movements is done in order and season; therefore let method and order be considered important. A place for everything and everything in its time and place, are good family mottos.

Farmer's Almanack, 1842, Robert B. Thomas

FRICANDEAU WITH SPINACH

Neatly trim a nice piece of fillet or cushion of veal. Place in a large stew-pan a layer of slices of bacon, then some carrots and onions, cut in slices, with a bundle of sweet herbs, pepper, salt, and spices to taste; lay the piece of veal in the middle, and moisten with about a pint of stock. Let the meat stew gently for three or four hours, basting the top occasionally. Then strain off the gravy, put it into a small saucepan, skim off superfluous fat, add to it a little butter, mixed smooth with a small quantity of flour, and let the gravy reduce nearly to a glaze; pour it over the meat, the top of which should be previously browned with a salamander if necessary, and serve with a border of spinach.

Godey's Lady's Book and Magazine, 1862

BEEF SANDERS

Mince cold beef small with onions, add pepper and salt, and a little gravy; put into a pie-dish until about three parts full. Then fill up with mashed potatoes. Bake in the oven or before the fire until done a light brown. Mutton may be dressed in the same way.

Peterson's Magazine, March 1866

LOVE

We distinguish four seasons in love. First comes love before betrothal, or spring; then comes the summer, more ardent, and fiercer, which lasts from our betrothal to the altar; the third, the richly laden, soft, dream autumn, the honey-moon; and after it the winter, bright, clear winter—when you take shelter by your fireside from the cold world without, and find comfort and pleasure there. In each season the beauties seem supremely beautiful, and add to life all its sweetness.

Farmer's Almanac, 1869, Samuel Hart Wright

EASTER CAKES

One pound flour, nine ounces of butter, five ounces currants, five ounces white sugar, the yolks of three and white of two eggs, cinnamon and nutmeg to flavor. Bake as flat biscuits in a moderate oven.

New England Fireside, September 1880

HOUSECLEANING

The following remark we consider worth fifty dollars in any family, in city or country, and we commend it to all housekeepers, old and young: "The best way to clean a house, is to keep it clean by a daily attention to small things, and never allow it to get into such a state of dirtiness and disorder as to require great and periodical cleanings, which turn comfort out of doors."

The Old Farmer's Almanack, 1855, Robert B. Thomas

Polishing the andirons

SPRING HOUSECLEANING

In all households there are certain periods in which the comfort of the family is subordinate to the good of the cause. One of these periods has arrived. Certain housekeepers take work, as some children do the measles, "hard." Others go through with a vast amount without allowing the machinery to be visible.

There is no need of turning everything upside down at once. Clean little by little, finishing one room before beginning another, even if it is more convenient to have all the carpets taken up at the same time.

Do not be afraid to give away or sell cast off clothing for which you have no need. Too much trash is carefully hoarded each year, on the chance that "it may come in handy some day," and old clothing is stored away in drawers and boxes to become a nest in which moths may breed, which ought to have been given away.

Household, April 1884

FOR THE COMPLEXION

If ladies use anything, the following are the best and most harmless: Blanch one-fourth pound best Jordan's almonds, slip off the skin, mash in a mortar, and rub together with the best white soap for fifteen minutes, adding gradually one quart of rose-water;

or clean fresh rain-water may be used. When the mixture looks like milk, strain through fine muslin. Apply after washing with a soft rag. To white the skin and remove freckles and tan, bathe three times a day in a preparation of three quarts of alcohol, two ounces cologne, and one of borax, in proportion of two tea-spoons mixture to two table-spoons of soft water.

Ladies' Home Cook Book, 1896

HEAVE OFFERING

A Quaker invited a tradesman to dine with him, whom he treated with an excellent dinner, a bottle of wine, and a pipe of tobacco. His guest, after drinking pretty freely, became extremely rude to his host, insomuch that the Quaker's patience was at length exhausted, and he rose up and addressed him in the following words—"Friend, I have given this meat offering and drink offering, and burnt offering, and for thy misconduct, I will give thee a heave offering" and immediately threw him into the street out of the parlor window.

New Jersey Almanac, 1832, David Young

HOPPING JOHN

It is said in the South that without a dish of Hopping John, which is a combination of rice and black-eyed peas and bacon, on New Year's Day, a year of bad luck will follow. The name may have been derived from a custom that children must hop once around the table before the dish is served.

DUTCH OVEN

The Dutch oven was another place for baking bread. This was the shallow, three-legged kettle with a bail handle and a cover with a rim. Placed in the embers and covered over with them, it baked in the same slow way as the brick oven.

Baking in embers was the earliest and only way known to primitive people. The Dutch oven was one of the first kettles and appeared before the brick oven was added to the open fireplace.

A NEW OVEN: *A Letter from Ruth*

Dear Hannah:

I must tell you how we happen to have an oven, when there has been only the big fire-place in which to cook our food. Mistress White and Mistress Tilley each brought from Leyden, in Holland, what some people call a "roasting kitchen," and you can think of nothing more convenient. It is made of thin iron like unto a box, the front of which is open, and the back rounded as is a log. It is near to a yard long, and stands so high as to take all the heat from the fire which would otherwise be thrown out into the room. In it we put our bread, pumpkins, or meat and set it in front of and close against a roaring fire. The back or rounded part is then heaped high with hot ashes or live embers, and that which is inside must of necessity be cooked. At the very top of the oven is a small door which can be opened for the cook to look inside, and one may see just how the food is getting on without disturbing the embers.

We often borrow of Mistress Tilley hers, and father has promised to send by the first ship that comes to this harbor for one that shall be our very own.

Ruth

BUNDLING

Early marriage was encouraged and there was a tolerance of premarital intimacy in the early days of the colonies.

Whether the Dutch or the English invented bundling nobody seems quite certain, but by the late eighteenth century, it was an accepted part of courtship in New England and the middle colonies.

In warm months, lovers could walk off into the woods or meet in the barn or the spring house, but on cold or stormy nights they could be together only indoors—and it was pretty crowded around the fireplace. As a result of a genuine wish to hasten the courtship, an invitation might have been given to the young man to stay and share the girl's bed; it was usually the only place where the boy could have slept, and the center board kept for such occasions theoretically discouraged close intimacy.

One obvious advantage was that the parents knew where the girl was and who was with her, whether or not the center board remained in place. If the bride was pregnant at her wedding, the ceremony sanctified it and, besides, bearing children was a woman's duty.

In colonies where bundling was not a practice, "natural children" were quite numerous.

A BRIDE IN NEW YORK, 1800

My head is almost turned, and yet I am very happy. I am enraptured with New York. You cannot imagine anything half so beautiful as Broadway, and I am sure you would say I was more romantic than ever, if I should attempt to describe the Battery, —the fine water prospect,—you can have no idea how refreshing in a warm evening. The gardens we have not yet visited; indeed, we have so many delightful things to see 'twill take me forever. My husband declares he takes as much pleasure in showing them to me as I do in seeing them; you would believe it if you saw him.

I went shopping yesterday, and 'tis a fact that the little white satin Quaker bonnets, cap-crowns, lined with pink or blue or white, are the most fashionable that are worn. But I'll not have one, for if any of my old acquaintance should meet me in the street, they would laugh: I would if I were they.

I have been to two of the Columbia gardens, near the Battery, a most romantic place, it is enclosed in a circular form and has little rooms and boxes all around, with chairs and tables, these full of company; the trees are all hung with lamps, twinkling through the branches; in the centre is a pretty little building with a fountain playing continually, and the rays of the lamps on the drops of water gave it a cool sparkling appearance that was delightful. This little building, which has a kind of canopy and pillars all around the garden, had festoons of colored lamps, that at a distance looked like large brilliant stars seen through the branches; and placed all around were marble busts, beautiful little figures of Diana, Cupid and Venus, which by the glimmering of the lamps, partly concealed by the foliage, give you an idea of enchantment.

As we strolled through the trees, we passed a box that Miss Watts was in. She called to us, and we went in, and had a charming refreshing glass of ice cream, which has chilled me ever since. They have a fine orchestra and have concerts here sometimes.

We went on toward the Battery. This is a large promenade by the shore of the North River: there are rows and clusters of trees in every part, and a large walk along the shore, almost over the water, gives you such a fresh delightful air, that every evening in summer it is crowded with company. Here, too, they have music playing in boats on the water of a moonlight night.

I am in raptures, as you may imagine, and if I had not grown sober before I came to this wonderful place, it would have turned my head.

Reprinted from an Old Valentine Manual

ODD SCRAPS FOR THE ECONOMICAL

If you would avoid waste in your family, attend to the following rules, and do not despise them because they appear so unimportant: 'many a little makes a mickle.'

Look to the grease-pot, and see that nothing is there which might have served to nourish your own family, or a poorer one.

As far as is possible, have bits of bread eaten up before they become hard. Spread those that are not eaten, and let them dry, to be pounded for puddings, or soaked for brewis. Brewis is made of crusts and dry pieces of bread, soaked a good while in hot milk, mashed up, and salted, and buttered like toast.

Make your own bread and cake. Some people think it is just as cheap to buy of the baker and confectioner; but it is not half as cheap. True, it is more convenient; and therefore the rich are justifiable in employing them; but those who are under the necessity of being economical should make convenience a secondary object. In the first place, confectioners make their cake richer than people of moderate income can afford to make it; in the next place you may just as well employ your own time, as to pay them for theirs.

Indian meal and rye meal are in danger of fermenting in summer; particularly Indian. They should be kept in a cool place, and stirred open to the air, once in a while. A large stone, put in the middle of a barrel of meal, is a good thing to keep it cool.

Spots in furniture may usually be cleansed by rubbing them quick and hard, with a flannel wet with the same thing which took out the color; if rum, wet the cloth with rum, &c. The very best restorative for defaced varnished furniture, is rotten-stone pulverized, and rubbed on with linseed oil.

New iron should be very gradually heated at first. After it has become inured to the heat, it is not as likely to crack.

If you happen to live in a house which has marble fire-places, never wash them with suds; this destroys the polish, in time. They should be dusted; the spots taken off with a nice oiled cloth, and then rubbed dry with a soft rag.

If you wish to preserve fine teeth, always clean them thoroughly after you have eaten your last meal at night.

Keep a bag for odd pieces of tape and strings; they will come in use. Keep a bag or box for old buttons, so that you may know where to go when you want one.

Use hard soap to wash your clothes, and soft to wash your floors. Soft soap is so slippery, that it wastes a good deal in washing clothes.

The American Frugal Housewife, 1844

MENUS FOR SPRING EATING

APRIL

MONDAY. *Breakfast*—Rolls, veal chops, fried raw potatoes. *Dinner*—Rice soup, roast beef, turnips, potatoes, tomato sauce, pickled oysters, baked custard pie. *Supper*—Cold rolls, omelette, cold beef sliced, cake and jam.

TUESDAY. *Breakfast*—Muffins, fried liver, fried potatoes. *Dinner*—Mutton soup, mutton garnished with eggs, pickles, creamed potatoes, canned tomatoes, bread pudding with sauce. *Supper*—Toasted muffins, sliced mutton, sponge cake and jelly.

WEDNESDAY. *Breakfast*—Flannel cakes, minced mutton or broiled chops, breakfast potatoes. *Dinner*—Roast pork, apple sauce, mashed potatoes, fried parsnips, lettuce, lemon pudding, jelly cake. *Supper*—Yankee dried beef, soda biscuit and honey, floating island.

THURSDAY. *Breakfast*—Sally Lunn, veal cutlets, potato cakes. *Dinner*—Baked stuffed heart, potatoes, turnips, canned corn, pickled eggs, cup custard, peach tapioca pudding. *Supper*—Light biscuit, cold sliced heart, bread fritters with sugar, cake and sauce.

FRIDAY. *Breakfast*—French rolls, broiled fish if salt, fried, if fresh, fried raw potatoes, tomato sauce. *Dinner*—Soup, baked or boiled fresh fish, mashed potatoes, canned peas or beans, lettuce, onions, English pudding, jelly tarts. *Supper*—Cold rolls, bologna sausage sliced, steamed crackers, cake and preserved fruit.

SATURDAY. *Breakfast*—Batter cakes, broiled chops, scrambled eggs, potato rissoles. *Dinner*—Bean soup, broiled beefsteak, spinach, potatoes, pickled beets, pudding with sauce, oranges and cake. *Supper*—Toasted bread, cold tongue sliced, hot buns and marmalade.

SUNDAY. *Breakfast*—Baked beans and Boston brown bread, omelette with parsley. *Dinner*—Vermicelli soup, baked shad or croquettes of canned lobster, broiled squabs or pigeon pie, mashed potatoes, turnips, asparagus, spring cresses, dressed lettuce, grape jelly, custard pie. *Supper*—Plain bread, canned salmon, cold buns, jelly, sponge cake.

MAY

MONDAY. *Breakfast*—Gems, dry toast, potato cakes, broiled beefsteak. *Dinner*—Roast of mutton with potatoes, canned tomatoes, rhubarb sauce, baked custards, fruit cake. *Supper*—Cold biscuit, sliced mutton, currant jelly, sweet buns, cream.

TUESDAY. *Breakfast*—Corn cakes, fried pickled tripe, scrambled eggs, potatoes. *Dinner*—Boiled beef with soup, whole potatoes, asparagus with eggs, cocoanut pudding, jelly. *Supper*—Plain bread, cold beef, toasted buns with strawberry jam or canned fruit, cake.

WEDNESDAY. *Breakfast*—Dropped eggs on toast, broiled ham, potatoes. *Dinner*—Boiled tongue with Chili sauce, fricasseed potatoes, cresses, boiled asparagus, ice-cream, sponge cake. *Supper*—Tea biscuits, shaved tongue, sago jelly, lady cake.

THURSDAY. *Breakfast*—Graham bread, fried mutton chops, fried raw potatoes. *Dinner*—Asparagus soup, roast of veal with potatoes, stewed onions, pickled beets, cake, orange float. *Supper*—Toasted Graham bread, sliced veal, tea rusk, lemon jelly.

FRIDAY. *Breakfast*—Muffins, broiled beefsteak, poached eggs, chipped potatoes. *Dinner*—Baked or boiled fish (if large, or fried small fish), boiled potatoes in jackets, lettuce salad, custard pie. *Supper*—Toasted muffins, cold rusk with strawberries, or marmalade, cake.

SATURDAY. *Breakfast*—Bread puffs with maple syrup, fricasseed potatoes, croquettes of fish. *Dinner*—Boiled leg of mutton, mint sauce, asparagus, boiled macaroni, potatoes, bread pudding. *Supper*—Cold rolls, cold mutton sliced, plain boiled rice with cream and sugar.

SUNDAY. *Breakfast*—Rice waffles, mutton croquettes, boiled eggs, fried raw potatoes. *Dinner*—Soup, roast beef, clam pie, new potatoes, tomatoes, dressed lettuce, young beets, strawberry cream and snow custard, coffee and macaroons. *Supper*—Light rolls, cold beef, cake and jelly, or strawberries.

JUNE

MONDAY. *Breakfast*—Oranges, French rolls, broiled liver, scrambled eggs. *Dinner*—Roast beef, mashed potatoes, beets, salmon salad, boiled rice with cream. *Supper*—Plain bread, Graham bread, bologna sausage, rusk with berries.

TUESDAY. *Breakfast*—Rice cakes, lamb chops, boiled eggs, fried potatoes. *Dinner*—Boiled beef's tongue (fresh) served with Chili sauce, baked potatoes, young beets, lettuce dressed, raspberry cream, cake. *Supper*—Rolls, sliced beef's tongue, cheese, toasted rusk, berries.

WEDNESDAY. *Breakfast*—Graham gems, muffins, beefsteak, potato cakes. *Dinner*—Soup of stock boiled yesterday with tongue, chicken pie, mashed potatoes and turnips, spinach, lettuce, cream fritters with sauce. *Supper*—Toasted muffins, cold chicken pie, cake and strawberries.

THURSDAY. *Breakfast*—Sally Lunn, veal cutlets, potatoes, radishes. *Dinner*—Ragout of lamb, mashed potatoes, asparagus, lettuce, lemon pudding, pie. *Supper*—Rolls, bread, cold sliced lamb, sliced tomatoes, Swiss cakes, berries.

FRIDAY. *Breakfast*—Rolls, breakfast stew, potatoes or tomatoes. *Dinner*—Soup, fresh fish fried or baked, mashed potatoes, asparagus, beet salad, rice pudding with sauce and cake, oranges. *Supper*—Cold rolls, dried beef chipped, custard cake with fruit or berries.

SATURDAY. *Breakfast*—Graham gems, croquettes of fish or breaded veal cutlets, potatoes, escaloped eggs. *Dinner*—Ham boiled with greens, potatoes, beets, young onions, Eglantine pudding, Italian cream. *Supper*—Toasted gems, cold ham, oatmeal with cream, cake and jelly.

SUNDAY. *Breakfast*—Light rolls, broiled beefsteak, sliced tomatoes, omelets. *Dinner*—Vegetable soup, baked chicken, mashed potatoes, green pease, pickled beets, Bavarian cream with strawberries. *Supper*—Cold rolls, cold chicken, toast with jelly, fruit.

Queen of the Household, 1906

MENUS FOR PEOPLE OF LIMITED MEANS

Sunday's Dinner: Roast beef, potatoes, greens, and yorkshire pudding.
Monday's Dinner: Hashed beef, potatoes, and bread pudding.
Tuesday's Dinner: Broiled beef and bones, vegetables, apple pudding.
Wednesday's Dinner: Fish, if cheap, chops, vegetables, pancakes.
Thursday's Dinner: Boiled pork, pea pudding, greens, rice pudding.
Friday's Dinner: Pea soup, remains of pork, and baked batter pudding.
Saturday's Dinner: Stewed steak with suet dumpling, and rice in a mould with sauce.

The Practical Housekeeper, Mrs. Ellet, 1857

Author's note: Imagine a family of limited means trying to tackle the above.

MENUS FOR THE HOLIDAYS

LENTEN DINNER

Clam and corn soup, bread rings, egg and pimento tamales, baked stuffed haddock, hollandaise sauce, French fried potatoes, boiled Brussels Sprouts, apple and chestnut salad, danish custard, crackers, cheese, coffee.

EASTER BREAKFAST

Strawberry and rhubarb cup, fried chicken, Julienne potatoes, fresh asparagus, hollandaise sauce, tomato and pineapple salad, hot biscuits, sponge cake baskets filled with caramel flavored whipped cream, coffee.

EASTER DINNER

Chicken soup, bread rings, broiled trout, roast spring lamb, mint sauce, new potatoes, boiled green peas, dressed lettuce, cheese eggs, lemon ice, currant wafers, boiled salted almonds, bonbons, coffee.

What to Have for Dinner, Fannie Farmer, 1905

GRANDMA MOSES: *July Fourth.*

Summer

THE QUAKERS

The Quakers broke away from the Church of England because they felt that all men were equal before God and that no man could set himself above his fellowmen. This meant that they would not take off their hats even to the King. They felt no need for the sacraments of Communion and Baptism, and these beliefs outraged almost everyone.

William Penn, the son of a prominent admiral of the Royal Navy, was converted to this belief in 1667, and his father was both shocked and angry when he heard the news of his conversion, for the Quakers at this time were one of the most disliked religious groups in England. But Penn went his own way. His father finally forgave him and left him a large inheritance.

Part of Penn's inheritance was a debt that Charles II had owed his father. In place of the money, the King in 1681 gave Penn a charter granting him full ownership, thus making him proprietor, of a huge grant of land in the New World. On this land Penn founded a colony to which the King gave the name Pennsylvania. As a proprietor, Penn had power over this proprietary colony almost as great as the King's power over the Royal colonies.

Pennsylvania had no coastline. Penn solved this problem in 1682 by asking for, and receiving, another grant of land to the south, on the west bank of Delaware Bay. This new land, later called Delaware, was for many years referred to as "the lower counties." Until the Revolutionary War, both grants remained in the hands of the Penn family, which governed them as Separate Colonies.

Penn settled Philadelphia first with the Quakers. Philadelphia was planned according to Quaker principles, with each man having space and freedom, and no man's house being larger than his neighbor's. However, by the middle of the eighteenth century, Philadelphia was the largest city in the English colonies, and much of the simplicity and soberness of the Quaker town was forgotten.

The first Quaker colonists dug themselves caves in the river bank where Philadelphia was to be. As the town grew, it was laid out in neat rectangular blocks. The early Quaker dwelling usually had four rooms and an attic, with perhaps a separate kitchen out back. It was built of brick with painted woodwork. The windows were some of the first sash windows in America that slid up and down.

The Quaker was by preference a town dweller and was usually engaged in business or in some other distinctly town occupation. A description of Philadelphia: "There were many drab-coated men, and there were elderly women, in gowns of drab or gray, with white silk shawls and black silver-covered cardboard bonnets. Here and there a man or woman was in gayer colors or wore buckles, and some had silver buttons; but these were rare."

THE HOUSEHOLD AND FOOD IN PHILADELPHIA

The women who were at the head of the old Philadelphia homes were usually good housewives, for in that day more attention was paid to educating a girl in housework and homemaking than in studies at school. It was considered to be of far greater value for a young girl to know how to spin, knit, sew, and cook than that she should be familiar with literature or be able to scan a line of Latin verse. The average mother took great pride in having her floor spotless, in making the clothing for her children as well as for her husband, and in collecting china, brass, pewter, or possibly silver for her pantry shelves.

The ordinary kitchen was apt to contain some modest supply of furnishings such as that sold in 1760 to Thomas Potts, owner of the house in which Washington later made his headquarters at Valley Forge: "A large copper sauce pann; a small dome, 8 shillings; a pair of Brass Candlesticks, 15 shillings; a pair of Rose Blanketts, 46 shillings; 6 china bowls, 23 shillings 6 pence; a pr. of Snuffers, 2 shillings 6 pence; 2 Brush, 2 shillings 9 pence; a pr. Iron Candlesticks, 2 shillings; 2 China bowles, 5 shillings; 3 saucers, 2 shillings 3 pence; a Looking Glass, 54 shillings; a dozen Knives and Forks, 7 shillings; 6 yards of Drapery, 11 shillings; a dozen Plates, 32 shillings; 6 hardkettle porringers, 15 shillings; a dozen spoons, 6 shillings; a trunk, 18 shillings; a cotton Counterpane, 57 shillings; ½ dozen Chairs, 40 shillings; 3 galls. of Spirit, 22 shillings; 3 silver spoons, 66 shillings 10 pence; a Bedsted, 40 shillings; Fire shovel and Tongs, 10 shillings."

The cleanliness of Philadelphia homemakers is shown by this excerpt from a magazine article of the early 1800's: "There is another cherished custom peculiar to the city of Philadelphia and nearly allied to the former. I mean that of washing the pavement before the doorway every Saturday evening. I at first took this to be a regulation of the police, but, on further enquiry, find it to be a religious rite in which the numerous sectarians of the city profoundly agree.

"The ceremony begins about sunset, and continues till about ten or eleven at night. It is very difficult for a stranger to walk the streets on these evenings. He runs a continual risk of having a bucket of water thrown against his legs, but a Philadelphia born is so accustomed to this danger that he avoids it with surprising dexterity. It is from this circumstance that a Philadelphian is known anywhere by his gait."

The Quakers got on extremely well with the Indians and soon learned to use Indian corn and cornmeal in their cookery, as well as elk, venison, wild turkey, passenger pigeons, and water-fowl, all of which were plentiful in the region.

The opportunities in Philadelphia to enjoy the pleasures of the table were soon unlimited. Farm, garden, and dairy products, vegetables, poultry, beef, and muttons were produced in immense quantity and variety and of excellent quality. Madeira obtained in trade with Spain was the popular drink even at the taverns. Various forms of punch and rum were common, but the modern light wines and champagne were not then in vogue.

Main room of an 18th-century Pennsylvania house

The Quakers were known to have had gout. Food in great quantity and variety seems to have been placed on the table at the same time with little regard to formal courses. Beef, poultry, and mutton would all be served at one dinner. Fruit and nuts were also placed on the table in great quantities, as were puddings and desserts, of which there were many. Dinners were usually served in the afternoon.

Chastellux, a Frenchman who visited the country and then wrote about its people and customs, complained that the breakfasts were very heavy. Loins of veal, legs of mutton, and other substantial dishes at an early hour in the morning were rather staggering to a Frenchman who was accustomed to a cup of coffee and a roll. One of these breakfasts lasted an hour and a half, according to him.

In 1786, a quiet family meal consisted of roast turkey, mashed potatoes, whipped syllabubs, oyster pie, boiled leg of pork, bread pudding, and tarts, to be followed by an "early dish of tea for the old folks."

GULIA PENN

William Penn's first wife, Gulia, kept a handwritten book of family recipes which had been handed down from her mother and grandmother. In 1702, a manuscript copy of them was made and brought to America for use in the Penn household.

TOO MAKE A PUDING IN MUTTEN: Take grated bread, yeolks of eggs Rosted hard and sliced very fine, corants, parsly, time, Rosmary shreed youre herbs very fine, put a Litell sugar Cloves mace put all these together between the skin and the flesh of the mutton and so Rost it with the meat.

TOO MAKE A COLLWORT OR CABIDGE PUDING: Take a pound of beefe and ½ pound of suett shred them small season them with peper salt nutmegs sweet herbs work it up with some yeolks of eggs, boyle it in a Collwort or Cabidge Leafe when it is boyled putt in sum butter and eat it—

TRIP TO PHILADELPHIA MARKETS

"You may be Supply'd with every Necessary of Life throut the whole year, but Extraordinary Good and reasonably Cheap, and it is allow'd by Foreigners to be the best of its bigness in the known World, and undoubtedly the largest in America; I got to the place by 7; and had no small satisfaction in seeing the pretty Creatures, the Young Ladies, traversing the place from Stall to Stall, where they could make the best Market, some with their Maids behind them with a Basket to carry home the Purchase. Others that were designed to buy but trifles, as a little fresh Butter, a Dish of Green Peas, or the like, had Good Nature and Humility enough to be their own Porter."

William Black, 1744

JOHN ADAMS ON FOOD IN PHILADELPHIA: 1787

(Of the home of Miers Fisher, a young Quaker lawyer.)
"This plain Friend, with his plain but pretty wife with her Thees and Thous, had provided us a costly entertainment; ducks, hams, chickens, beef, pie, tarts, creams, custard, jellies, fools, trifles, floating islands, beer, porter, punch, wine, etc."

(Of the home of Chief Justice Chews.)
"About four o'clock we were called to dinner. Turtle and every other thing, flummer, jellies, sweetmeats of twenty sorts, trifles, whipped sillabubs, floating islands, fools, etc., with a dessert of fruits, raisins, almonds, pears, peaches.
"A most sinful feast again! everything which could delight the eye or allure the taste; curds and creams, jellies, sweetmeats of various sorts, twenty kinds of tarts, fools, trifles, floating islands, whipped sillabubs, etc., Parmesan cheese, punch, wine, porter, beer."

THE HOLY EXPERIMENT

Pennsylvania, which Penn liked to call the "Holy Experiment," attracted many settlers. One of Penn's first acts was to write and publish in English, French, Dutch, and German a pamphlet describing the colony he proposed to build. In the pamphlet he invited honest, hard-working settlers to come, promising them religious toleration, representative government, and cheap land. To every settler who would establish his home and family in the colony, Penn offered 500 acres of free land, with the right to buy additional land at one shilling an acre.

The Welsh Quakers came to Philadelphia and its surrounding area. There were Germans from the Palatinate, and the Scotch-Irish, each settling in a different section of the area.

THE SCOTCH-IRISH

This group came to Pennsylvania early in the eighteenth century and eventually spread throughout the colonies. They were primarily spinners and weavers by trade. They did not have the Quaker calm or German thrift. They took any land they wished and dared anyone to move them. They were independent and belligerent, ready to fight anyone, any place, for any reason.

They did little farming at first in the frontier homes that they established in the Allegheny Mountains.

In the daily life of the Scotch-Irish there were just four things essential—the rifle, the backwoods axe, the fort or blockhouse, and the trail, later to become a road connecting them with their source of supplies and their markets back East and following their spearhead farther and farther on toward the Ohio and the West.

Their homes were grouped around "forts" built where three or four cabins were close together and where a good spring could be enclosed. The forts were nothing more than log fences with one or more blockhouses. Their entire cabin was built of logs, the floor of half-logs with their flat sides upwards. The puncheons also made the tops of the tables and benches. When a cabin was to be built, the neighbors gathered and within three days the house was up and furnished. Before the family moved in, there was a housewarming, which was a dance lasting all night long.

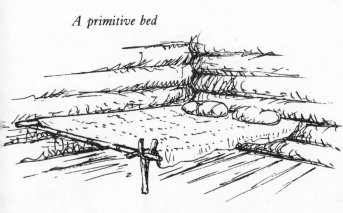

A primitive bed

The Scotch-Irish settler lived by hunting, and bought only such things as salt and iron. He scratched out a living by making whiskey, collecting pelts, and making alum from the burning of wood, leaching the ashes, and boiling down the residue.

However, soon every cabin had a truck garden which the wife and children took care of. Later a small field of grain brought real bread to the table. From the first settling they had potatoes, pumpkins, beans, and corn, and soon a cow and a few pigs gave them milk and pork. So the table afforded them a diet of "hog and hominy," johnny cake, corn pone, and mush and milk within a short time. Supper usually consisted of mush and milk. When milk was in short supply, mush was eaten with sweetened water, molasses, bear's oil, or the gravy of fried meat. The standard fare for every log-rolling, house-raising, harvest day, or whenever the neighbors got together, was a pot pie!

With so many trees about, the dishes were mostly woodenware. Utensils of gourds and squashes were made. They had neither tea, coffee, nor china at first.

Clearing the land

SCRAPPLE

Scrapple was invented by the Mennonites, who were sometimes called the German Quakers. They spread out into the wilderness surrounding Philadelphia, which they soon transformed into farmlands. Scrapple was the wedding of German sausage skills and American Indian corn meal.

THE MORAVIANS

The Moravians also came from Germany and believed in peace not only with others but also among themselves. The Moravian settlements were as truly church settlements as were those of the Puritans in New England.

They settled in the area of Pennsylvania known later as the city of Bethlehem. Their first buildings were the church buildings, with the Bell House, completed in 1745, as the center.

Moravians were music-loving people, and Bethlehem had the first symphony orchestra in America.

At harvest time, the men mowed the oats, while the women pulled the flax.

Education became one of their first interests once they were settled. They were also interested in the care of their sick, and established one of the first hospitals, in 1742.

During the Revolutionary War, practically the entire town became a hospital, since the Continental Army was in the vicinity from December 3, 1776 to March 27, 1777, and then from September 17, 1777 to April 14, 1778.

PENNSYLVANIA DUTCH

In the early days of the eighteenth century, nearly all the first settlers in eastern Pennsylvania came from the Palatinate in Germany. They selected pieces of land, built log houses, and began to clear and cultivate the soil. Though these good people came from Germany, they came to be known as "Dutch." These same people developed a language—a mixture of their mother tongue in the Old World and that spoken in their new homeland, America—which came to be known as Pennsylvania Dutch.

They were the best farmers in the colonies, but, since they had been so poor in Germany, many of them mortgaged their own labor and that of their children to pay for passage across the ocean.

In those early days, the Germans sacrificed not only luxury but comfort in order to gain profit. Their barns were usually larger and finer than their homes. The German houses were generally built of logs, although some were half timber, framed and braced with hewn beams, and the spaces filled with brick. By the middle of the 1700's, their houses were made of thick fieldstone, built into the sides of a hill and over a spring so that the cellar could be used as a milk-cooling room.

Although they were simple people, once they prospered, the interiors of their houses were often quite elaborately finished. The kitchen was the main room of the house, and many fine things were to be found there. Where a stairway led to a second story, the staircase often had such carved bannisters that one might expect to see it in a mansion instead of a farmer's dwelling.

Many of them decorated their houses by painting flowers and decorations on the window shutters. The rose and the tulip were their traditional emblems and were painted on chests, benches, and even on some dishes.

THE KLOSTER OF THE SEVENTH-DAY BAPTISTS

Many sects of Germans came to Pennsylvania, among whom was a group headed by Johann Conrad Beissel. He founded a sort of farm community at Ephrata, Lancaster County. It was a community growing up among "the hands," without a family unit as the nucleus. The people believed in the spiritual superiority of celibacy.

Although they were extremists, they were excellent farmers, and their buildings were extremely well built. They lived very simply and dressed very simply, the men in shirt, trousers, and vest under a long gown to which was attached a pointed cowl or hood. The women wore shirts and narrow skirts with a long gown covering all, to which was attached a rounded cowl or hood.

They supplied most of the paper, and did some of the best printing, in colonial America. They had a bookbindery which was the largest and best in all the colonies.

PENNSYLVANIA DUTCH AND GOOD FOOD

In anything pertaining to food, the Pennsylvania Dutch were inventive. To bring home more game, they designed a longer, more accurate rifle. The first American cookstove was cast at Mary Ann Furnace in 1765. They also made a long-handled waffle iron, imprinting a tulip design, for use on the open hearth. Instead of diamonds, young men gave their sweethearts handsomely carved rolling pins as engagement presents.

Many of their early stoves were decorated with biblical scenes that are today called "The Bible in Iron." And Henry William Stiegel, the glassmaker, was Pennsylvania Dutch. The Conestoga wagon is another of their inventions which was originally used to transport their produce to fairs and farmers' markets.

Christopher Ludwick, a baker, was commissioned to be baker general of the Continental Army, while the famous Philadelphia Pepper Pot is supposed to be another delicacy invented by a German at Valley Forge in answer to General Washington's plea for some good food.

In the early days, the housewives had brought with them the recipes of the traditionally famous German cooks. Life was hard, and at first the land yielded but little return. There were few roads, and towns were far apart. It was not always possible to secure the prescribed ingredients, and it became necessary to develop new recipes to utilize the plainer foods in the creation of tasty dishes. Necessity was again the mother of invention, and these good women became famous for their fine cooking. The Pennsylvania Dutch created the colored Easter egg, shoofly pie, and apple butter.

HAM WITH GREEN STRING BEANS *(Speck und Beans)*

3 pounds smoked ham, water, 1 quart green string beans; 5 medium-sized potatoes; salt and pepper.

Cover the piece of ham with cold water and set over a low flame to cook for three hours. Add water from time to time during the cooking in order to have at least one quart of broth at all times. Wash and clean the string beans, break into small pieces and add to the ham. Continue cooking about 25 minutes. Pare and quarter the potatoes; add to the beans and ham and cook about 25 or 30 minutes, or until beans and potatoes are tender. About 15 minutes before serving, add salt and pepper to taste. Serve hot, providing vinegar for those who like the dish strongly flavored.

MOULDASHA *(Parsley Pie)*

Mash and season with butter and salt half a dozen boiled white potatoes, add a little grated onion and chopped parsley. Sift together in a bowl 1 cup of flour, 1 teaspoon baking powder and a little salt. Add one egg and a small quantity of milk if not enough liquid to mix into a soft dough. Roll out like pie crust, handling as little as possible. Cut into small squares, fill with the potato mixture, turn opposite corners over and pinch together all around like small three-cornered pies. Drop the small triangular pieces into boiling salted water a few minutes, or until they rise to top; then skim out and brown them in a pan containing a tablespoon each of butter and lard. Stale bread crumbs, browned in butter, may be sprinkled over these pies when served. Serve hot.

MORE ABOUT PENNSYLVANIA DUTCH FOOD

The Pennsylvania Dutch believed in "plain and plenty" food, and so they had all sorts of pot-roasted meats and stews as well as plenty of chicken, especially as chicken pot pie.

Many of their dishes are still eaten today, such as sauerbraten, Boova shenkel (beef stew with potato dumplings), noodles, and dumplings, which form a substantial part of many of their dishes.

Dried apples were used for all sorts of pies and other desserts.

The early Pennsylvania Dutch settlers built huge outdoor ovens of stone. The interiors of these ovens were sometimes seven feet wide and could accommodate five or six loaves of bread, seven or eight pies, half a dozen crumb cakes, and several batches of cookies all at one time.

Corn was an important crop, and the housewife dried it for use throughout the winter months. To dry it, the kernels were cut from the ripe ears and dried in a very slow oven, or out of doors in the sun on a cloth-covered screen suspended from wooden posts.

The Germans brought the art of pretzel-making to the New World. It is said that the shape of the twisted pretzel symbolizes the position of the arms crossed in prayer, and that pretzels date back to the time of the Crusades.

Raisin pie was known as "funeral pie," since it was traditionally served along with a nourishing meal to mourners who had come a long distance to attend a funeral.

Christmas dinner always had roast duck or goose as its main dish.

The Pennsylvania Dutch had many superstitions and one is that at a company or holiday meal there must be exactly "seven sweets and seven sours" on the table. The Pennsylvania Dutch housewife did not dream of asking her family, much less guests, to sit down to a table that didn't have at least the "seven sweets and seven sours" on it. Rhubarb jam, rhubarb marmalade, lemon honey, cherry relish, pear marmalade, and quince marmalade were some of the more unusual "sweets," although all sorts of preserves were served. As for the "sours," they included such dishes as green tomato relish, cucumber relish, onion, pepper, pickle relish, and vegetable catsup, as well as all the other relishes.

A FRONTIER WEDDING

In the first years of the settlement of the frontier, a wedding engaged the attention of a whole neighborhood and was anticipated by young and old alike. The wedding was almost the only gathering held in this area that was not accompanied by the labor of reaping, log rolling, building a cabin, or planning some sort of campaign.

The groom and his attendants assembled at the house of his father early in the day, since he had to reach the home of his bride before noon, which was the usual time for celebrating the nuptials.

The men were dressed in mocassins, leather breeches, leggings and linsey hunting shirts, all homemade. The ladies were dressed in linsey petticoats and linsey or linen gowns, coarse shoes, stockings, handkerchiefs, and buckskin gloves.

The party marched off to the bride's house, and when it was about a mile from her home, two young men would single out to run for the whiskey bottle; the worse the path, the more logs, brush, and deep hollows, the better. The start was announced by an Indian yell. The first who reached the door was presented with the prize, which he returned to the company. He then gave the bottle first to the groom and his attendants and then to each pair in the succession to the rear of the line, saving the rest for himself.

The ceremony of the marriage preceded the dinner, which was a substantial backwoods feast of beef, pork, fowls, and sometimes venison and bear meat roasted and boiled, with plenty of potatoes, cabbage, and other vegetables. If there were not enough plates and knives, fingers did very nicely.

After dinner there was dancing which generally lasted till the following morning, with refreshments throughout the night. About nine o'clock a deputation of young ladies stole off the bride and put her to bed; this was followed by a deputation of young men stealing off the groom and placing him snugly by the side of his bride. All the while, the dancing went on. During the night, food and drink were sent up to the bride and groom which they were compelled to eat and drink.

The feasting and dancing often lasted for several days, at the end of which the whole company was so exhausted with lack of sleep that several days of rest were needed to return them to their ordinary daily chores.

FARMER'S HOUSEWIFE

The main entrance to her farmhouse was the kitchen door, since no housewife in her right mind would allow farm mud and grasses to be tracked into her parlor. The children generally made use of the shed door so that they could leave their dirty shoes there. The kitchen usually was filled with aromas—the pleasant ones of baking bread or gingerbread, bubbling stew, or roasting meat; mundane ones of wax melting for candle-making, apple slices and herbs drying before the fire, coffee beans roasting, or sausage being stuffed; or the unpleasant ones of the dyepot and its indigo mixture, the products of slaughtering, or milk souring for cheese-making.

Cooking was done at the large fireplace, where pots and kettles, toaster, waffle iron, oven peel, tin roaster, and all the other cooking paraphernalia were stored. On the mantel were pressing irons, candle molds, lamps, and other gear. The big table was used for both work and dining, and might have been set with a hand-loomed linen cloth, blue Staffordshire ware, white napery, and bone-handled knives and forks.

The cupboard contained all the necessary kitchen equipment. Beyond it on one side was the buttery, where much food preparation took place. Here the housewife churned her butter, pressed and cared for her cheeses, kneaded her dough, put up her preserves, and filled her pie shells and bean pot.

There was a long ell-room between kitchen and shed where equipment not in daily use was stored. There might be spare pots and kettles to be used for extra mouths to feed, wool and flax waiting to be spun and dyed.

The kitchen of the 1700's

The parlor beyond the kitchen was never used except for weddings and funerals. The room usually had stencilled walls, a rag carpet, and gay curtains. There also was a desk, chest, and sewing table rarely used.

The housewife had her bedroom on the downstairs floor, while the children slept up on the second floor. Under her bedstead was a trundle bed where the current toddler slept while the infant was in a cradle by the side of the bed.

A FARMER'S DAINTY DISH

Peel and slice thin potatoes and onions (five potatoes to one small onion); take half a pound of sweet pork (in thin slices) to a pound of beef, mutton, or veal; cut the meat in small pieces; take some nice bread dough and shorten a little; line the bottom of the stewpan with slices of pork, then a layer of meat, potatoes and onions, dust over a little pepper and cover with a layer of crust; repeat this until the stewpot is full. The size of the pot will depend on the number in the family. Pour in sufficient water to cover and finish with crust. Let it simmer until meat, vegetables, etc., are done, but do not let it boil hard. Serve hot. This we are assured by one who knows is a dish fit to set before a king.

The Successful Housekeeper, 1885

In 1686, James Harrison, a Quaker minister, praised the new land: "The Peach-Trees are much broken down with the weight of Fruit this Year . . . Rasberries, Goosberries, Currans, Quinces, Roses, Walnuts and Figs grow well . . . Our Barn, Porch and Shed, are full of Corn this year."

FARM WIVES—THEIR DAY

Farm wives before 1820 rose long before dawn to begin their day's chores. They were married at twenty or earlier and produced large families. They had no leisure and often died young.

At this time, the housewife had no cookstove, so in the morning she had to revive the fire on the kitchen hearth and prepare a breakfast of cornmeal mush, bread or toast, and a hot drink. Occasionally there was a bit of bacon or sausage for the adults, leftover potatoes fried up, or doughnuts. In some families there was pie.

After breakfast she cleared up and got her dinner under way. If she had spare time, she might weave linen for sheets or some cloth for clothing.

The noon meal was a boiled dinner—salted beef or pork boiled with potatoes, carrots, turnips, onions, and whatever else she chose to put into the pot. There was cider for drinking, and gingerbread, apple pie, or a baked Indian pudding for dessert.

She then cleaned up again and either worked in her garden in the summer or at her loom or wheel or ironing in the winter. Her evening meal served at five or six o'clock was simpler. The evening was spent in supervising the children and then back again to the things that had to be done for the house and family.

When finally in bed after her prayers, it seemed as if she had just fallen asleep when the daily round began again.

APPLE BUTTER

Apple butter has always been associated with the Pennsylvania Dutch, and it has a special meaning for one particular group, the Schwenkfelders. Every September this group holds a Thanksgiving service. In July 1734, they left Germany for America, and they finally anchored on September 21, 1734, near New Castle. There they obtained their first fresh water in weeks out of the river, while the captain rowed over and brought back a supply of apples from the shore. This was their first meal of fresh food, along with some rolls that the Schwenkfelders had, and their traditional Thanksgiving, water, bread, butter, and apple butter, commemorates that fact each year.

Making apple butter

THE HOUSEWIFE'S WORK WEEK

MONDAY: Monday was washday. Everyone would rise early and, before the sun was up, carry the water in and build up a fire. The water would be put into the boiler to boil while breakfast was being prepared. After that the women of the family would get to the clothes and would continue for the next five or six hours. Usually by noontime the clothes were being dried either on lines or over the bushes, and our housewife would now attend to the noon meal and then get back to the clothes, folding each item and putting it away either to iron or in storage.

TUESDAY: Tuesday was ironing day, and with the type of equipment at hand, ironing for the average family was an all-day, morning-to-night affair. The oldest girls in the family helped their mother, each one working at her own ironing board.

WEDNESDAY: Wednesday was usually known as mending or sewing day. If there were new clothes to cut out and put together by basting or on the small hand-operated sewing machine, this would be one of the days to do it. Also, all the mending was supposed to be done on this day.

Women made their own clothing and the clothing for the family unless they were more affluent and could afford the services of a seamstress, one who either stayed at the house for a while or one to whom the housewife went with her material and ideas. Men's clothing was usually handled by a local or itinerant tailor.

Women and girls also made their own stockings or later on bought cotton stocking by the yard and cut it off in sections and sewed a toe on it.

The small pieces of cloth left over from sewing were used to make quilts.

THURSDAY: Thursday was odd-job day. This was the day that our housewife might do her gardening in the summer or sharpen knives or do quilting. Whatever task that she could not categorize into another day was done on Thursday, so that often this day was one in which lots of little jobs were done. It could be a most tiring day.

FRIDAY: Friday was cleaning day for the entire house. Although wash was done on Monday, linen was changed on Friday since the beds were supposed to be thoroughly cleaned and brushed on that day.

Friday was the day that the broom and dustpan were in constant use. Rugs were not beaten unless it was spring and spring-cleaning was under way. Spring-cleaning meant everything, including curtains and rugs and other dust-catchers which were divested of their accumulated dust.

SATURDAY: Saturday was baking and bath day. The children were home from school and helped with the baking and watched the process so that nothing would burn. Baking was often done for the following week and consisted of bread, cakes, pies, cookies, beans, and meats. Cooking and baking was done for Sunday since no one worked on Sunday. It was a day of rest.

On Saturday afternoon and evening there would be bath time. The children took their baths as soon as baking was over, and after an early supper, they went to bed. The adults took their baths after supper and then went to bed.

SUNDAY: Sunday was church day. Everyone went to church. It was a religious obligation and at the same time it was a day to catch up on all local news and gossip. For the housewife it was a day of pleasure and rest from her hard work. One week was gone and the other was first thing tomorrow. Sunday was her day of peace and quiet.

FRESH AIR AND HEALTH

Very many persons, especially ladies, have a horror, in winter, of going out-of-doors for fear of taking cold. If it is a little damp, or a little windy, or a little cold, they wait, and wait; meanwhile, weeks and even months pass away, and they never, during the whole time, breathe a single breath of pure air. The result is they become so enfeebled that their constitutions have no power of resistance; the least thing in the world gives them a cold, even going from one room to another; and before they know it, they have a cold all the time, and this is nothing more or less than incipient consumption. Whereas, if an opposite practice had been followed of going out for an hour or two every day, regardless of the weather, except actually falling rain, a very different result would have taken place.

Peterson's Magazine, 1875

KIND OF WIFE

Hannah More says, that when a man of sense comes to marry, it is a companion whom he wants, and not an artist. It is not merely a creature who can paint, play, dress and dance; it is a being who can comfort and console him.

The Old Farmer's Almanac, 1858, Robert B. Thomas

TO FRESHEN BAKED GOODS

Doughnuts and cookies, as well as crackers, can be freshened by heating them thoroughly in a moderate oven, after which they should be cooled in a dry place before serving.

Household, 1869

NO MARRIAGE LICENSES

"As no Licenses for Marriage could be obtained since the first of November for Want of Stamped paper, we can assure the Publick several Genteel Couples were publish'd in the different Churches of this City last Week; and we hear that the young Ladies of this place are determined to Join Hands with none but such as will to the utmost endeavour to abolish the Custom of marrying with License which Amounts to many Hundred per annum which might be saved."

New York Gazette and Postbody, December 6, 1709

A FARMER'S BREAKFAST

For those of our readers who live in the city and wondered about the breakfast eaten by a farmer, here is a menu sent to us by one of our readers along with various recipes for the breakfast. No doubt you will enjoy it.

Buckwheat cakes	Coffee	Fried Mush
Potatoes	Ham and Eggs	Apple Sauce
Graham Gems	Maple Syrup	Doughnuts

Household, 1884

A HOUSEHOLD ABC

As soon as you are up, shake blankets and sheet;
Better be without shoes than sit with wet feet;
Children, if healthy, are active, not still;
Damp sheets and damp clothes will both make you ill;
Eat slowly, and always chew your food well;
Freshen the air in the house where you dwell;
Garments must never be made to be tight;
Homes will be healthy if airy and light;
If you wish to be well, as you do, I've no doubt,
Just open the windows before you go out;
Keep your rooms always neat, and tidy, and clean;
Let dust on the furniture never be seen;
Much illness is caused by the want of pure air,
Now to open your windows be ever your care;
Old rags and old rubbish should never be kept
People should see that their floors are well swept;
Quick movements in children are healthy and right;
Remember the young cannot thrive without light;
See that the cistern is clean to the brim;
Take care that your dress is all tidy and trim;
Use your nose to find out if there be a bad drain,
Very sad are the fevers that come in its train;
Walk as much as you can without feeling fatigue—
Xerxes could walk full many a league;
Your health is your wealth, which your wisdom must keep;
Zeal will help a good cause, and the good you will reap.

Peterson's Magazine, June 1888

A frontier kitchen

THE OLD EAGLE COFFEE HOUSE AT CONCORD, N.H.

Author's note: This was a famous country inn, noted for its food in the mid-1800's.

In this kitchen the mistress of the house reigned supreme. Working *with* her, not *under* her (for we write of the days when *help* was hired, not *servants*), were a meat cook, one who attended to the vegetables, a "kitchen colonel," kitchen boy, and a little girl who made herself generally useful. There were others, but these are the ones we know most about. The mistress herself made all the pies, cake, and most of the puddings, in a room adjoining the kitchen, and on great occasions she would be up at four in the morning to make at least a hundred pies. The "kitchen colonel's" duties must have been arduous with all the wood to bring for the fireplace and oven, and the latter to clean out every time it was heated. The kitchen boy was expected to scour the knives, blacken the boots of the guests, and to trim and fill the whale oil lamps used in lighting all the rooms.

What were some of the dishes which made our old tavern famous? Meats roasted in tin kitchens before the fireplace—in the common size tin kitchens for ordinary occasions, but when preparations were made for a great feast in "double-decked" ones, as they were called. Meats cooked in this way were never surpassed, each kind retaining its own flavor. Vegetables of all kinds boiled over the fireplace in kettles suspended from the crane; pies (famous ones too); the rich old-fashioned cakes; little cheese cakes; bread and Indian puddings; and those who washed the dishes remember well the great number of custard cups to be washed when "June Court" was in session; so cup custards must have been a favorite dainty with those who came to make the laws.

Potatoes were at first served plain, but the mistress, going away for a visit, came back with a new and wonderful rule for preparing them, and afterwards mashed potatoes were also served. Another time it was a new recipe for puddings, "packed puddings" she called them, thick slices of bread, buttered, packed into the deep brown earthen pudding pots with alternate layers of apples, spices, and sugar, covered and baked in the brick oven until they were red and delicious. One of the duties of the useful little girl was to beat the butter and sugar together in a broad earthen milk pan, for the sauce to serve with these puddings; then to mould it in a little old china cup kept for that purpose, and after turning the balls out on small saucers, to mark them with a knife to somewhat resemble a pineapple, and to finish by grating nutmeg over them. Another of her duties was to line all the pans used in baking sponge cake with a thick paste of ryemeal and water. When the cake was baked it came out of the paste without a crust, soft and delicious. The pound cake was so light that those who ate it could not believe it was pound cake, so tradition says. All the eggs were beaten in a tall earthen jar with a beater which resembled a bunch of wires fastened to a handle.

For Saturday dinner boiled salt codfish was served, as a special dish. It made its reappearance Sunday morning in fish hash, beefsteak being also served on that morning. For dinner on Sunday there would be brown bread, beans, and Indian puddings. These would be prepared the day before and put into the brick oven by four o'clock on Sunday morning. Poor kitchen colonel! No Sunday morning nap for him. Sunday nights for supper hot biscuits and "flapjacks" were the chief substantials. The "flapjacks" were made as large as a plate, buttered and sugared while warm, piled on top of one another, and served in wedge-shaped pieces, cut from the pile.

Georgia L. Green, in Concord Monitor.
American Kitchen, September 19, 1882

MAPLE BISCUIT

2 cups flour; ½ teaspoon salt; 4 teaspoons Rumford Baking Powder; 2 table-spoons shortening; about ¾ cup milk or milk and water, mixed; softened shortening; crushed maple sugar.

Sift together the flour, salt and baking powder; cut or rub in the shortening until the fat is thoroughly blended with the flour, then mix to a very soft dough with the liquid, having this as cold as possible. After mixing, divide into two portions and roll out each not over a half an inch thick, keeping the shape of the dough as square as possible. Brush over one portion with softened shortening, spread thickly with crushed maple sugar, cover with the second portion of dough and cut into squares that they may be no left-over fragments for re-rolling. Bake in a quick oven [450° F] twelve to fifteen minutes.

The Rumford Cook Book, Fannie Merrit Farmer

SAUERKRAUT

Sauerkraut is a Pennsylvania Dutch staple. It is so popular that it is said that when General Lee captured Chambersburg on his way to Gettysburg, one of the first things he demanded for his army was twenty-five barrels of sauerkraut.

HOMEMADE RECEIPT BOOK

Have at hand a blank book in which to paste or copy valuable recipes. Cover this with white oilcloth neatly pasted on. Have a special part of this book or a separate book for menus. This will help to solve the problem of what to have for dinner.

Household Discoveries, 1905

A REAL OVEN: *A Letter from Ruth*

Dear Hannah:

Father brought in the vessel as many bricks as would serve to make an oven by the side of our fireplace, and thus it was that we were the first family here who could bake bread or roast meats as do people in England.

This oven is built on one side of the fireplace, with a hole near the top for the smoke to go through. It has a door of real iron, with an ash pit below so that we may save the ashes for soap-making without storing them in another place.

At first the oven was kept busily at work for the benefit of our neighbors, being heated each day, but for our own needs it is used once a week. Inside a great fire of dried wood is kindled and kept burning from morning until noon, when it has thoroughly heated the bricks. Then the coals and ashes are swept out, the chimney draught is closed, and the oven filled with whatsoever we have to cook. A portion of our bread is baked in the two pans which mother owns, but the rest of it we lay on green leaves, and it is cooked quite as well, although one is forced to scrape a few cinders from the bottom of the loaf.

Ruth

THE ARRIVAL OF THE GERMANS

When the ships have landed at Philadelphia after their long voyage, no one is permitted to leave them except those who pay for their passage or can give good security; the others, who cannot pay, must remain on board the ships till they are purchased, and are released from the ships by their purchasers. The sick always fare the worst, for the healthy are naturally preferred and purchased first; and so the sick and wretched must often remain on board in front of the city for 2 or 3 weeks, and frequently die, whereas many a one, if he could pay his debt and were permitted to leave the ship immediately, might recover and remain alive.

Journey to Pennsylvania, 1750

GODEY'S LADY'S BOOK

It has been said that the era of the American magazine began with *Godey's Lady's Book,* which was founded in 1830 and ran almost to the end of the nineteenth century.

Godey's, like the happy little man, Louis A. Godey, who owned it and like Mrs. Sarah Josepha Hale, the feminist from Boston, who edited it from 1837 to 1877, was marvelous. It may not have been as academic a magazine as *North American Review* or as brilliant as the magazine *Graham's,* or as readable as the *Knickerbocker Magazine,* but the popular *Godey's Lady's Book* under the militant Sarah Josepha Hale had more real influence on American life than any other magazine of the same period.

Godey's was directed entirely to the woman and as a result it affected the manners, morals, tastes, fashions, homes, and diets of generations of Americans. It did much to form the American woman's idea of what she was like, how she should act, and how she should insist that she be treated. It had no interest in political or intellectual subjects.

It is said that Sarah Josepha Hale wrote the American classic:

> Mary had a little lamb;
>> Its fleece was white as snow;
> And everywhere that Mary went
>> The lamb was sure to go.

This great woman's magazine of the mid-century captured its audience through its superbly detailed engravings of long-gowned and gusseted ladies, whose carefully tinted regalia made them suitable for framing as well as imitation. Along with the patterns for these dresses went a regular ration of sentimental fiction in which the main concern was whether the heroine was marrying beneath or above her station. Much of the verse and more of the fiction reads like drivel today, but they must have been adored in their day, for *Godey's* claimed a circulation of 25,000 in 1839—which might well mean 100,000 readers since the magazine was passed around to friends, neighbors and relatives—and the magazine reached a circulation of 100,000 before the Civil War.

Besides fashions, fictions, and feminine verse, *Godey's* published recipes, embroidery patterns and instructions, beauty and health hints, and elaborate illustrations called "embellishments."

Every issue also contained complete plans and illustrations for a model cottage, together with the prices of materials needed in its construction.

Mrs. Hale was a determined individual and campaigned for the recognition of women writers. Before that time many women writers used masculine pseudonyms or initials. She had them boldly sign their names. She introduced Harriet Beecher Stowe when still an unknown writer. Mrs. Hale believed in educational opportunities and physical exercises for women and argued for national recognition of Thanksgiving Day until President Abraham Lincoln proclaimed it on October 20, 1863.

Sarah Josepha Hale gave up the editorship of *Godey's* two years before her death, and Louis A. Godey died in 1878, but *Godey's Lady's Book* continued until 1898, when it finally vanished.

PETERSON'S MAGAZINE

The other popular woman's magazine of the 1800's was *Peterson's Magazine*, founded in January 1842 as *Ladies National Magazine*. It was founded by Charles J. Peterson and George R. Graham of *Graham's Magazine* to cut into the rising circulation of *Godey's Lady's Book*.

It had the same features as *Godey's* but was a slimmer edition since it was one dollar cheaper per year. It, too, had the colored fashion plates and mezzotints. By the Civil War, it had surpassed *Godey's Lady's Book* in circulation.

By 1870, the magazine had serials, monthly departments of fancywork, recipes, etc., including some music. The stories were very much alike: virtue in poverty, a broken heart, the dangers of frivolity.

However, there was some humor injected into the magazine with Marietta Holley's stories of "Josiah Allen's Wife."

Charles Peterson died in 1887 and his widow took over, but the magazine gradually went downhill and by 1895 it was out of existence. Yet this magazine together with *Godey's Lady's Book* influenced the women of America and indirectly the entire country in the mid-1800's.

FARMING VILLAGES, 1750

Not far from the coast, and particularly in New England, New Jersey, and Pennsylvania, there were many small farming villages of fifty or a hundred families, with a church or meetinghouse, a school, and several shops. The villagers might go to a cobbler to have their shoes made, to a blacksmith to have their wagons fixed, to

a doctor for medical attention, or to a general store to buy sugar, spices, or English fabrics for dresses. Traveling barbers also came to the villages to cut hair and pull teeth. Everything else was performed by the householder.

To pay for these services, the farmers of the village and the surrounding territory hauled their surplus tobacco, grain, cattle, and hogs to the nearest seaboard or river-port town. There they sold their products.

Before they returned home, the farmers often stopped to make purchases in the shops displaying goods from England. Thus the settlers who lived in areas where it was possible to market their surplus produce were able to live better than their more isolated fellows.

TO PRESERVE EGGS

It is only necessary to close the pores of the shell. This may be done by varnishing, or by dipping in melted suet, and then packing them in salt with the small end downward.

Mrs. Rorer's Philadelphia Cook Book, 1886

Washing clothes—1880's

THE WELL-TO-DO FAMILY

As families began to prosper, the houses were built with better accommodations. In the course of time there was a pantry, a buttery, a milk room, a shed, a shed chamber, and an attic. The first appearance of these homes came at the end of the eighteenth century, but it was not for another hundred years that it was a general thing to see.

The pantry was added to the one-room house as the first necessity, and every kitchen had its pantry, whether it was large or small.

The buttery served as an overflow of the pantry. Originally this room was used as a storeroom for provisions but eventually it held everything not found in the pantry, such as sap pail, butter boxes, butter tubs, the molasses keg, salt barrels, and the various cereals.

The third room added was the milk room where were found the butter churn, the cheese press, the racks for the buckets, and the cheese closet.

PERSPIRATION

The unpleasant odor produced by perspiration may be removed by putting a spoonful of spirits of ammonia in a basin of water and bathing in this. This is especially good for bathing the feet.

Sense in the Kitchen, 1881

GRANITEWARE

Graniteware was found in almost every American kitchen at the turn of the century. Essentially these are metal pieces with a coating of glass or enamel that has been fused onto the metal surface.

The term "graniteware" is in a sense wrong because the ware has no connection with the material granite except, in some cases, for a similarity in appearance. Although the enameled surface is very hard, it is also, unfortunately, brittle, so that it is easily chipped.

This nineteenth-century innovation was popularized by the Philadelphia Centennial Exposition of 1876. Here, many people were shown the sanitary advantages of glass combined with the strength of metal; compared to the older cast iron, copper, brass, and crockery utensils, it was more healthful and easier to handle and to care for. If it had lacked these qualities, its beauty alone would probably have made it popular.

In the 1890's the work of Charles Martin Hall with aluminum replaced graniteware with aluminum ware.

FOOD FOR THOUGHT

From the first cookbook published in 1742 at Williamsburg, Virginia, up to the newest published in our day, there have been so many that an entire book would be needed just to list them all.

Cherry-stoner

Apple-corer

GADGETS

The nineteenth-century inventor concentrated his efforts on the various household problems. As a result, he came up with gadgetry galore for food processing, internal communications, baby care, household chores, and pest control. However, all or most of the gadgets were "woman-powered," and so few of them are recognizable to us today.

There were all manner of parers, graters, beaters, home canners, etc. No matter what job was to be done in the home, there was a gadget to make it "easier." But the poor housewife had to use all her energy in working these "conveniences," so as soon as electric power came into existence, many of the gadgets just disappeared from the shelves of the general or hardware store and became items for the collector of today to ferret out.

SPICED SALT FOR SOUPS AND STUFFINGS

4 ounces of salt
2 ounces of celery salt
1 ounce each of white pepper and ground thyme
1 ounce each of marjoram and summer savory
½ ounce of sage
1 saltspoonful of cayenne pepper
½ teaspoonful each of cloves, allspice, and mace.
Mix, sift, and keep closely covered.

New Household Receipt Book, Sarah Josepha Hale, 1853

NEW KINDS OF FOOD: *A Letter from Ruth*

Dear Hannah:
Often my mother prepared nassaump, which is nothing but corn beaten into small pieces and boiled until soft, after which it is eaten hot, or cold, with milk or butter.

I wrote to you about nookick and save for the flavor lent to it by the roasting, I can see no difference between nookick and the meal made from the ground corn.

Mother makes a mixture of oatmeal, milk, sugar, and spice, which is much to my taste, although father declares it is not unlike oatmeal porridge such as is eaten in some parts of England; but it hardly seems to me possible, because of one's not putting sugar and spice into porridge.

We often have bread made of pumpkins boiled soft, and mixed with the meal from Indian corn, and this father much prefers to the bread of rye with the meal of corn, but the manner of cooking pumpkins most to my liking is to cut them into small pieces, when they are ripe, and stew during one whole day upon a gentle fire, adding fresh bits of pumpkin as the mass softens. If this be steamed enough, it will look much like baked apples, and, dressed with a little vinegar and ginger, is to me a most tempting rarity. But we do not often have it upon the table because of so much labor being needed to prepare it.

Yokhegg is a pudding of which I am exceedingly fond, and yet it is made of meal from the same Indian corn that supplies the people hereabout with so much of their food. It is boiled in milk and chocolate, sweetened to suit one's taste after being put on the table, and while to English people, who are not accustomed to all the uses which we make of this wheat, it may not sound especially inviting, it most truly is a toothsome dainty.

The cost of setting one's table here is not great as compared with that in England, for we may get a quart of milk by paying a penny, or a dozen fat pigeons, in the season, for three pence, while father has more than once bought wild turkeys, to the weight of thirty pounds, for two shillings, and wild geese are worth but eight pence.

Ruth

APPLE SAUCE OMELET (BAKED)

Beat the yolks of seven eggs light, sift into them five spoonfuls of powdered sugar and a cupful and a half of sweetened apple sauce. Beat long and hard, stir in the stiffened whites, beat for a minute longer and turn into a greased pudding dish. Bake, serve at once with whipped cream. It is also good served with a hot sauce made by the following recipe.

Into a pint of boiling water stir a half-cupful of sugar, and when this dissolves add a teaspoonful of butter, the juice and the grated rind of a lemon and the stiffened white of an egg. Beat for a minute over the fire, but do not let the sauce boil.

Marion Harland's Complete Cook Book, 1903

BISCUITS

The Marquis de Chastellux, traveling through North America in the early 1780's, wrote of a meal he had at the Bullion Tavern in Basking Ridge, New Jersey: "Our supper was very good; only bread was lacking; but inquiring of us what sort we wanted, in an hour's time they served us what we had asked for. This speed will appear less extraordinary, if one knows that in America little cakes, which are easily kneaded and baked in half an hour, often take the place of bread. Possibly one might tire of them, but I always found them to my taste whenever I met with them."

Churning butter—1890's

CRACKNELS

Two cups of rich milk, four tablespoonfuls of butter and a gill of yeast, a teaspoonful of salt; mix warm, add flour enough to make a light dough. When dough is ready, roll thin and cut in long pieces three inches wide, prick well with a fork and bake in a slow oven. They are to be mixed rather hard and rolled very thin, like soda crackers.

The White House Cook Book, 1887

THE SCHOOLMASTER 'BOARDING ROUND'

Extract from the Journal of a Vermont Schoolmaster.

Monday.—Went to board at Mr. B—'s, had a baked goose for dinner; supposed from its size, the thickness of its skin, and other venerable appearances, to have one of the first settlers of Vermont—made a slight impression on the patriarch's breast. *Supper*—cold goose and potatoes; family consisting of man, good wife, daughter Peggy, four boys, Pompey the dog, and a brace of cats, fire built in the square room about 9 o'clock, and a pile of wood laid by the fire place; saw Peggy scratch her fingers, and couldn't take the hint—felt squeamish about the stomach, and talked about going to bed; Peggy looked sullen, and put out the fire in the square room; went to bed, and dreamed of having eaten a quantity of stone wall.

Tuesday.—Cold gander for breakfast, swamp tea and some nutcakes; the latter some consolation. *Dinner*—The legs, &c. of the gander done up warm, one nearly dispatched. *Supper*—The other leg, &c. cold; went to bed as Peggy was carrying the fire to the square room, dreamed I was a mad turtle, and got on my back and could not get over again.

Wednesday—Cold gander for breakfast; complained of sickness, and could eat nothing. *Dinner*—Wings, &c. of the gander warmed up; did my best to destroy them for fear they should be left for supper, did not succeed; dreaded supper all the afternoon. *Supper*—Hot Indian Johnny cakes, and no goose; felt greatly relieved, thought I had got clear of the gander, and went to bed for a good night's rest; disappointed; very cold night, and couldn't keep warm in bed; got up, and stopped the broken windows with my coat and vest; no use; froze the tip of my nose a little before morning.

Thursday—Breakfast; cold gander again! felt very much discouraged to see the gander not half gone; went a visiting for dinner and supper; slept abroad and had pleasant dreams.

Friday—Breakfast abroad. Dinner at Mr. B—'s; cold gander and hot potatoes; last very good; eat three, and went to school quite contented. *Supper*—Cold gander, and no potatoes; bread heavy and dry; had the head ache and couldn't eat; Peggy much concerned; had a fire built in the square room and thought she and I had better sit there out of the noise; went to bed early; Peggy thought too much sleep bad for the head ache.

Saturday—Breakfast, cold gander, and hot Indian Johnny-cake; did very well; glad to come off so. *Dinner*—Cold gander again; didn't keep school this afternoon; weighed, and found I had lost six pounds the past week; grew alarmed; had a talk with Mr. B. who concluded I had boarded out his share; made no objection—bid the family and gander 'good bye,' and went to Mr. C's.

Farmer's Almanac, 1845

FOOD, 1860–1900

Although the city man was beginning to acquire a taste for new foods, outside of the city the frying pan was still the most used kitchen pan. Isolated in winter, the

Ordering from the grocer

farmer tried to make up in warmth on the inside what he lacked on the outside by stuffing himself with poultry and game. Then in the spring he trekked off to the village druggist for the spring dose of sulphur 'n' molasses.

After 1870, with the refrigerator cars now in operation, food was brought from other places, not all locally. From factories came canned tomatoes and milk, canned corn and beef, canned peas and beans, canned tuna and sardines. Forerunners of a long line of packaged cereals, Quaker Oats and Wheatena took the place of the traditional cornmeal mush at breakfast.

Meanwhile there was a surge of immigration from the European countries and each of the immigrants brought their native dishes. While German sauerkraut and the white potato had been familiar for many years, the Italians contributed spaghetti, the Hungarians, goulash.

Appliances—the steam cooker, the double boiler, the Dover egg beater, the gas toaster, the asbestos stove mat, the cake tin with removable bottom—invaded the kitchen in such bewildering variety that the housekeeper had to learn cooking all over again. Schools were organized throughout the country for just this purpose. Another revolution occurred in the nineties with the introduction of light, non-poisonous, heat-conductible, and easily handled aluminum ware.

HOUSEHOLD CONVENIENCE: *A Letter from Ruth*

Dear Hannah:

Do you know what a Betty lamp is? We have two in our house, which were brought over by Captain Pierce as a gift for my mother.

You, who have more or less trouble with your rushlights, cannot fancy how luxurious it is to have one of these Betty lamps, which cost in care no more than is required to fill them with grease or oil.

Fearing lest you may not know what these lamps are, which Sarah's mother says should be called brown-Bettys, I will do my best to set down here such a description as shall bring them before you.

The two which we have are made of brass; but we were told that they are also to be found in pewter or in iron.

These are round, and very much the shape of half an apple, save that they have a nose an inch or two long, which sticks out from one side. The body of the bowl is filled with tallow or grease, and the wick, or a piece of twisted cloth, is threaded into the nose, with one end hanging out to be lighted.

Ours hang by chains from the ceiling, and the light which they give is certainly equal to, if not stronger than, that of a wax candle; but they are not so clean, because if the wick be ever so little too long, the lamps send forth a great smoke.

Father says he has seen a Phoebe lamp, which is much like our Betty lamps, save that it has a small cup underneath the nose to catch the dripping grease, and that I think would be a great improvement, if indeed it is possible to improve upon so useful an article of household furniture as this.

Speaking of our Betty lamps reminds me that Sarah's mother had sent over to her a set of cob irons, which are something after the fashion of andirons, or fire dogs, save that they are also intended to hold the spit and the dripping pan. She has also a pair of "creepers," which are small andirons, and which she sometimes uses with the cob irons.

The andirons which we brought from England are much too fine to be used in this fireplace, which is filled with pothooks, trammels, hakes, and other cooking utensils.

They were a wedding present to my mother, and are in what we call "sets of three," meaning that on each side of the fireplace are three andirons; one to hold the heavy logs that are at the bottom of the fire, another raised still higher to bear the weight of the smaller sticks, and a third for much the same purpose as the second; or, perhaps, to make up more of an ornamentation, for they are of iron and brass, and are exceedingly beautiful to look upon.

Ruth

FOOD FOR THE VEGETARIAN

The subject of vegetarianism is coming more and more to the front, and is no longer treated with ridicule by thoughtful people. Fifty years ago the vegetarian required courage to face the attitude of contemptuous incredulity attached to his peculiar mode of living, but we of to-day have grown broader in our opinions and less ready to condemn our neighbors because they differ in theories or methods of living from ourselves . . .

To be a vegetarian means the abjuring of all flesh that has given up its life for food. The use of eggs and milk is allowed, and inconsistent as it seems, fish is sometimes eaten . . . Milk and eggs are called animal products. Their use does not require the taking of life. Strictly speaking they are not vegetable foods and a considerable number of vegetarians exclude them. On the other hand a few include oysters and some, fish with milk and eggs . . .

The vegetarian needs to know how to combine food so that the body will be nourished without the use of meat. Fruit and nuts should largely enter into a menu that excludes flesh . . . Peas, beans and lentils are also especially nourishing. It is said that the Pyramids of Egypt were built by men who could have had little else to sustain them than lentils.

The Delineator, June 1883

MAGAZINES

In the twenty years following the Civil War, 9,000 different magazines were printed; yet in no single year were there more than 3,300 in existence. However, in 1900 there were about 5,500 magazines, many of which were magazines slanted to the woman. In fact, about half a dozen periodicals had passed the 500,000 circulation mark by 1900 and of these *Comfort, Ladies' Home Journal,* and *Hearthstone* were the leaders.

JUICE PIE

Two cups of fruit juice, one cup of sugar, let come to a boil, stir in two tablespoons of cornstarch dissolved in a little juice, boil from three to five minutes, set off the fire, add a lump of butter the size of an egg, one half teaspoon of Buckeye cinnamon, one half teaspoon of vanilla, yolks of two eggs. Bake with one crust, using the two whipped whites for frosting.

Cherry City Cook Book, 1898

HUNGER IS THE BEST SAUCE

As a rule a person who has a good appetite has good health. But how many there are who enjoy nothing they eat, and sit down to meals only as an unpleasant duty. Nature's antidotes for this condition are so happily combined in Hood's Sarsaparilla that it soon restores good digestion, creates an appetite, and renovates and vitalizes the blood so that the beneficial effect of good food is imparted to the whole body. Truly hunger is the best sauce, and Hood's Sarsaparilla induces hunger.

Good Bread, published by C.I. Hood & Co
Proprietors of Hood's Sarsaparilla

BREAKFAST

Breakfast may be made the pleasantest meal of the day. In some families it is so; it ought to be in all. The table should be made attractive in appearance; luncheons and dinners should not alone absorb all attention and ornamentation . . .

As to what should be eaten, that must be left to the tastes of each family, modified, of course, by the season. But as a rule, there should be fruit, in some shape, at least. An old proverb says that fruit in the morning is golden, but in the evening is lead. A dish of it ought always to be on the table in the morning, so that we may at any rate have the chance of indulging in the gold. In summer, fresh fruit is attainable by everyone; in the winter stewed fruit should replace the fresh . . . Some people indulge in different sorts of breakfast cakes and hot breads, although they are generally unhealthy and indigestible. Why not be content with good crisp toast? or, if dry toast be objected to, do not make it dry. New rolls, if quite cold, are not so unwholesome as hot bread and cakes. Bread a day old, or brown bread, are far better than the smoking rolls, etc., one so often sees. We often hear people wondering why they have dyspepsia, after they have eaten enough hot rolls, at breakfast, to kill anything, but an ostrich. Of course, if you take a good deal of exercise, you may eat even hot cakes with impunity. But sedentary people cannot indulge in these dishes without dyspepsia.

Peterson's Magazine, January 1865

EVERYONE HAS ARRIVED

For a family gathering, the housewife would usually prepare a week or two in advance. Fruitcakes and tins of puddings were prepared, pies of every kind baked. The turkeys were taken from the fattening pen, butchered, stuffed, and roasted, and whole hams were studded with cloves, maple sugar-glazed, and baked. When the family got together for Thanksgiving or Christmas, it was not just for the day. Travel was hard, and once one arrived at his destination he made a long visit.

The housewife also had to prepare for a crowd on threshing day, when all the neighbors came to help in the field and the women helped in the kitchen. Every farmer cooperated with his neighbor. There was a holiday atmosphere and a square dance and refreshments served at the day's end.

Barn raisings, house raisings—practically any type of help was cooperative, and mountains of food were prepared with the workers and the guests. Neighbors were neighbors and always ready and willing to cooperate with one another. "Love thy neighbor" was in effect.

GRINDING CORN: *A Letter from Ruth*

Dear Hannah:

When I heard Squanto telling father that corn must be ground, I said to myself that we were not like to know how it might taste, for there is not a single mill in this land; but Squanto first cut a large tree down, leaving the stump a full yard in weight. Then by building a fire in the stump, scraping away with a sharp rock the wood as fast as it was charred, he made a hollow like unto a hole, and so deep that one might put in half a bushel of this turkie wheat.

From another portion of the tree, he shaped a block of wood to fit exactly the hole in the stump, and this he fastened to the top of a young slender tree, when even we children knew that he had made a mortar and pestle, although an exceedingly rude one.

We had only to pull down the heavy block with all our strength upon the corn, thus bruising and crushing it, when the natural spring of the young tree would pull it up again. In this way did we grind our Guinny wheat until it was powdered so fine that it might be cooked in a few moments.

Ruth

CORN ON THE COB

When Fredrika Breme visited America in 1850, she was amazed when she saw: "Some people take the whole stem and gnaw out with their teeth: two gentlemen do so who sit opposite myself at the table, and whom we call 'the sharks,' because of their remarkable ability in gobbling up large and often double portions of everything which comes to table, and it really troubles me to see how their wide mouths ravenously grind up the beautiful, white, pearly maize ears."

TO DRY PEACHES

Take the fairest and ripest peaches, pare them into fair water; take their weight in double refined sugar. Of one half make a very thin syrup; then put in your peaches, boiling them till they look clear, then split and stone them.

Boil them till they are very tender, lay them a-draining, take the other half of the sugar and boil it almost to a candy. Then put in your peaches and let them lie all night. Then lay them on a glass, and set them in a stove till they are dry. If they are sugar'd too much wipe them with a wet cloth a little; let the first syrup be very thin, a quart of water to a pound of sugar.

The Frugal Housewife, 1772

HERB DYES OF THE 1700'S

The housewife did her own dyeing of cloth and therefore used whatever she·had at hand.

Blue, in all shades, was the favorite color, and was dyed with indigo. So great was the demand for this dyestuff that indigo-peddlers traveled over the countryside selling it.

Madder, cochineal, and dogwood dyed beautiful reds. The bark of red oak or hickory made very pretty shades of brown and yellow. Various flowers growing on the farm could be used for dyes. The flower of the goldenrod, when pressed of its juice, mixed with indigo, and added to alum, made a beautiful green. The juice of the pokeberry boiled with alum made crimson dye, and a violet juice from the petals of the iris, or "flower-de-luce," that blossomed in June meadows, gave a delicate light purple tinge to white wool.

The bark of the sassafras was used for dyeing yellow or orange color, and the flowers and leaves of the balsam, also. Fustic and copperas gave yellow dyes. A good black was obtained by boiling woolen cloth with a quantity of the leaves of the common field sorrel, then boiling again with logwood and copperas.

Elderberry was also used for blue, while parsley made a lovely shade of green, and hop-stalks dyed the wool brown.

TIN UTENSILS

When tin found its way into the homes, there was another array of cooking utensils. There was a tin bird roaster and a tin apple roaster. The bird roaster was an upright support holding six hooks, onto which bobwhites were hung by their breasts. The bottom part of this small roaster, ten inches wide and eight inches high, was shaped like a pan into which the juices ran. The apple roaster was made with two shelves, holding four apples each. This stood before the fire, resting on one support at the back and two small front feet. A biscuit oven was made in sizes to accommodate various sizes of family. It was in two parts, one hinged to the other, so that the biscuits might be watched as they baked in front of the hot embers. A sheet of tin held the biscuits, resting on supports at the sides of the lower part of the oven. Small biscuit ovens were made of one piece.

EARLY HERBS

As the early ships from Europe landed along the Atlantic Coast, colonists brought their cherished seeds and plants with them because of the "vertues" attributed to them in Old World medicine and cooking. The people believed that many plants indicated their usefulness to health by some particular sign, such as color, texture, or shape.

Herbals published in England before 1650 formed the basis for "Physick" during the following century. In America, the early colonists used their gardens to furnish both food and remedies.

Many secrets bubbled in colonial kitchen pots. A good cook knew her fruits, vegetables, and herbs—and interesting things to do with them. She prepared teas, wines, or remedies ("Simples") as easily as a meal.

Herbs were gathered as follows: flowers in summer; leaves and bark in spring; and roots in spring and fall. To dry the herbs, the colonists hung them from the rafters of the kitchen in bundles.

The small colonial herb garden was cultivated carefully as a kitchen necessity. Herbs, fresh or dried, were used in daily cooking to improve flavor, and because it was believed that herbs aided in digestion and health. A colonial woman often established her reputation as a homemaker by her knowledge of the flavoring magic of herbs as well as their medicinal value.

When a colonial hostess served a "dish of tea," she brewed it carefully in a non-metal pot, allowing 1 teaspoon dried herb to a cup of boiling water. It was steeped until as strong as desired, then served with honey or lemon. Long before the Boston Tea Party, certain teas were thought to have mildly medicinal values and could refresh, quieten, or warm the blood on a cold day.

While colonial cooks knew nothing about vitamins, or nutrition as we know it today, they knew what foods were considered necessary to maintain good health. Children were told to eat a certain food because it was a specialty food for a certain part of the body.

Although nuts and seeds were used from Biblical times, in 1608 a Virginia colonist wrote home to London of the strange uses the Indians made of the simple seeds and nuts gathered in the woods and fields. He said that the Indians used acorns to furnish a sweet oil which they kept in gourds to anoint their "heades and joynts."

It was believed that spices had almost magical powers for preserving foods and meat, stimulating the body, and protecting against illness. When the colonists came to America, spices were still being used as antiseptics, pain killers, and stimulants. Cooks used spices to flavor foods, and also believed that they added protection against gas, colic, and poor digestion.

HONEY

Honey could be gathered wild in the forests and used as a sweetener, but the supply was limited and the long hours of searching needed to find a single comb could be spent on other tasks.

GLASS

Glass was made in the colonies of silica (sand) and two alkaline bases, either soda (found in salt water) or potash (leached from wood ashes) and lime (found in oyster shells). There was much and varied need for glass in the form of beads, window glass, bottles, and other utensils. The Wistars of Philadelphia were good businessmen and the first American glass manufacturers to make flint glass. They had competition from Henry William Stiegel, mentioned earlier, who arrived in Philadelphia from Rotterdam on August 31, 1750.

SEVERAL SAUCES FOR ROAST HENS

Take beer, salt, the yolks of three hard eggs minced small, grated bread, three or four spoonfuls of gravy; and being almost boiled, put in the juice of two or three oranges, slices of a lemon and orange, with lemon peel shred small.

Beaten butter with juice of lemon or orange, white or claret wine.

Gravy and claret wine boiled with a piece of onion, nutmeg, and salt; serve it with slices of oranges or lemons, or the juice in the sauce.

Or with oyster liquor, an anchovy or two, nutmeg, and gravy, and rub the dish with a clove of garlic.

Take the yolks of hard eggs and lemon peel, mince them very small, and stew them in white wine, salt, and the gravy of the fowl.

The Accomplisht Cook, 1678

TO STEW PEARS

Pare six pears, and either quarter them or do them whole; they make a pretty dish with one whole, the rest cut in quarters, and the cores taken out. Lay them in a deep earthen pot, with a few cloves, a piece of lemon peel, a gill of red wine, and a quarter of a pound of fine sugar.

If the pears are very large, they will take half a pound of sugar, and a half a pint of red wine; cover them close with brown paper, and bake them till they are done enough.

Serve them up hot or cold, just as you like them, and they will be very good with water in the place of wine.

The Frugal Housewife, 1772

TO POT LOBSTERS

Take a dozen of large lobsters; take out all the meat of their tails and claws after they are boiled; then season them with pepper, salt, cloves, mace, and nutmeg, all finely beaten and mixed together; then take a pot, put therein a layer of fresh butter, upon which put a layer of lobster, and then strew over some seasonings, and repeat the same till your pot is full, and your lobster all in; bake it about an hour and a half, then set it by two or three days, and it will be fit to eat. It will keep a month or more, if you pour from it the liquor when it comes out of the oven, and fill it up with clarified butter. Eat with vinegar.

The Complete Housewife, E. Smith, 1766

PLUM-POTTAGE

Take two gallons of strong broth; put to it two pounds of currants, two pounds of raisons of the Sun, half an ounce of Sweet Spice, a pound of Sugar, a quart of claret, a pint of Sack, the juice of three oranges and three lemons; thicken it with grated biskets, or rice flour with a pound of pruants.

Author's note: Pruants are prunes, Sweet Spice is cloves, mace, nutmeg, cinnamon, sugar, and salt.

Receipts of Pastry and Cookery, c. 1730

TO MAKE A CATCHUP TO KEEP SEVEN YEARS

Take two quarts of the oldest strong beer you can get, put to it one quart of red wine, three quarters of a pound of anchovies, three ounces of shalots peeled, half an ounce of mace, the same of nutmegs, a quarter of an ounce of cloves, three large races [roots] of ginger cut in slices. Boil all together over a moderate fire, till one third is wasted. The next day bottle it for use; it may be carried to the East Indies.

The Experienced English House-Keeper, 1778

MUSTARD OF DIJON, OR FRENCH MUSTARD

The seed being cleansed, stamp it in a mortar with vinegar and honey. Then take eight ounces of seed, two ounces of cinnamon, two of honey, and vinegar as much as will serve good mustard not too thick. And keep it close covered in little oyster-barrels.

The Accomplisht Cook, 1678

CORN PUDDING

The Early American housewife was particularly ingenious at inventing variations for what became a standard table item—corn pudding. The six most common recipes all involved meal and liquid, which were mixed in differing proportions and cooked various lengths of time. The most popular concoctions were:

Hasty pudding, a quickly cooled gruel of cornmeal boiled in almost equal parts with milk or water. Hasty pudding was also called loblolly.

Indian pudding, a slightly more liquid version of hasty pudding which was boiled in a bag containing various spices.

Suppawn, a thick mixture of cornmeal and milk, eaten either hot or cold from the pot, or allowed to cool. Then it could also be sliced and fried in deep fat.

Mush, a watery type of suppawn eaten with sweetened fruit or molasses.

Samp porridge, an Indian goulash featuring cornmeal cooked for a minimum of three days with meats and vegetables. After the prolonged simmering, this mixture became so thick that it could be removed from the pot in one solid chunk.

HOME REMEDIES

Descriptions of popular household remedies of the seventeenth century are to be found in a volume entitled *The Queen's Closet Opened, or The Pearl Of Practice*, published in 1656. For example, "Bruise a handfull of aniseeds, and steep them in Red Rose Water. Make it up in little bags, and bind one of them to each nostril, and it will cause sleep."

Again, to cure deafness, "Take Garden Daisie roots, and make juice thereof. Lay the worst side of the head low upon the bolster, and drop three or four drops thereof into the better ear. This do three or four days together."

SALADS

Mixed greens and vegetable salads, topped with oil and vinegar dressings, were well known to the colonists. Wild greens, such as leeks, pigweed, cowslip, cress, milkweed, ferns, purslane, swamp cabbage, and the leaves of the pokeberry bush, were often eaten raw in what was then called "sallet." In some cases, these were supplemented with radishes, violets, sorrel, sunflowers, spinach, savory, wild rhubarb, mushrooms, endive, and turnip greens. Beet tops, dandelions, and lettuce were all important salad greens. Cucumbers, believed valuable in unstopping the liver, were also used in salads.

FASHIONS IN PHILADELPHIA *by Dolly Madison* (1791)

And now, my dear Anna, we will have done with judges and juries, courts, both martial and partial, and we will speak a little about Philadelphia and the fashions, the beaux, Congress, and the weather. Do I not make a fine jumble of them? What would Harper or beau Dawson say were they to know it, ha, ha,—mind you laugh here with me. Philadelphia never was known to be so lively at this season as at present; for an accurate account of the amusements, I refer you to my letter to your sister Mary.

I went yesterday to see a doll, which has come from England, dressed to show us the fashions, and I saw besides a great quantity of millinery. Very long trains are worn, and they are festooned up with loops of bobbin and small covered buttons, the same as the dress; you are not confined to any number of festoons, but put them according to your fancy, and you cannot imagine what a beautiful effect it has. There is also a robe which is plaited very far back, open and ruffled down the sides, without a train, even with the petticoat. The hats are quite a different shape from what they used to be: they have no slope in the crown, scarce any rim, and are turned up at each side, and worn very much on the side of the head. Several of them are made of chipped wood, commonly known as cane hats; they are all lined: one that has come for Mrs. Bingham is lined with white, and trimmed with broad purple ribbon, put round in large puffs, with a bow on the left side. The bonnets are all open on the top, through which the hair is passed, either up or down as you fancy, but latterly they wear it more up than down; it is quite out of fashion to frizz or curl the hair, as it is worn perfectly straight. Earrings, too, are very fashionable. The waists are worn two inches longer than they used to be, and there is no such thing as long sleeves. They are worn half way above the elbow, either drawn or plaited in various ways, according to fancy; they do not wear ruffles at all, and as for elbows, Anna, ours would be alabaster, compared to some of the ladies who follow the fashion; black or a colored ribbon is pinned round the bare arm, between the elbow and the sleeve. Some new-fashioned slippers for ladies have come made of various colored kid or morocco, with small silver clasps sewed on; they are very handsome, and make the feet look remarkably small and neat. Everybody thinks the millinery last received the most tasty seen for a long time.

All our beaux are well; the amiable Chevalier is perfectly recovered, and handsomer than ever. You can have no idea, my dear girl, what pleasant times I have; there is the charming Chevalier, the divine Santana, the jolly Vicar, the witty and agreeable Fatio, the black-eyed Lord Henry, the soft, love-making Count, the giggling, foolish Duke, and sometimes the modest, good Meclare, who are at our house every day. We have fine riding parties and musical frolics.

Traveling in style

SUMMERTIME IN THE LATE 1800'S

Summertime was a time for heavy work if one lived on a farm. There was planting, haying, harvesting, and threshing. Fruit was gathered and preserved, while the vegetables were also preserved for use in the coming winter.

However, it was also the time for visiting, family reunions, and home picnics. There were country fairs to be visited, and the farm wife looked forward to exhibiting her quilts and pies and preserves. Perhaps she would get a ribbon for one of her exhibitions.

BAKED BEETS

Beets retain their sugary delicate flavor to perfection if they are baked instead of boiled. Turn them frequently while in the oven, using a knife, as the fork allows the juice to run out. When done, remove the skin and serve with butter, salt and pepper on the slices.

Ladies' Home Cook Book, 1885

FEMALE PHYSICIANS

A very influential Boston paper submits the following opinions, as those now popular in New England:—

That the medical profession is hereafter to consist of women as well as men, is no longer a matter of doubt, judging from the strong setting of public sentiment in this direction. The preference for females in some departments of practice is becoming so general, we understand that the few who are educated are overtasked with labor, and many incompetent women are prompted to advertise themselves, and, for the want of those better qualified, they are employed. To prevent the evils from this source, it is important that the Female Medical College in this city, designed to accommodate the whole of New England, should be placed in a condition to afford a thorough scientific and practical education to a sufficient number of suitable females.

Godey's Lady's Book and Magazine, 1853

MADEMOISELLE HAZARD,—This young lady succeeds her mother, lately deceased, in the tuition of dancing, at the corner of Twelfth and Chestnut Streets, Sime's Building. We cheerfully recommend her as one well versed in the art, and worthy of the support of Philadelphians, with whom her mother was so deservedly a favorite.

Godey's Lady's Book and Magazine, 1853

FISH A L'ORLY

Bone, skin and cut the fish in pieces; beat two eggs and a pinch of salt together and dip each piece of fish in it; roll in browned bread crumbs; fry in hot fat; turn the sauce on a platter and lay the fish in it. The sauce is made by putting half a can of tomatoes in a saucepan with a little onion, two or three stalks of parsley, thyme, one bay leaf, one clove, six pepper corns and salt; reduce, by boiling, one-third; strain gently through a collender, and return to the fire with half a spoonful of butter, a little water and flour mixed smoothly.

Everyday's Need, 1873

CLAMS

First catch your clams,—along the ebbing edges
Of saline coves you'll find the precious wedges,
With backs up, lurking in the sandy bottom;
Pull in your iron rake, and lo! you've got 'em.
Take thirty large ones, put a basin under,
Add water, (three quarts) to the native liquor,
Bring to a boil (and, by the way, the quicker
It boils the better, if you do it cutely).
Now add the clams, chopped up and minded minutely,
Allow a longer boil of just three minutes,
And while it bubbles quickly stir within its
Tumultuous depths, where still the mollusks mutter,
Four tablespoons of flour and four of butter,
A pint of milk, some pepper to your notion,—
And clams need salting, although born of ocean.
Remove from fire (if much boiled they will suffer,—
You'll find that Indian-rubber isn't tougher);
After 'tis off, add three fresh eggs well beaten,
Stir once more, and it's ready to be eaten.
Fruit of the wave! Oh, dainty and delicious!
Food for the gods! Ambrosia for Apicius!
Worthy to thrill the soul of sea-born Venus,
Or titillate the palate of Silenus!

The Household Friend, 1879

HOUSES, 1825–1860

What had been beautiful when applied to religious architecture became grotesque when applied to houses. Householders, decorators, and most architects attempted to make up for lack of imagination in style and design by lavishness of decoration. A bare spot was not to be endured. Pointed gables, towers, and oriel windows broke the outline of roof and facade. Bay windows were supported by heavy decorative brackets. Hollow brick walls, often painted a dark brown, were adorned with elaborate stone trimmings on the slightest provocation. Behind the flamboyant curves of cast-iron ornaments gleamed small, diamond-paned casement windows.

Inside, softwood floors were entirely covered with carpets in brightly flowered patterns. There was a fireplace in every room. Flowered paper covered the walls to within two or three feet of the floor. A stained or gilded wood molding separated the wallpaper from the plain strip beneath, which was painted a uniform color. Thick satins, draped to the jambs and crowned with festooned lambrequins, did their best to shut out light and air.

LETTER FROM MARTHA WASHINGTON TO HER SISTER

Mt. Vernon, Aug. 28, 1762

My Dear Nancy,—I had the pleasure to receive your kind letter of the 25 of July just as I was setting out on a visit to Mr. Washington in Westmoreland where I spent a weak very agreably I carried my little Patt with me and left Jackey at home for a trial to see how well I could stay without him though we are gone but wone fortnight I was quite impatient to get home. If I at aney time heard the doggs barke or a noise, out I though thair was a person sent for me. . .

We are daly expect[ing] the kind laydes of Maryland to visit us. I must begg you will not lett the fright you had given you prevent you comeing to see me again—If i could leave my children in as good Care as you can I would never let Mr. W. . .n come down without me— Please to give my love to Miss Judy and your little babys and make my best compliments to Mr. Bassett and Mrs. Dawson.

I am with sincere regard

dear sister
Yours most affectionately
MARTHA WASHINGTON

ROASTING

Roasting was a third method of fireplace cooking, but one usually reserved for cuts of domestic stock or the most tender sections of game animals.

Andirons, or fire dogs, were equipped with special notches for supporting the spit on which meats were skewered for roasting. If andirons were lacking, the meat was wrapped in a rope sling and hung from the lug pole. Using either method, the meat was turned periodically to assure even cooking, and a pan was placed just below the roast to catch the drippings for use in basting or in flavoring other dishes.

Children were often assigned the job of turning the spit, but more elaborate roasting mechanisms were devised as the country became more advanced technologically.

With time, less cumbersome methods of roasting were introduced in America. Many homes used portable metal ovens called roasting kitchens. These were shaped like rectangular boxes but were open on the side that was placed before the fire. Smaller versions of this appliance were used to prepare any small game or bird.

Roasting meat—colonial days

A SALMON PYE

Take a convenient piece of fresh Salmon, 2 quarts of Shrimps or prawns, & ye like quantity of Oysters, Half a Quarter of an ounce of whole Mace, ye like of Beatton Pepper, & 4 Anchovies, Spread Your pye Bottom with a good piece of Butter, then lay in your Salmon, first Laid 3 or 4 hours in white Wine, then Strane your Seasoning upon it, lay good store of Butter on ye Topp then cover it & Bake it.

Manuscript of 18th Century at Tryon Palace, New Bern, N.C.

MISS BEECHER'S DOMESTIC RECEIPT BOOK, 1846

The temperance movement was founded in this country in the early years of the century and by the 1830's had attracted more than a million members. Some cookbooks stumped for the cause and Catherine Beecher, noted educator, was one of the most effective members of the temperance movement.

However, she held out for temperance in everything, not only alcohol, but tea, coffee, and food in general. She objected to fried foods, especially fried in animal oils. She was also materialistic, though, and realized that a cookbook without "receipts" for rich dishes would not be a best-seller; therefore, she did have some in the book, such as veal cutlets and fried mush.

TO PICKLE MUSHROOMS

Take your mushrooms as soon as they come in; cut the stalks off and throw your mushrooms into water and salt as you do them; then rub them with a piece of flannel, and as you do them, throw them into another vessel of salt and water, and when all is done, put some salt and water on the fire, and when it is scalding hot, put in your mushrooms, and let them stay in as long as you think will boil an egg; but first put them in a sieve, and let them drain from the hot water, and be sure to take them out of the hot water immediately, or they will wrinkle and look yellow. Let them stand in the cold water till next morning, then take them out, and put them into fresh water and salt, and change them every day for three or four days together; then wipe them very dry, and put them into distilled vinegar; the spice must be distilled in the vinegar.

The Complete Housewife, E. Smith, 1766

KEEPING FOOD FRESH

In the early days, the householder spent a lot of his time and energy just trying to keep food fresh.

If he was an early settler in his area, his first concern was to locate as near as possible to a cold, flowing spring, at which he built a "spring house," a low building with a stone trough running through it. The housewife was then able to set her bowls of milk and cream, and crocks of butter and cheese near or in its shaded icy water.

However, not every settler was lucky enough to have a stream on his property, but he did have a well, and it was the well that was used for refrigeration. The spoilables were put into a large bucket, or into a wooden frame with shelves, which was lowered into the well on a rope slung over a pulley until it hung just over the water level, where the air was quite cold.

The luckiest man of all was one who lived on land near a lake, pond or river that froze deeply in the winter. He built an ice house, a wooden building with double walls between which he stuffed sawdust for insulation. In the middle of the winter, he cut blocks of ice from the water and lugged it back to the ice house for use the following summer. Usually the ice-cutting was a community affair.

HOW TO BATHE PLANTS

Large-leaved plants, either the smooth- or the hairy-leaved, may be easily bathed in the windows where they stand, if the pots are too heavy to be removed, or if for any other reason it may seem best.

A soft cloth or sponge, well wet in slightly warm water, may be used to gently wipe off the upper and under sides of each leaf and wash down each stem. But a soft brush, similar to the hair brushes for babies, is better, especially for rough- or fuzzy-leaved plants.

If the leaf is corrugated it is yet more necessary that each depression be reached.

Household, 1875

Weeding the flax

FLAX: *A Letter from Ruth*

Dear Hannah:

It would be strange indeed if I failed to set down anything concerning the flax which we spin, because save for it we would have had nothing of linen except what could be brought from England.

Flax is sown early in the spring, and when the plants are three or four inches long, we girls are obliged to weed them, and in doing so are forced to go barefooted, because of the stalks being very tender and therefore easily broken down.

I do not believe there is a child in town who fails to go into the flax fields, because of its being such work as can be done by young people better than by older ones, who are heavier and more likely to injure the plants.

I have said that we are obliged to go barefooted, but where there is a heavy growth of thistles, as is often the case, we girls wear two or three pairs of woolen stockings to protect our feet.

If there is any wind, we must perforce work facing it, so that such of the plants as may by accident have been trodden down, may be blown back into place by the breeze.

Wearying labor it is indeed, this weeding of the flax, and yet those who come into the new world, as have we, must not complain at whatsoever is set them to do, for unless much time is expended, crops cannot be raised, and we children of Boston need only to be reminded of the famine, when we are inclined to laziness, in order to set us in motion.

Of course you know that flax is a pretty plant, with a sweet, drooping, blue flower, and it ripens about the first of July, when it is pulled up by the roots and laid carefully out to dry, much as if one were making hay. This sort of work is always done by the men and boys, and during two or three days they are forced to turn the flax again and again, so that the sun may come upon every part of it.

I despair of trying to tell anyone who has never seen flax prepared, how much and how many different kinds of labor are necessary, before it can be woven into the beautiful linen of which our mothers are so proud.

First it must be rippled. The ripple comb is made of stout teeth, either wood or iron, set on a pouch, and the stalks of the flax are pulled through it to break off the seeds, which fall into a cloth that has been spread to catch them, so they may be sown for the next year's harvest.

Of course this kind of work is always done in the fields, and the stalks are then tied in bundles, which are called "bates," and stacked up something after the shape of a tent, being high in the middle and broadened out at the bottom.

After the flax has been exposed to the weather long enough to be perfectly dry, then water must be sprinkled over it to rot the leaves and such portions of the stalks that are not used.

Then comes that part of the work which only strong men can perform, called breaking the flax, to get from the center of the stalks the hard, wood-like "bun," which is of no value. This is done with a machine made of wood, as if you were to set three or four broad knives on a bench, at a certain distance apart, with as many more on a lever to come from above, fitting closely between the lower blades. The upper part of the machine is pulled down with force upon the flax, so that every portion of it is broken.

After this comes the scutching, or swingling, which is done by chopping with dull knives on a block of wood to take out the small pieces of bark which may still be sticking to the fiber.

Now that which remains is made up into bundles, and pounded again to clear it yet more thoroughly of what is of no value, after which it is hackled, and the fineness of the flax depends upon the number of times it has been hackled, which means pulling it through a quantity of iron teeth driven into a board.

Breaking the flax

After all this preparation has been done, then comes the spinning, which is, of course, the work of the women and girls. I am proud to say that I could spin a skein of thread in one day, before I was thirteen years old, and you must know that this is no mean work for a girl, since it is reckoned that the best of spinners can do no more than two skeins.

Of course the skeins must be bleached, otherwise the cloth made from them would look as if woven of tow. This portion of the work mother is always very careful to look after herself.

The skeins must stay in warm water for at least four days, and be wrung out dry every hour or two, when the water is to be changed. Then they are washed in a brook or river until there is no longer any dust or dirt remaining, after which they are bricked, which is the same as if I had said bleached, with ashes and hot water, over and over again, afterward left to remain in clear water a full week.

Then comes more rinsing, beating, washing, drying, and winding on bobbins, so that it may be handy for the loom.

The chief men in Boston made a law that all boys and girls be taught to spin flax, and a certain sum of money was set aside to be given those who made the best linen that had been raised, spun, and woven within the town.

I am told that in some villages nearabout, the men who make the laws have ordered that every family shall spin so many pounds of flax each year, or pay a very large amount of money as a fine for neglecting to do so.

Ruth

Bleaching the flax

GARDENING FOR LADIES

Make up your beds early in the morning; sew buttons on your husband's shirts; do not rake up any grievances; protect the young and tender branches of your family; plant a smile of good temper in your face, and root out all angry feelings, and expect a good crop of happiness.

The Old Farmer's Almanac, 1862, Robert B. Thomas

Charles Joseph Latrobe in 1836 said: "No where is the stomach of the traveller or visitor put in such constant peril as among the cake-inventive housewives and daughters of New England. Such is the universal attention paid to this particular branch of epicurism in these states, that I greatly suspect that some of the Pilgrim Fathers must have come over to the country with Cookery Book under one arm and the Bible under the other."

CHEESE-MAKING: *Diary of An Early American Housewife*

August 5th, 1772—This is a good time to begin making our cheese. We are now waiting for some of the vegetables to ripen before preserving them for the winter. I hope that we shall have enough cheese to sell some to Abner Smith at the corners.

CHEESE-MAKING

Butter was not made during the hot summer months of July and August, but during these months the cheese was made, and the task was a hard one, requiring daily attention.

The first step was to prepare the rennet, or runnet. The stomach of a young calf which had never taken anything but milk was used. It was washed, turned, and washed again and put into a strong brine. When well salted, it was taken out and stretched over a stick to dry. It was then cut into small pieces and placed in jars or a bag called a "cheeselep." The liquid obtained was poured into the milk or cream, standing in tubs, and then stirred with wooden paddles. Coagulation took place and the curds which hardened had to be cut several times. The following morning the curds were put into the cheese drainer.

The drainer was placed on a rack or tongs, also called a cheese ladder, which rested on a tub. Cheesecloth was laid in the drainer and the mixture poured in, filling the drainer. The whey then drained through and was given to the pigs, while the curds were tied in the cloth and hung up to drain thoroughly. This mass again had to be cut with a curd knife made of wood, or run through a curd breaker, which was a box-shaped grinder with wooden teeth. This broken mass was then put into a wooden bowl, salted, and worked again, and thus made ready for the cheese press.

The purpose of the cheese press was to press and drain the curds of all the whey. There were many kinds. The press generally consisted of two uprights placed on a "floor" which was called the cheese board. The cheese board had a circular groove in it with a snout in front. As the top and bottom were pushed together, the balance of the whey was forced down the snout into a tub.

The following morning the cheese was taken out to be pressed. The cheesecloth was taken off and the cheese pared with a wooden knife and made smooth. It was then buttered, and a band of cloth, an inch wider than the cheese, was wrapped around it, lapping over fully four inches. The top and bottom were left exposed so that as the cheese was cured it could be turned and buttered every day. This last process took two weeks, the cheese having been put into the cheese closet. The air could come in and the flies kept out of the cheese because the front had cheesecloth.

Dutch cheese was made by crumbling cottage cheese and working in butter, salt, and chopped sage. Formed into pans, it was set to ripen. Cottage cheese was eaten with molasses on bread, like the Yankee combination of pork and molasses.

Cheese was often made with juices, which gave it different flavors, adding also to its appearance. Sage cheese was a common variety and was made by adding the juice of sage leaves or the leaves themselves, chopped fine. Other flavors were made from various herbs and herb teas, and from teas made by boiling young, green corn husks or spinach, which gave a fine green color. Pigweed water was used to color the cheese green without giving it any taste.

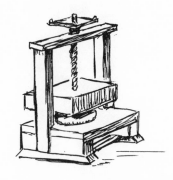

The cheese press

ICEBOXES

The first primitive refrigerator was patented in 1834 by Jacob Perkins, although at that time there were many large storehouses for ice throughout the country. No matter how well the housewife covered the ice in her cellar pantry, it melted very quickly. So she hailed the invention of the icebox, designed to make the ice last longer.

The first refrigerators were little more than lined boxes which held ice. The manufacturers also made refrigerators that looked like sideboards or lowboys.

The German Revolution of 1848 sent many German emigrants to the United States, and many of them were butchers who settled in and around Cincinnati, which had developed into a significant meat-packing area. Besides bringing with them the frankfurter, the weiner, and the hamburger, they also became involved with the process of refrigeration for train cars with blocks of ice. The first practical refrigerator car was built in the 1860's with ice bunkers lined with lead. From these cars the first models of home iceboxes emerged and rapidly found acceptance among homeowners.

Early home models were priced as low as $2.75 for a chest model to $56.00 for a large upright model.

After 1870 the ice was not always natural, since artificial ice was now being made in ice plants.

With the coming of the icebox, the milkman emerged as an important part of food delivery. The housewife also found that she could buy and store a greater variety of fresh foods and foods out of season.

FRYING

Frying was not one of the daily cooking techniques in most homes prior to 1850. A primary reason was the basically dangerous nature of open hearth cooking. Skillets with handles up to three feet in length were needed to reach into the fire if the housewife was to stand in a safe position on the hearth.

Frying pans could be set on long-legged trivets, but the action of turning the food without upsetting the skillet required a steady hand. This problem was solved to some degree by the manufacture of spiders, special skillets with legs attached to the bottom of the pan which were specifically used for frying over an open fire.

Splattering fat or flammable grease into the fire was an additional hazard in frying, as were the long-handled wooden spoons or turning spatulas that could catch fire at any moment. Finally, frying required much closer attention than other cooking methods, a distinct drawback for the harried colonial cook.

COOKBOOKS AND COOKSTOVES

After 1850, the compilers of cookbooks generally assumed that a woman who would buy a cookbook would be using a wood range that was economical in its fuel consumption and easy—well, relatively—to clean.

However, many good cooks believed that the cookstove worsened the American cuisine. Mrs. Harriet Beecher Stowe put into words what others felt when she wrote that "an open fireplace is an altar of patriotism. Would our Revolutionary fathers have gone barefooted and bleeding over snow to defend air-tight stoves and cooking ranges? I trow not. It was the memory of the great open kitchen-fire . . . its roaring, hilarious voice of invitation, its dancing tongues of flame, that called to them through the snows of that dreadful winter. . . ."

TRAINING DAY: *A Letter from Ruth*

Dear Hannah:

I must tell you of our Training Day and I am setting down what happened on that particular day, because of its being the largest and most exciting training ever held in Boston, so everyone says.

Sarah believes Training Day should come oftener than four times a year, so that we young people may get some idea of what gay life is in the old countries, where they make festivals of Christmas, and other Saint Days. It does truly seem as if we might see our soldiers perform quite often, for it is a most inspiring spectacle, and especially was it on last Training Day, when, so father says, there were upwards of seven hundred men marching back and forth across the Common in a manner which at times was really terrifying, because of their fierce appearance when fully armed.

Imagine, if you can, a row of booths along the Common, in which are for sale ground nuts, packages of nookick, sweet cakes, pumpkin bread roasted brown and spread with maple syrup, together with dainties of all kinds lately brought over from England.

Between these booths and the water are many tents, which have been set up so that the people of quality may entertain their friends therein with toothsome food and sweet waters.

The middle of the Common, and a long space at either end, is kept clear of idle ones, so that the soldiers may exercise at arms, and these do not appear until the on-lookers are in their places. Then we hear a flourish of trumpets, the rolling of drums, and from the direction of the Neck comes our army, a mighty array of seven hundred or more men, all armed and equipped as the law directs.

When this vast body of warlike men have marched into the vacant space, they are drawn up in line, there is another flourish of trumpets, together with the rolling of drums, and a prayer is offered by Master Cotton.

On this day, moved by the sight of the great throng, the prayer was long and fervent, whereat some of the younger soldiers, having not the fear of God in their hearts, pulled long faces, one to another, or shifted about uneasily on their feet, as if weary with long standing, and I trembled lest the Governor, seeing such levity, might rebuke them openly, which would be a great disgrace at such a time.

After the prayer, the soldiers began to march here and there in many ways until one's eyes were confused with watching them, and then came the volleys, as the men shot straight over the heads of the people; but father says one need not fear such warlike work, for there were no bullets in the guns. However, I could not but shudder when so many guns were fired at one time, while the smoke of powder in the air was most painful to the eyes.

After the soldiers had marched back and forth in the most ferocious manner possible until noon, they were allowed a time for rest, and then it was that those who set up tents entertained their friends at table with stores upon stores of dainties of every kind.

Ruth

HOUSEKEEPING

I love the good old-fashioned word
    "Housekeeping"—whatsoe-er they say;
There is another we have heard
    To take the place of it to-day.

It is a word that's long and dry,
    But everywhere they're preaching it;
Co-operation is the cry,
    It may be hard to practice yet.

Might we not call it *Coop*-eration,
    And each construct herself a tub,
Diogenes our mediation,
    And rest from all the fret and rub?

Ah, we are all of us to blame,
    For we are faint, and out of heart;
The homely ways we put to shame,
    And everyday we shirk our part.

The little cares that make the sum,
    Of our accustomed days and hours,
If we are faithful when they come,
    Will sweeten life like humble flowers.

Bathroom—1890's

So let us learn to live aright,
　　　To guide our homes with grace and power;
　Then shall we grow in depth and height,
　　　And ripen for the coming hour.

by Martha Perry Lowe, *American Kitchen Magazine,* July 1889

CANNING

Summertime was canning time—and a busy time for the housewife until she had the cellar filled with hundreds of jars full of fruits and vegetables. There were steamer cookers and pressure cookers invented and marketed as early as 1870, but most of the steamer cookers were ineffectual, while the pressure cookers were dangerous.

Therefore the housewife resorted to boilers of all sizes that could hold up to eighteen jars at a time. These came equipped with a metal rack to hold the jars a little above the bottom surface. Vegetables were usually precooked for a short time and packed in jars sterilized by boiling. The hot jars were sealed and placed on the rack in the boiler and covered with water to about two inches below the top; they were then boiled for as long as three or four hours.

Fruits did not require a water bath. Once the fruits were boiled in a sugar and water syrup they were placed in sterilized jars and the jars were sealed and set aside to cool.

However, the problem then as now was getting the jar to be perfectly airtight after filling. A little air in the jar and that was the end of the food in that jar.

ICE CREAM FREEZER

Ice cream used to be made only in the home, in an ice cream freezer that consisted of a wooden tub containing a metal can equipped with a crank and a paddle that were turned by hand. The freezing was accomplished with the aid of crushed ice, rock salt, and plenty of muscle. But muscle power was not lacking, as the reward for turning the crank was the privilege of licking the paddle after the job was done.

The variety of flavors was limited to vanilla, chocolate, fresh peach, and fresh strawberry.

DAMPNESS IN THE CLOSET

Place a bowl of quicklime in a damp pantry, cupboard, or closet. This not only removes dampness but kills all odors.

Household Discoveries, 1903

CHINA: *Diary of An Early American Housewife*

August 10, 1772—I have ordered some dishes which Captain Abner will bring back to me when he returns from his latest trip.

CHINAWARE

There was no china in common use on the table, and even little was owned by persons of wealth, throughout the seventeenth century, either in England or America. It was not until the late 1700's that china became a common table commodity and began to crowd out pewter. The sudden and tremendous spurt in East Indian commerce, along with the vast cargoes of Chinese pottery and porcelain brought to American ports, had given rise to ample china for every housewife. The first china used for general tableware was the handleless tea cup as tea became a necessity in the more affluent homes.

At first, china was not universally accepted because it broke so easily and dulled the edge of the knife as compared with woodenware.

Americans appreciated good china whether Oriental or European in origin and it was not uncommon to send special orders to be completed on an individual basis. Often monograms or armorial bearings on each piece were requested.

A very popular pattern then and still popular today was the Willow Pattern, which was designed by Thomas Turner in England in 1772 from a design of Chinese antiquity. The pattern caught on immediately and has been made ever since.

A GOOD BISQUE OF LOBSTER

Chop one pound of lobster meat very fine, melt two ounces of butter, adding three tablespoonfuls of sifted flour; when smooth add one pint of rich stock or soup; when boiled up add the lobster meat, one tablespoonful of fresh butter, one pint of cream, salt, pepper and mace to taste.

Culinary Helps and Hints,
Ladies' Home Journal, 1892

EXPERIENCE TALKS: EGGS

Eggs, in an emergency, will stamp or seal letters. Will seal the paper jelly-glass cover. Will render corrosive sublimate harmless, if half a dozen be given after an emetic. Will soothe a burn, if several applications of the white be put on to exclude the air. Will not permit a plaster to blister, if the mustard be mixed with egg instead of water. Will remove a fishbone from the throat, if the white be beaten and given at once.

Household, 1877

HOME MEDICINE

In an era when doctors, trained nurses, and well-equipped hospitals were still relatively scarce, childbearing and the treatment of sickness typically took place in the home. An ailing member of the family was bundled up in bed in the guest room or, in winter, on a daybed in the living room, and home remedies were applied: hot and cold compresses, immersion of the feet in hot water, drinking of special teas and herb brews—remedies that had not changed much for centuries. It was an age when the editor of a leading women's magazine could claim that dizziness, unsettled nerves, and female disorders could be cured by sleeping with the head of the bed northward.

The housewife would use one of the many patent medicines advertised in her magazines with complete confidence in its remedial powers. Only when home and patent remedies had failed was the doctor summoned, and his arrival was a signal for concern. Neighbors brought prepared food, with offers to attend the ailing one, and with the inevitable morsels of advice and recountings of personal experiences, most of them bad.

WHAT A YOUNG GIRL DOES AT HOME:
A Letter from Ruth

Dear Hannah:

Living here, if we do not know how to make what is needed, then we must go without, because one cannot well afford to spend the time, nor the money, required to send to London for whatever may be desired, and wait until it shall be brought across the sea.

I wonder if it would interest any of you to know what Sarah and I are obliged to do in our homes during each working day of the week?

I can remember a time when we were put to it to perform certain tasks within six days, and have set down that which we did.

It was on a Monday that Sarah and I hackled fifty pounds of flax, and tired we were when the day had come to an end. On Tuesday we carded tow, and on Wednesday each spun a skein of linen thread. On Thursday we did the same stint, and on Friday made brooms of guiney wheat straw. On Saturday we spun twine out of the coarser part of flax, which is called tow.

All this we did in a single week, in addition to helping our mothers about the house, and had no idea that we were working overly hard.

And now about tow: When flax has been prepared to that stage where it is to be hackled, the fibers pulled out by the comb are yet further divided into cobweb-like threads, and laid carefully one above the other as straight as may be. To these a certain yellow substance sticks, which we call tow, and this can be spun into coarse stuff for aprons and mats, or into twine, which, by the way, is not very strong.

It would surprise you, when working flax, to see how small a bulk may be reduced. What seems like an enormous stack, before being made ready for spinning, is lessened to such extent that you may readily take it in both hands, and then comes the next surprise, when you see how much cloth can be woven out of so small an amount of threads.

As for myself, I am not any too fond of working amid the flax, save when it comes to spinning; but such labor is the greatest pleasure as compared with soap-making, which is to my mind the most disagreeable and slovenly of all the housewife's duties.

Ruth

FROZEN COFFEE

Put one quart of cream in a bowl; add a pint of granulated sugar and half pint of cold, black coffee, very strong; whip until a stiff froth, then pour into a freezer and pack in salted ice; let stand two hours. Serve in little glass cups.

The Woman's Magazine, June 1903

THE WOMAN WHO LAUGHS

For a good, everyday household angel, give us the woman who laughs. Her biscuits may not be always just right, and she may occasionally burn her bread, and forget to replace dislocated buttons; but, for solid comfort all day and every day, she is a very paragon. The trick of always seeing the bright side, or, if the matter has no bright side, of shining up the dark one, is a very important faculty; one of the things no woman should be without. We are not all born with the sunshine in our hearts, as the Irish prettily phrase it; but we can cultivate a cheerful sense of humor, if we only try.

The Old Farmer's Almanac, 1889, Robert B. Thomas

DR. KING'S NEW DISCOVERY

William H. Mullen of 255 Wabash Avenue, Chicago, has no desire to stand as close to the awful brink of death as he had to before he was induced by a friend to try that marvelous cure, Dr. King's New Discovery. Mr. Mullen says that for a long time he suffered intensely from a very serious bronchial and lung trouble. He had tried six physicians, but without avail. They all gave him up. Then he followed his friend's advice and commenced to use Dr. King's New Discovery. After taking five bottles he was entirely cured, and felt as well as he ever did. He says he owes his life to this greatest of all cures.

Dr. King's Guide to Health and Family Cook Book, 1890

KEROSENE LAMPS

One of the daily chores for the farm boy and girl was taking care of the kerosene lamps—filling them with kerosene, trimming the wicks, and cleaning the glass chimneys. Kerosene lamps were widely used before electricity.

Some of the lamps were quite ornate, and many have been saved and converted to electricity for use today. In larger homes there was a chandelier or a large kerosene lamp hanging from the ceiling.

Child's carriage—1880's

A RECIPE FOR A WIFE

As much of beauty as preserves affection,
As much of cheerfulness as spurns detection,
Of modest deference as claims protection,
Yet stored with sense, with reason and reflection.
And every passion held in due subjection,
Just faults enough to keep her from perfection;
Find this, my friend, and then make your selection.

The Old Farmer's Almanac, 1858, Robert B. Thomas

BOILED FOWL WITH OYSTERS

Ingredients: One young fowl, three dozen oysters, the yolks of two eggs, quarter pint of cream.

Mode: Truss a young fowl as for boiling; fill the inside with oysters which have been bearded and washed in their own liquor; secure the end of the fowl, put it into a jar and plunge the jar into a saucepan of boiling water. Keep it boiling for one hour and a half, or rather longer, then with the gravy that has flowed from the oysters and fowl, of which there will be a good quantity, stir in the cream and yolks of the eggs, add a few oysters scalded in their liquor; let the sauce get quite hot, but do not allow it to boil; pour some of it over the fowl, and send the remainder to table in a tureen.

A blade of pounded mace added to the sauce, with the cream and eggs, will be found an improvement.

Time: One hour and a half. Sufficient for three or four persons.

Godey's Lady's Book and Magazine, 1861

Feeding the fowl

TO CLEAN BRUSHES

The best way in which to clean hairbrushes is with spirits of ammonia as its effect is immediate. No rubbing is required, and cold water can be used just as successfully as warm. Take a tablespoonful of ammonia to a quart of water, dip the hair part of the brush without wetting the ivory, and in a moment the grease is removed; then rinse in cold water, shake well, and dry in the air, but not in the sun. Soda and soap soften the bristles and invariably turn the ivory yellow.

Ladies' Home Cook Book, 1890

TO MAKE THE TEETH WHITE

A mixture of honey with the purest charcoal will prove an admirable cleanser.

MacKenzie's Five Thousand Receipts, 1848

THE TONGUE

A white fur on the tongue attends simple fever and inflammation. Yellowish of the tongue attends a derangement of the liver, and is common to bilious and typhus fevers. A tongue vividly red on the tip and edges, or down the centre, or over the whole surface, attends inflammation of the mucuous membrane of the stomach or bowels. A white velvety tongue attends mental disease. A tongue red at the lips, become brown, dry and glazed attends typhus fever.

Arts Revealed, 1859

FRIED ASPARAGUS

Wash and scrape the asparagus, cover with boiling water and let it stand five minutes; drain and dry on a soft towel. Sprinkle well with salt and pepper. Beat an egg until very light, add to it a half cup of milk and sufficient flour to make a thin batter, add a half teaspoonful of salt and beat the batter until smooth. Dip the asparagus one piece at a time into this batter, and drop at once into hot fat, and fry until a golden brown. When done, drain on brown paper and serve hot.

Hot Weather Dishes, 1888

CANNED BANANAS

Grate rind of four lemons into their juice and let soak over night. Boil two cups sugar and two cups water to a syrup. Add the lemon juice strained and one dozen bananas peeled and cut in pieces three-fourths of an inch long. Cook until of a semi-transparent appearance. Put into self-sealing glass jars which have been scalded.

For immediate use make half the above quantity, lift the fruit carefully into a glass fruit dish, boil the syrup very thick and pour over them. It will jelly when cold.

For variety substitute for the juice of each lemon one tablespoonful of cider jelly which is made by boiling cider fresh from the press without sugar until it jellies.

American Kitchen Magazine, 1872

EMBROIDERY: *Diary of An Early American Housewife*

August 25, 1772—I have asked Joshua to bring me some patterns to embroider when he next goes to Boston. Mrs. Allen who is located near the Old North Meetinghouse has put notices into the Boston Gazette about the new patterns she has. I would like some patterns of animals since I see boats whenever I look out of my window. Tomorrow I will finish embroidering the flowers on my new stockings. I am making a cap for Joshua to wear on his head at night when it gets so cold in the winter.

EMBROIDERY

Crewel work was a big thing at that time, as was needlepoint. Wools for needlepoint and crewels were known as worsted. The *Boston News Letter* of April 28, 1743, advertises: "Shaded crewels, blue, red, and other colours of Worsteds." At about the same time, another advertisement read: "Imported white thread and white chapple needles."

Although patterns could be bought ready-made, as seen in the advertisement of Mrs. Condy in the *Boston News Letter:* "All sorts of beautiful figures on Canvas, for Tent Stitch," others advertised at the same time that they made "All sorts of Drawing for Embroider." There were also advertisements from women who wanted to give instruction in the art of embroidery "and other Works proper for young Ladies." The tent stitch was usually the first stitch taught to very young girls as they attended the Dame Schools.

Silk stockings which were worn by the wealthier were frequently more costly than the attire on their backs and were elaborately embroidered on the instep in florals in silk. Nightcaps were also very elaborately made of silk and embroidered with flowers and gold lace effects.

BAKING BREAD

Although it was cheaper to buy bread than to make it (the fuel for the stove cost more than the flour at the end of the nineteenth century), most American housewives still preferred to make their own loaves. It was a time-consuming process, as indicated by a warning from a popular cookbook, *Practical Housekeeping* (1883): "Knead for from forty-five minutes to one hour . . . Any pause in the process injures the bread."

REFRIGERATORS

A refrigerator should be examined daily and kept thoroughly clean. If a suitable brush cannot be had, a long stiff wire with a bit of cloth on the end should be used to clean the drain pipe. Pour boiling washing-soda water through it every other day; and do not forget to wash off the slime that adheres to the water pan. Fish, onions, cheese, any strong vegetables, lemons, or meat not perfectly sweet, should not be kept in the same icebox with milk or butter.

Boston Cook Book, 1883

THE ICE WAGON

One of the most frequently seen vehicles on the street in the summertime was the ice wagon. Pulled by one or more horses, it delivered blocks of ice to stores and homes. The ice wagon was usually driven by a husky individual, who also had to cut and weigh the ice and carry it, by means of ice tongs, to the icebox. To keep from freezing his shoulder and getting himself wringing wet, the iceman placed a leather blanket over the shoulder on which he carried the ice.

To simplify the process of delivering ice to city homes, each home had a card with large numbers, visible from the street, telling the iceman how many pounds of ice was wanted on that particular day. If the card did not appear in the usual window, the iceman drove on, assuming no ice was wanted.

Usually the same driver delivered coal in winter.

FOOD: 1825–1860

Although people in the growing Republic lived frugally, as we can see from the cookbooks of the era, they did not deny themselves the joys of a good table. The English writer Harriet Martineau, who traveled in the United States in 1834, described an average breakfast as consisting of a pie dish full of buttered toast, hot biscuits and coffee, beefsteak, apple sauce, hot potatoes, cheese, butter, and two large dishes of eggs. No true New Englander denied himself the joys of pie at breakfast.

The entire family sat down for breakfast at seven o'clock. Dinner was served at noon except on festive occasions and consisted of chops, steaks, or roast, with potatoes, green corn, and peas, finished off with pudding, pie, and coffee. In wealthy homes the principal dish might be home-raised chicken and a Virginia ham, preceded by okra soup and followed by orange fritters to the accompaniment of wine, champagne, liqueur, and coffee.

People were constantly eating and insisted upon meat three times a day to be followed by all sorts of snacks, especially fruit between meals.

In 1840 a man in Connecticut, Sylvester Graham, fell ill and blamed it on his bread. He tried unbolted bread and his health improved. As a result he became a vegetarian and a teetotaler and ate bread made only from the unbolted flour. This flour became known as Graham flour.

BAKING-POWDER AND COCOA CANS

One of these cans, with a few nail holes in each end, is a good soap shaker. This will utilize all the scraps of soap.

Household Discoveries, 1903

MONDAY: WASHDAY

Getting water from the well

Throughout the world the task of washing clothes has always been the woman's lot. Until the modern washing machines came into use, this was a back-breaking task which entailed long hours of carrying water to a tub after heating it in boilers, tea kettles, stove reservoirs, and even over the open outdoor fire.

When the water was hot, our housewife placed her tub on a wooden bench, filled it with hot water, placed a washboard in it, and reached for a bar of homemade lye soap.

White articles were always washed first, then the colored clothing was done. Each item was rubbed well with a bar of soap, treated to a good scrubbing on the washboard, and then tossed into one of the pots of boiling water. Here more soap was added and the clothes were stirred with a long wooden paddle or stick. After boiling, they were transferred by means of the stick to a pot of clean boiling water and finally to a wash tub filled with cold water. The clothes were then wrung out by hand and hung up to dry.

"Automatic" washtub—1880's

However, in the late 1800's a hand-operated wringer was devised to make the job easier, and a number of various types of washing machines came onto the market. These machines were sold primarily through mail order and ranged in price from about two to five dollars.

Washing clothes took from five to six hours, so the housewife had breakfast prepared earlier than usual.

TUESDAY: IRONING DAY

Our housewife of the 1800's did not save her ironing to do on a rainy day or on a day when she had some free time. She knew that as sure as Monday was Washing Day, Tuesday was Ironing Day, and ironing was not any simpler than was the washing the day before.

We know that at one time there were no irons, but that a smoothing board was used to get some of the wrinkles out of the clothes. However, somewhere along the line, the iron was invented. It was called the "sad iron." The iron was stuck into the hot ashes of the fireplace or, later on, put on the stove to heat; it was then used to smooth out a newly washed piece of clothing. There were several sizes and shapes kept hot and brought to the ironing board just short of scorching temperatures.

It has been said that women pushed the sad iron a mile or two in the course of doing the ironing on a Tuesday. When the iron grew too cold to remove wrinkles, it was exchanged for one fresh off the stove. At first the iron was of one piece with the handle, so that it was impossible to touch unless one used a pot holder of sorts. Eventually, however, came the removable handle of wood, which could be taken off one cool iron and placed into a new, hot one.

There was also a flatiron which contained a compartment into which live charcoal was placed. This type was handy when there was no stove or when the pressing was to be done at a distance from the stove.

These irons held their heat so well that it has been said that many a house burned down because the iron was left standing on the ironing board after the one who was doing the ironing walked away.

At first, ironing was done on the broad wooden kitchen table. Then an ironing board without legs was devised which was supported by the kitchen table at one end and a kitchen chair at the other. This was not too convenient, since it was not simple to slip anything over the board to iron.

There were all sizes of ironing boards to be used for various pieces of clothing. Each of the boards was padded with an old blanket or something similar tacked to it and covered with muslin.

It was a while before the folding ironing board came into use.

HINTS ON THE PRESERVING OF FRUIT

The first and most important thing to be attended to is the selection of the fruit. This, to insure the finest flavor, should have been gathered in the morning of a bright, sunny day; but as this is an advantage which none but the country housewife can be sure of, she who is not blessed with a rural home must take her chances in this particular. She should see, however, that the fruit is sound, perfectly clean and dry, and, as a general rule, thoroughly ripe. These are essentials which her own judgment will find but little difficulty in securing. If not used immediately the fruit should be kept in a cool, dark place until wanted. At the same time it is well to remember that the sooner it is boiled after gathering the better.

... Fruits vary much in the amount of acidity they contain, and it is this variation that regulates the amount of sugar that should be used. The preserving pan may be either an enameled one or made of brass or copper. If either of the latter metals, great care should be used to keep it bright and clean.

In selecting preserve jars have none but glass. They are far preferable, because they allow the examination of the preserves from time to time, a precaution which it is well to take during the first month or two, in order to discover whether they show any indication of fermentation or mould. If they do, they should be at once removed from the jars, and re-boiled.

In storing preserves, a dry, cool place should be selected, and one to which the fresh air can have access, for dampness will soon mould the fruit and heat cause it to ferment.

Jams and marmalades are similar in their character, and are prepared from the pulp of the fruits, and sometimes the proteins of the rinds, by boiling them with sugar. The chief difference between the marmalade and the jam is that the former is made from the firmer fruits, while the latter is prepared from that which is more juicy, such as the strawberry, raspberry, currant, etc.

A very important thing in the preserving of fruits in syrup is to have the latter of proper strength. Sugar, we know, ferments readily, but only when dissolved in a sufficient quantity of water. When the quantity is just sufficient to render it a strong syrup it will not ferment at all. The right degree of strength for the preserving of fruits, so that there may be neither fermentation nor crystallization, may be obtained by dissolving double refined sugar in water in the proportion of two parts of sugar to one of water, and boiling it a little. The degree thus obtained, which is the proper one for the preserving of fruits, is technically known as smooth. In preserving fruits whole it is necessary that this syrup should penetrate every portion of it, therefore, to aid this, the fruit should be blanched before it is boiled in the syrup.

Fruit jellies are made by so combining the juices of fruits with sugar by boiling that the product, when cold, becomes a quivering, translucent mass, the consistency of which is neither that of a solid or liquid. The jelly must be gratifying to the eye as well as the palate.

The Successful Housekeeper, 1885

THE HOME IN 1890

The home in this period was comfortably warm in the winter because of the use of wood- and coal-burning stoves.

A typical parlor had a marble-top table, an organ in the corner, and an array of treasures on the mantle. It was a gay room for the holidays and guests, and a somber one in times of illness and death. It was also used as a visiting room for the minister.

The kitchen was the housewife's special room. The huge stove was there, with something always in the oven sending out an aroma.

The pantry had all sorts of round wooden boxes of spices, pails of lard, colorful boxes of oatmeal, red tins of coffee and tea, as well as all types of boxes, tins, and crocks for cookies.

Food was plentiful, either fresh from one's own garden and yard or else just delivered to one's back door from the local farm.

The pace was slower than today's in spite of all the work the housewife had to do; she seemed to enjoy her work, her house, and her family.

The sewing machine—1890's

MENUS FOR SUMMER EATING

JULY

MONDAY. *Breakfast*—Griddle cakes, broiled ham, tomato omelette, radishes. *Dinner*—Baked lamb, green pease, baked potatoes, squash, rice custard, berries with cream. *Supper*—Biscuit, cold lamb sliced, cake, ripe currants with cream.

TUESDAY. *Breakfast*—Rice muffins, hash on toast, tomatoes. *Dinner*—Economical soup, stuffed fillet of veal, green pease, mashed potatoes, beet salad, blackberry pudding with sauce, cake. *Supper*—Buttered toast, cold sliced meat, blackberries with cream.

WEDNESDAY. *Breakfast*—Rolls, vegetable hash, broiled beefsteak, cottage cheese. *Dinner*—Mock (or real) turtle soup, baked heart, baked potatoes, stewed beans, chocolate pudding, cocoanut cake. *Supper*—Cold rolls, sliced heart, cottage puffs, berries.

THURSDAY. *Breakfast*—Cream toast, fried liver, dropped eggs, fricasseed potatoes. *Dinner*—Clam pie, boiled ham, mashed potatoes, string beans, lettuce, blackberry pie. *Supper*—Plain bread, dried beef frizzled, rice batter cakes with sugar, cake and berries.

FRIDAY. *Breakfast*—Muffins, broiled beefsteak, fried potatoes. *Dinner*—Soup, fish, fresh or canned, whole potatoes, pease, squash, lettuce, chocolate cream. *Supper*—Toasted muffins, cold pressed meat, corn meal mush with cream, cake and fruit.

SATURDAY. *Breakfast*—Plain bread, veal sweetbreads, fried mush, boiled eggs. *Dinner*—Boiled ham with potatoes, cabbage, string beans, warm gingerbread, pie. *Supper*—Dry toast, cold ham shaved, rusk, blackberries and cream.

SUNDAY. *Breakfast*—Vienna rolls, fried chicken with cream gravy, fried tomatoes, cottage cheese. *Dinner*—Barley soup, roast of beef with potatoes, stewed tomatoes, cucumber, wilted lettuce, charlotte russe. *Supper*—Cold rolls, sliced beef, blackberries, cake.

AUGUST

MONDAY. *Breakfast*—Dropped eggs on toast, roast beef warmed up with gravy, tomato omelette. *Dinner*—Baked lamb, creamed cabbage, stewed tomatoes, cream pudding. *Supper*—Buns, cold lamb sliced, preserve puffs, apple sauce.

TUESDAY. *Breakfast*—Plain bread, hash, stewed tomatoes. *Dinner*—Corn soup, beef *a la mode,* boiled potatoes, green corn pudding, sliced tomatoes, tapioca cream. *Supper*—Milk toast, cold pressed meat, chocolate custard.

WEDNESDAY. *Breakfast*—French rolls, broiled beefsteak, baked potatoes, cottage cheese. *Dinner*—Soup with chicken, celery, mashed potatoes, stewed beans, sliced cucumbers and onions, watermelon. *Supper*—Cold rolls, chicken salad, apple sauce, schmier kase.

THURSDAY. *Breakfast*—Cream toast, fried liver, potato cakes, stewed tomatoes. *Dinner*—Roast leg of mutton with potatoes, green corn, tomatoes, musk melon. *Supper*—Plain bread, dried beef with gravy, boiled rice with cream, berries.

FRIDAY. *Breakfast*—Rice cakes, waffles, mutton stew, fried potatoes. *Dinner*—Meat pie, young corn, boiled cauliflower, grapes, plain cake. *Supper*—Toast, cold pressed meat, Graham mush with cream, cake and berries.

SATURDAY. *Breakfast*—Bread, broiled bacon, Graham mush fried, boiled eggs. *Dinner*—Soup, boiled ham with potatoes, cabbage, string beans, lemon pie. *Supper*—Light biscuit, cold ham shaved, cake and peaches.

SUNDAY. *Breakfast*—Nutmeg melons, fried chicken with cream gravy, fried tomatoes, cottage cheese, fritters. *Dinner*—Soup, roast loin of veal, mashed potatoes, creamed cabbage, tomatoes, tapioca pudding, watermelon. *Supper*—Cold rolls, sliced veal, cake and fruit.

SEPTEMBER

MONDAY. *Breakfast*—Graham bread, rolls, fried liver, fried tomatoes. *Dinner*—Soup, roast beef, potatoes, green corn, fried egg plant, salad, watermelon. *Supper*—Toasted biscuit, cheese, cold beef, fruit.

TUESDAY. *Breakfast*—Buttered toast, hash, green corn, fried oysters. *Dinner*—Meat pie, potatoes, young turnips, stewed onions, pickled beets, apple dumplings with cream sauce, peach pie. *Supper*—Canned salmon, cold roast beef, biscuit and jam, cake.

WEDNESDAY. *Breakfast*—Hot muffins, broiled chicken, cucumbers. *Dinner*—Roast mutton, baked sweet potatoes, green corn, apple sauce, slaw, bread pudding with sauce. *Supper*—Toasted bread, sliced mutton, baked pears.

THURSDAY. *Breakfast*—Corn gems, rolls, stew of mutton, tomatoes. *Dinner*—Chicken pot pie, Lima beans, baked egg plant, peach meringue, lady cake. *Supper*—Pressed chicken, omelet, biscuit, baked sweet apples.

FRIDAY. *Breakfast*—Batter cakes, veal croquettes, fried apples, potatoes. *Dinner*—Soup, boiled or baked fish with potatoes, green corn, tomato slaw, peaches and cream, cake. *Supper*—Cold tongue, light biscuit, bread and iced milk, cake and fruit.

SATURDAY. *Breakfast*—Short cake, mutton chops, potatoes. *Dinner*—Soup, boiled leg of mutton, caper sauce, potatoes, squash, pickled beets, apple meringue, cake. *Supper*—Cold meat, warm rolls, grapes, cake.

SUNDAY. *Breakfast*—Rolls, breakfast stew, potatoes, stewed okra. *Dinner*—Broiled chicken, sweet potatoes, boiled cauliflower, plum sauce, cabbage salad, ice-cream, cake. *Supper*—Sliced veal, biscuit, floating island, baked pears.

Queen of the Household, 1906

FOURTH OF JULY COLLATION

Let the centre of the table be ornamented by a pyramid of evergreens or laurel, which may be made thus: make a stand or frame not less than three feet high, make a long wreath of the richest laurel or evergreens, and beginning at the top, wind it around the frame until the bottom is reached; at the summit, let there be a miniature flag of our country, or a small bust or statue of Washington, and at regular distances downward, small silk flags with the coat of arms and mottoes of each several State in the Union; or instead of the flags, take as many streamers of different shades of colored ribbons as there are States, or stars cut from gold or silver paper. The flags may be painted by ladies whose national feelings and talents inspire them to the work.—A cold boiled ham and cold roasted poultry may be placed on one end of the table, or at the middle of one side, and lobster and chicken salads at the sides or end, with bread and butter sandwiches and crackers and soda biscuits; such pastry, jelly tarts, jellies, floating island or blancmange and baskets of cut cake and maccaroons, as may be desired, may be distributed around the table; and syrup water and lemonade, with a fine bowl of temperance beverage and bottled soda, which will generally leave a more clear recollection, than wines, cordials, and champagne.

American Lady's System of Cookery, 1850

Early photography

WARM WEATHER DINNER

Chicken soup, creamed sweetbreads, salmon loaf with frozen horseradish sauce, potatoes, boiled green peas, asparagus salad in lemon rings, vanilla ice cream in cantaloupe cases, oatmeal snaps.

What to Have for Dinner, Fannie Farmer, 1905

ITEMS OF ADVICE

If you keep an account of your stores, and the dates when they are bought, you can know exactly how fast they are used, and when they are wasted, or stolen.

Grate up dry cheese, and cheese crusts, moisten it with wine or brandy, and keep it in a jar for use. It is better than at first.

When you clean house, begin with the highest rooms, first, so that clean rooms be not soiled when done.

Repair house linen, turn sheets, and wash bedclothes in summer.

Buy your wood in August or September, when it usually is cheapest and plenty.

In cities, nothing is more pernicious to a housekeeper's health, than going up and down stairs, and a woman who has good taste and good sense, will not, for the sake of *show* keep two parlors on the ground floor and her nursery above and kitchen below. One of these parlors will be taken for her nursery and bedroom, even should all her acquaintance wonder how it can be, that a wife and mother should think her health and duties of more importance than two dark parlors shut up for company.

Do not begin housekeeping in the style in which you should end it, but begin on a plain and small scale, and increase your expenditures as your experience and means are increased.

Be determined to live within your income, and in such a style that you can secure time to improve your own mind, and impart some of your own advantages to others.

Eating too fast is unhealthful, because the food is not properly masticated, or mixed with the saliva, nor the stomach sufficient time to perform its office on the last portion swallowed before another enters.

Beef and mutton are improved by keeping as long as they remain sweet. If meat begins to taint, wash it and rub it with powdered charcoal and it removes the taint. Sometimes rubbing with salt will cure it.

A thick skin shows that the pork is old, and that it requires more time to boil.

It is best to fry in lard not salted, and this is better than butter. Mutton and beef suet are good for frying. When the lard seems hot, try it by throwing in a bit of bread. When taking up fried articles, drain off the fat on a wire sieve.

The best method of greasing a griddle is, to take a bit of salt pork, and rub over with a fork. This prevents adhesion, and yet does not allow the fat to soak into what is to be cooked.

The art of keeping a good table, consists, not in loading on a variety at each meal, but rather in securing a successive variety, a table neatly and tastefully set, and everything that is on it, cooked in the best manner.

Miss Beecher's Domestic Receipt Book, 1846

GRANDMA MOSES: *Pumpkins*.

EARLY DAYS IN VIRGINIA

When the little band of colonists landed on the banks of the James in 1607, their first thought was to protect themselves from what Captain John Smith called the "salvages." Within a month they had built a triangular enclosure of sturdy eight-foot poles, with half-moon-shaped bulwarks at each corner in which they mounted their four or five pieces of artillery. Without John Smith it is doubtful whether there would have been any settlement established in Virginia. He writes that four months after landing "we had no houses to cover us, Our Tents were rotten, and our cabins worse than nought."

The dampness of the Virginia climate was not for the houses of flimsy materials that had first been raised. For this reason, in 1611, Sir Thomas Dale built the new town of Henrico, near what is now Richmond, where he had kilns set up; thus the foundations and first-floor walls of some of the houses were built of brick.

Plenty of bricks were made, so that the authorities in January 1639 arbitrarily instructed Governor Wyatt "to require every land owner whose plantation was five hundred acres in extent (and proportionally for larger or lesser grants) to erect a dwelling house of brick, to be twenty-four feet in length, and fifteen feet in breadth, with a cellar attached." However, few heeded this law, so that there are few or no houses of wood still standing that were built in that period.

Tobacco was the main crop, and the planters became more and more affluent. As they did so the houses grew, but they still resembled the more modest English manor houses of Tudor days. The building formed a rectangle from twenty to forty feet in length on the long side, from fifteen to thirty on the short. At each end of the house was a big outside chimney of stone or logs-and-clay. The front door was in the middle of the long side, opening on a hall, or "Great Room," where the family lived and ate. The house was commonly of the two-story and dormer type, with about six rooms. The partitions were covered with a thick layer of dried mud, which had been "daubed and white limed, glazed and flowered." The steep-pitched roof was covered with cypress shingles and had attractive long dormer windows with sharp-peaked gables. Windows were glazed, with small panes set in lead, and were sometimes protected by shutters "which are made very pretty and convenient."

When his tobacco brought him a profit, the planter ordered many of his necessities and all of his luxuries from England, and only when it didn't arrive would he consent to take an interest in having things made at home. Often in debt, and often unable to afford travel, he found his chief distraction was his ungrudging hospitality to visitors.

At first there would be a long table for eating purposes in the Great Room, but it was little more than a few boards laid across trestles. Only the master of the house, or perhaps a distinguished guest, was entitled to use a chair, which was a heavy, impressive affair of paneled oak, with a solid wooden seat. Stools, and forms, as benches were then called, were the seats of everyday life.

By the late 1700's, a certain amount of comfort had begun to creep in. Besides the dining table there were small tables, some of which were known as "flap tables" since they had flaps, or leaves, which could be let down when the table was not in use.

SETTING THE TABLE IN THE EARLY SOUTH: 1700'S

In the early part of the century, the dining table boasted almost no china and no more than a tankard or two of silver. There were wooden trenchers, however, and the plates and dishes were made of pewter. Spoons, bowls, jugs, sugar pots, castors, and porringers were also made of pewter, as were the cups, flagons, tankards, and beakers. A pewterer at this time was a very important person. Wooden and pewter spoons were in common use, but knives and forks were rarely used.

In the latter part of the century, the wealthier planters bought more and more silver, not only because they liked it, but also because it was considered a safe investment. Forks and table knives were now in use. Spoons, dishes, plates, "hand wash bowls," tankards, candlesticks, and candle snuffers were all made of silver, and were often engraved with the arms of the owner.

The tablecloth for everyday use was of Holland linen, and, for special occasions, of damask. Napkins, often of excellent quality and beautifully embroidered, were plentiful. In fact, good linen was the pride of the Southern housewife.

FOOD IN THE EARLY SOUTH

"Virginia doth afford many excellent vegitables and living Creatures," wrote Captain Smith, and he sent home a coop of turkeys to prove it—the first ever seen in England. And before him, Sir Walter Raleigh had declared the soil of the colonies to be "the most plentifull, sweete, fruitful, and wholesome of the world."

The waters also yielded food, and George Percy, Smith's companion, said of oysters: "I have seen some thirteen inches long," and continued, "The salvages used to boile oysters and mussels together and with the broath they make a good spoone meal, thickened with the flower of their wheat; and it is a great thrift and husbandry with them to hang oysters upon great strings, being shauled [shelled] and dried in the smoake, thereby to preserve them all the year."

Despite all this abundance, the following winter starvation set in, and many died before the ships came with provisions in the spring.

However, since the forest teemed with bear, deer, wild turkey, quail, pheasant, and partridge, and the marshes and bays were cloudy with canvasbacks, mallards, and redheads, the planters soon were no longer starving. They had plenty of fish and shellfish, as well as hogs that rooted in the woods. They learned how to plant corn for flour and to use Indian recipes.

Chickens are believed to have been introduced into the colonies at Jamestown about 1607, and by 1700 were so plentiful that they no longer were listed as valuable property.

THE SOUTH, 1765

Since tobacco growing required plenty of land, the planter's house was a long way from that of his neighbor and soon grew into a little village in itself. Some of the houses were extremely beautiful, with lawns, big trees, and gardens. The interior was a profusion of richly carved woodwork, with great stairways and beautiful furniture.

Since the climate was warm and there was plenty of help to carry the cooked food to the dining room, the kitchen became a little, separate house. Also near the "great house" would be a large dairy and a laundry. There were stables for the

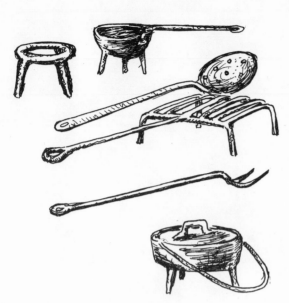

Kitchen utensils—colonial days

horses, pens and barns for the pigs and cattle, granaries for corn, and storehouses for tobacco.

With all the mouths to feed, the smokehouse had brick ovens for curing hams and bacon. There were no villages, so that each plantation had a blacksmith shop, a carpenter's shop, houses for spinning and weaving flax and hemp and for tanning leather for shoes. A malt house would complete the ensemble. The white indentured servants had cottages of their own, while the slaves had a little cluster of rudely built cabins.

DINING IN THE SOUTH, 1765

The napkins of the eighteenth century were nearly as big as a modern card-table cover and were customarily tied around the diner's neck to protect frills and furbelows. Forks appeared around the turn of the century, steel ones, with bone handles and only two tines. Their only purpose was to hold the meat down to be cut; to carry food to the mouth on a fork would have been bad manners. But that didn't last, and by 1750, finger-eating had become a taboo among the best people. Silver forks appeared then; they had three tines and were much smaller than a modern dinner fork. With silver forks came dinner knives. They had "pistol" handles, ending in a scroll. There were silver spoons, too, made with tapering "rat tails" on the backs of the bowls.

The big standing salt went out of fashion and the empty place in the center of the table was now filled with an elaborate silver epergne if one could afford it. It was ornamental and consisted of a central dish on a high stand, surrounded by three or four smaller dishes supported on arms attached to the pedestal. Fruit, flowers, or sweetmeats were put into the dishes. Silver candelabra were put on the table when needed, otherwise they stayed on the sideboard.

A few people began to use china plates for eating. These were imported from England and as rule were plain white "salt glaze" stuff, the glaze being produced by throwing pulverized salt into the kiln at a judicious moment.

In some of the plantation homes there was a separate dining room for the children, so that meals could be enjoyed in peace by adults and children alike. Dining was a fine art in Virginia, and the planters took great pride in setting their tables with more food than anyone could eat. Fruits and vegetables of every kind appeared on the table at a single meal, along with several different meats.

The colonists drank Sack Posset, which was made of sherry, ale, eggs, and milk dusted with nutmeg, and Syllabub, a frothy mixture of whipped cream and white wines. Then bourbon came into the picture, distilled from a corn mash, and the making of a mint julep became a ritual. One Virginia recipe called for cognac, Jamaica rum, port wine, and shaved ice, the drink topped by bruised mint leaves but no bourbon. In Kentucky, only bourbon was used for juleps.

Diamond-back terrapin was so plentiful in the early days that the kitchen help complained of having too much of it. Plentiful, too, were the shellfish, venison, bear steaks, and great hams.

In cool spring houses, cream, butter, and vegetables were kept chilled and fresh over the cold streams. Cellars were stocked with jars and crocks holding preserves, jams, and jellies of wild berries, peaches and pears. Cabbages, okra, carrots, kohlrabies, yams, and onions were packed in loose earth in the cellars throughout the winter.

Game, pork, and sausages hung over hickory smoke for weeks in stone houses built for that purpose. Game, pheasant, venison, beef, and muttons were seasoned by hanging in a dry place to age.

Lard and chicken fat and sweet country-churned butter were used lavishly in cooking.

They ate well in Virginia.

FOOD AND COOKING IN CHARLESTON

The records of early visitors to the province frequently refer to food. William Bartram, eighteenth-century botanist, told of the wild pigeons and of slaves hunting them by torchlight in the swampy section of southeastern Carolina. John F.D. Smyth, an English traveler, wrote of the wealthy widows of Edisto Island and suggested that the demise of their husbands was due partially to the rich food and drink in which they indulged.

Crabs and shrimp as well as oysters were abundant in the inlets and creeks of the Carolina coast, leading to a great variety of shrimp and crab dishes. "She-crabs" were preferred to "he-crabs" for soup because the eggs of the female added a special flavor. To make soup with "he-crabs," the cook crumbled hard-boiled egg yolk to simulate the eggs of the female. This was probably one of the rich soups that John F.D. Smyth wrote about.

Shrimp was eaten in all forms, including a paste made of ground shrimp with butter seasonings which was served at the breakfast table. The paste was so popular that it was eaten cold practically every day with hot buttered grits. Shrimp was also served sautéed in butter, and this was another popular breakfast dish.

Charleston used rice as a base for many of its dishes, such as purleaus (pilaus) of all kinds, hop-in-John (rice and peas), red rice, and rice wine. Many breads were made from rice flour.

Shrimp and rice croquettes were the Southern counterpart of New England codfish balls. There were other shrimp and rice dishes.

The African slaves introduced the planters to some exotic foods. The sesame seed was introduced into America by the Negro slaves in the late 1600's. In the South, sesame seeds are called benne seeds, and the Charlestonians used benne seeds to make cookies and a sort of benne brittle.

Calapash was a very common dish. It is turtle cooked in the shell. Many Charleston homes kept turtles in small "cooter" ponds covered with wire. The native yellow-bellied terrapin and the famous sea turtle were common dishes.

Some of the other local foods were: Pompey's head, tipsy pudding, jambalaya, panygetta, bogs, espetanga, corn bread, okra daube, ratifia pudding, and almond florentine.

Many forms of corn bread and corn dishes were part of the regular daily fare. Awenda was a hot bread made with hominy grits, corn meal. milk, eggs, and butter —no flour. It was of custard consistency. Carolina egg bread was a spoon bread made with many eggs separated and the white beaten to a stiff froth before being added to the batter. This caused the bread to rise high and puffy like a soufflé. It had to be eaten quickly, lest it fall.

CREOLE CUISINE

Creole cuisine, found in New Orleans, was a combination of the French and Spanish influence—the Spanish taste for strong seasoning of food combined with the French love for delicacies. The slaves of Louisiana had their share in refining the product, and likewise the Indians, who gathered roots and pungent herbs in the woods. No Creole kitchen was complete unless it had its iron pots, bay leaf, thyme, garlic, and cayenne pepper.

Louisianians had valuable natural resources which were a great asset in the preparation of food: partridge, snipe, quail, ducks, and rabbits; fresh- and salt-water fish of every description; numerous fruits, the outstanding being oranges and figs; many nuts, the most delicate being the pecan.

Creole menus could be very elaborate, with five to six courses. On occasion they were enriched by imported continental delicacies such as anchovies and brandied fruits. Creoles also imported, and drank, enormous quantities of wines which they bought in barrels at auction. Meals often included soups and stews composed of leftovers, for the Creole housewife threw nothing in the least edible away.

The Choctaw Indians were very friendly with the white men, and to them New Orleans is indebted for the filé, which is used in one of the best known Creole dishes—gumbo. The filé is made from dried sassafras leaves pounded to a powder. Gumbos of meats, poultry, or seafood were filling dishes and stretched a long way when unexpected guests were present.

The Mississippi River, Lake Ponchartrain, the Gulf of Mexico, the Mississippi Sound, and other nearby waterways furnished seafood of all flavors and varieties. Sheepshead, pompano, flounder, bluefish, silver and speckled trout as well as green trout and sacalit were taken from these waters. The protected bayous, coves, and small bays also furnished an inexhaustible supply of oysters as well as several varieties of shrimp and crab.

Madeline Hachard, the Ursuline nun, told of the magnificence of the fare that she found in 1727: "Buffalo, wild geese, deer, turkeys, rabbits, chickens, pheasant, partridge, quail; monstrous fish which I never knew in France" as well as other shellfish, and an array of fruits and vegetables, figs, watermelons, pecans, pumpkins. She also told how all drank chocolate and coffee with warm milk. Once she observed that though wild ducks were cheap and plentiful, "we scarcely buy any; we do not wish to pamper ourselves."

Removing the chaff from the wheat

THE FALL SEASON

In the fall of the year there were many jobs to be done. There was canning and food to be stored away for the coming cold weather. Apples were picked and either dried, stored away, or made into apple cider or apple butter. The housewife must dry the corn and get the potatoes, carrots, and beets into the root cellar.

The hogs were slaughtered and the sides of meat were smoked, pickled, and made into sausages and head cheese.

Because there were so few places to go, womenfolk would look forward from one fall to another to the fair. Like summer picnics, that and church were about all the recreation one had in the nineteenth century. Housewives would work the year through saving their money and building up their wardrobes for the County Fair. Exhibits were prepared for the various competitions and happy was the housewife who won a ribbon for it.

Finally, there was Thanksgiving and all its preparations, and then getting ready for Christmas.

AUTUMN FOOD

In the autumn, things had to be prepared for the winter. Fruits and berries were preserved in huge crocks or boiled into rich, spicy jams and marmalades. Apples were dried and strung up to be used the entire winter, while vast barrels of applesauce and apple butter were prepared. Meat and fish were salted down or smoked and packed into barrels. Cheese was pressed into flat wheels. Also, fancy pickles and relishes were made from such plants as nasturtium buds, green walnuts, barberries, marigolds, roses, violets, and peonies.

LIFE OF THE PLANTER'S WIFE

The mistress of a great house had to know every aspect of housekeeping. The training of servants required practical knowledge and skill. Few servants could read or write, and despite their vagaries cookbooks were a help in preparing very special dishes or some special fancy pudding. To teach the servant, the mistress had to be capable herself of making the dish.

Many housewives kept their own cookbooks and account books in order to have a smoothly run household.

Certain ingredients including sugar were expensive luxuries; to make preserves and jams over the open hearth meant lavish use of sugar, as they were made on a pound-to-pound basis. To prevent burning, scorching, or waste, the mistress of the household either made these luxuries herself or closely supervised the process.

The housewife also had to teach her daughters all domestic arts including the art of cookery and fine needlework against the time that they, too, would be running a large household.

There is an account of a day in the life of one of these wives which reads: "I would recall to you the picture of which I have often attempted to describe . . . . Of Aunt Helen, who was up by sunrise every day, making the rounds of the kitchen, the smokehouse, the dairy, the weaving room, and the garden, with a basket of keys on one arm, and of knitting on the other; whose busy fingers never stopped; and who, as the needles flew, would attend to every one of the domestic duties and give all the orders for the day, only returning to the house in time to preside at a bountiful breakfast table, then resuming her rounds to visit the sick, to give out work to the spinners and weavers, and those engaged in making clothes for the hands; prescribing for all the usual ailments of the young and old in the absence of the doctor, caring for her flowers, and then sitting down to her books and her music . . ."

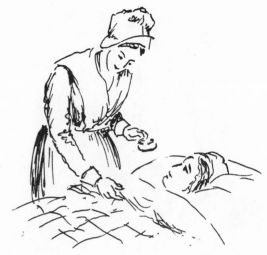

Taking care of the sick

CORN

The abundance, adaptability, and nourishing qualities of corn not only saved the colonists' lives, but altered many of their methods of living, especially their manner of cooking and their tastes in food.

If it had not been for the Indian corn, the history of the New England colonies might have read differently. The corn supplied what little food was available in the first winter, along with the fish from the sea, birds from the air, and wild animals. This corn had been buried with the Indian dead for their journey into other worlds.

Until Governor Bradford decided that "they should set corne every man for his

Pounding the corn

owne particuler, furnishing a portion for public officers, fishermen, etc., who could not work, and in that regard trust to themselves," corn growing was unsuccessful.

In Virginia, the early settlers starved before all were convinced that corn was a better crop for settlers than silk or any of the many hoped-for products which might be valuable in one sense, but which could not be eaten.

Powhatan, the father of the Indian princess Pocahontas, was one of the first to "send some of his People that they may teach the English how to sow the Grain of his Country." Captain John Smith planted forty acres of corn. A succeeding governor of Virginia, Sir Thomas Dale, assigned small farms to each colonist and encouraged and enforced the growing of corn.

The Indians taught the colonists much more than the planting and raising of corn; they showed how to grind the corn and cook it in many palatable ways. The various foods which we use today made from Indian corn are all cooked just as the Indians cooked them at the time of the settlement of the country; and they are still called with Indian names, such as hominy, pone, suppawn, samp, and succotash.

HUSKING CORN: *Diary of An Early American Housewife*

October 8, 1772—John Lake is having a corn husking tomorrow. All the young people of the neighborhood should be there. I expect to have my new pink calico dress finished before the day is over so that I can wear it to the husking.

A CORN HUSKING

Indian corn matured much later than the small grains. But by late autumn, after a frost or two, the ears hung heavy and brown on the dry stalks. They were then pulled and taken to the corncribs, where they were stored in the husks. Later in the season, when the more pressing work was over, corn shuckings would take place in the evenings. Cider or persimmon beer and cakes and cookies would be provided and everybody would turn out to help shuck corn and enjoy the frolic.

A moonlight night in November was a favorite time. A great pile of unshucked corn would be stacked on the ground at some convenient place and a bonfire would be lighted at a safe distance. Then the huskers would set to work. Most of the corn was yellow or white, but an occasional red ear would turn up, a sign of good luck to the shucker who found it.

Boys and girls liked corn shuckings, which gave them a chance to have a party—and perhaps evade the curious eyes of their elders as they sought out the shadows out of sight of the bonfires.

Reaping the harvest

TO KEEP WEEVILS OUT OF WHEAT

Put the wheat in barrels, smooth it, and sprinkle a layer of salt over the top. Keep the barrels well covered by tying cloths over them. A sure preventive.

Housekeeping in Old Virginia, 1879

PIES

Pies were a big item of food for the early settlers. It is hard to state when pies first appeared, but they must have been made when more thought could be given to the variety of food than in those first, more difficult days. The meat pie came first, used as a main dish, and the making of mince pies followed. At first, when meat from the farm animals was not obtainable, bear meat was a good substitute. Added to this were syrups and meat juices for liquids, dried fruit, and nuts, the whole seasoned highly with spices.

Pies made from fruits, squash, and pumpkins came in due time, and soon the pantry boasted of a continual row of pies. At Thanksgiving time many more pies were made than were to be used, and these were put away to "freeze" for the meals to come. They were called frozen pies and were stacked one on the other in the larder; sometimes there were as many as fifty.

A pie peel was a kitchen necessity in the days of brick ovens, to hold the pies as they were slid in or taken out. The pie peel had a short handle, whereas the bread peel had a long one.

THE FARMER'S WIFE

Some courteous angel guide my pen,
    While I describe a farmer's wife.
In her the poor do find a friend,
    To guide them through this life;
Before the king of day doth rise,
    To journey round the earth,
Before the stars fade from the skies,
    She quits her downy berth.
Then with a joyful, lovely song,
    She to her daily labor goes,
She never joins the idle throng,
    That seek their own repose.
Her mind is strong, and noble too,
    She judges all things right;
She hath her friends, a chosen few,
    And is to all polite;
She seeks not to adorn with gold,
    But looks upon the mind;
There nobler beauties doth behold,
    Than she in gold can find.

Farmer's Almanack, 1844, Robert B. Thomas

HOW TO COOK WATER

I must tell you the old story of how the late Charles Delmonico used to talk about the hot water cure. He said the Delmonicos were the first to recommend it to the guests who complained of having no appetite. "Take a cup of hot water and lemon and you will feel better," was the formula adopted, and the cup of hot water and lemon in it take away the insipidity. For this anti-bilious remedy the caterers charged the price of a drink of their best liquors—twenty-five cents or more—and it certainly was a wiser way to spend small change than in alcohol.

"Few people know how to cook water," Charles used to affirm. "The secret is in putting good fresh water into a neat kettle, already quite warm, and setting the water to boiling quickly, and then taking it right off for use in tea, coffee or other drinks, before it is spoiled. To let it steam and simmer and evaporate until the good water is all in the atmosphere, and the lime and iron and dregs only left in the kettle—bah! That is what makes a great many people sick, and is worse than no water at all." Every lady who reads this valuable recipe of a great and careful cook should never forget how to cook water.

Household, 1871

ABOUT VIRGINIA WOMEN

"The Women are not (as reported) put into the ground to work, but occupie such domestique imployments and housewifery as in England, that is dressing victuals, righting up the house, milking, imployed about dayries, washing, sowing, etc., and both men and women have times of recreations, as much or more than in any part of the world, besides, yet some wenches that are nasty, beastly, and not fit to be imployed are put into the ground, for reason tell us, they must not at charge be transported, and then maintained for nothing."

John Hammond, 1656

ANNE FOSTER'S PARTY: *A Letter from Ruth*

Dear Hannah:

There were good friends of ours in England who believed that we had come into a wilderness where was to be found naught save savages and furious beasts, and it would have surprised them greatly, I believe, if they could have known how much of entertainment could already be found.

It was while we were waiting in Charlestown for our new home to be built, that Anne Foster, whose father is one of the tithing-men, invited all of us young girls to spend an

*evening with her, and we had much pleasure in playing both the whistle and thread the
needle.*

*Anne was dressed in a yellow coat with black bib and apron, and she had black feathers
on her head. She wore both garnet and jet beads, with a bracelet, and no less than four rings.
There was a black collar around her neck, black mitts on her hands, and a striped tucker and
ruffles. Her shoes were of silk, and one would have said that she was dressed for some evening
entertainment in London.*

*Neither Sarah nor I wore our best, because of the candles here being made from a kind of
tallow stewed out of bayberry plums, which give forth much smoke, and mother was afraid
that it would soil our clothing. We were also told that because of there not being candles
enough, some parts of the house would be lighted with candle-wood, which last is taken from
the pitch of the pine tree, and fastened to the walls with nails. This wood gives forth a fairly
good light; but there drops from it so much of a black, greasy substance, that whosoever by
accident should stand beneath these flames would be in danger of receiving a most disagreeable shower.*

*This entertainment was not the only one which made for our pleasure while we remained
in Charlestown. However, it seemed almost a sin for us to be thus light-hearted while so many
were in dire distress.*

Ruth

APPLES

Apples supplied the table in many ways. There were pies made from dried
sliced apples, the apple butter and applesauce, as well as many barrels of cider for
drinking, and the vinegar for cooking. To pare three hundred bushels of apples was
a common occurrence, and this need brought about the apple-paring bees, which
usually turned into occasions of festivity.

The first paring machines show great ingenuity. Wooden parers were used for
many years until the patented machines of iron took their place. Those of iron
eventually cored as well as pared.

After the apples were pared, there were two different ways of cutting them for
dried apples. One way was to quarter them, remove the core, and then string them
on a heavy thread two yards long with a big needle. Such strings were draped over
tacks or hooks to dry. The other way was to core the apple and then slice it. These

slices were placed on apple driers. When one half was dried, the other half was turned outside. A bushel of apples made seven pounds of dried apples, and these not only supplied the family but were often taken to town and exchanged for necessary commodities.

An old rule for apple butter reads: "10 gallons sweet cider, 3 pecks of cored and quartered apples—do a few at a time—cook slowly. Add 10 pounds of sugar, 5 ounces of cinnamon. Stir for 5 or 6 hours with a wooden paddle." Often, pumpkins were substituted for apples.

Applesauce was flavored with molasses, apple-molasses, maple sugar molasses, or cider.

The apple barrel

Cider was the standard drink of all the early colonies, and inheriting barrels of cider in wills was as common as inheriting furniture or household supplies. Every family made its own cider, as apples were plentiful. Cider was used at the table and also taken to the fields in kegs, for water was not used much as a drink, perhaps because of the poor sanitation.

An old-time description of the old hand method of making cider was: Apple pomace was laid on a wooden slatted rack with layers of straw as a binder in between the layers of pomace. This was called a "cheese" when all set up. As the wooden screw pressed down on the "cheese" the juice was forced out while at the same time the pomace was squeezed out of the mass at the sides. This was cut down with a knife called a "cutting down" knife, having a long thin blade in an inverted position, on a short handle. The pomace was placed back on the top of the mass and another pressing took place. This was done two or three times, according to the amount of juice left in the pomace. The cider trickled out into buckets below the rack and the buckets were emptied into barrels. A bucket funnel was used, the size of an ordinary bucket, with a wooden funnel. This hand press produced about 2 gallons of cider to a bushel of apples.

After the cider was poured into barrels, the head was sealed. Near the bottom of the barrel was a bunghole, and in the early days this was sealed with a cluster of straw. This made a stopper and the straw was so deftly twisted that it was not only air-tight but moisture-tight and kept out all insects.

Vinegar was made from the inferior apple. Thus an orchard of apples provided raw fruit, apple butter, applesauce, cider for drinking, and vinegar for cooking and preserving.

THE CIDER PRESS

Almost every Northern farm had one or more apple trees, and many farmers either owned or borrowed a press with which to make cider for home consumption, if not for sale. The cider usually was consumed shortly after it was made, although the juice sometimes was allowed to harden until it developed an alcoholic content.

Making cider was one job that usually was not foisted off on the farm boy, as his elders preferred to do the work themselves so as to make sure that it was done right. The accidental inclusion of a rotten or wormy apple could alter the flavor of a whole batch of cider.

THE LARD KETTLE

Lard was made at butchering time, usually by the farm wife with the aid of any available male help. The process consisted of melting and rendering the fat of hogs over a hot wood fire, in a large iron kettle, usually out of doors. The kettle hung from a tripod and rested on the logs, or else was placed on a special fireplace built for that purpose.

PEDDLERS

In the days when most people lived on farms, often some miles from the nearest town, they obtained many of their everyday needs from peddlers, who brought the goods to them, instead of their having to take the time and trouble to go to town by horse and wagon or carriage, assuming they owned such equipment.

The old-time peddler transported his wares either in a trunk or knapsack that he carried on his back, in saddlebags if he rode a horse, or in a cart, wagon, or boat.

Peddlers sold almost every kind of movable commodity used by the public. They were most ingenious at condensing a maximum quantity of merchandise into a limited space, especially if they traveled on foot with their wares on their back or in a small wagon.

The foot peddler usually was obliged to confine himself to small, light items such as needles and pins, hooks and eyes, razors and razor strops, scissors, knives, etc.

Peddlers fortunate enough to have carts or wagons could handle heavier and bulkier goods ranging from Bibles, almanacs, and clocks to clothing, hardware, and housewares.

The peddler either was a self-employed individual or the employee of a small manufacturer, such as a maker of tinware. He obtained his stock from small producers in town, or it was taken in trade from farmers and their wives, who traded articles they made in their spare time for things they needed but could not make. Trades were more common than cash transactions.

The country peddler

BATTER BREAD

Break two eggs into a bowl. Beat to a stiff froth. Pour in one teacup of clabber or butter-milk, one of water, one of corn meal, one of flour, half teaspoonful of salt, a

Baking bread—1700's

heaping teaspoonful of butter melted. Beat all well together. Have already heated on the stove or range, iron-clad muffin moulds (eight or ten in a group). Grease them well with a clean rag, dipped in lard. Fill each one nearly full with the batter, first sifting in half a teaspoonful of soda. Set in a hot oven and bake a nice brown. Oblong shapes are the nicest. If preferred sweet milk may be used instead of sour milk and water. In this case add another egg and dispense with the soda.

Housekeeping in Old Virginia, 1879

THE SMOKEHOUSE

The small building where carcasses of pork were cut up and smoked was called the smokehouse. It was an active place at butchering time, which was usually in early winter when the outside temperature was low.

The smokehouse sometimes could be recognized by a chimney, but often there was none because it was desirable to keep the smoke from escaping. As a result, you can still smell the hickory smoke in an old smokehouse that has not been used as such for many years.

DUKE OF CUMBERLAND'S PUDDING

Six ounces grated bread, six ounces of sultana raisins, six ounces finest beef-suet, six ounces apples, chopped fine, six ounces loaf-sugar, six eggs, a very little salt, the rind of a lemon grated; add lemon, orange, and citron-peel. Mix all well together, put it in a basin covered loosely with a floured cloth, boil it three hours and a half. Serve with wine sauce.

Peterson's Magazine, November 1866

WOMEN'S HEALTH

Women must have some light work to do if they desire to remain healthy is a truth becoming generally known, even among those who are sometimes described as "devotees of fashion." Medical men constantly prescribe this remedy for their lady patients; one eminent physician in New York frequently insists on his patients making up their own beds, and arranging their rooms in imitation of their housemaids . . . .

Peterson's Magazine, November 1866

A SIMPLE PILAU

Crack a knuckle of ham and boil for one hour in three quarts of water, adding one-half teaspoonful of mixed spices, and one large pinch of black pepper. Remove the bone and all bits of fat. Pick carefully and thoroughly; wash by rubbing between the hands through two waters a cup of best rice. Boil until the grains are nearly three times their original size. Strain through a colander until all the liquor is drained off; return to the saucepan, which place uncovered over a slow fire for ten minutes, stirring frequently with a fork. Five minutes before serving sprinkle two table-spoonfuls of cold water over the rice; cover tightly, and remove from the stove. In preparing plain rice, follow the above directions, using plain, salted water, and leaving out meat, spice and pepper.

Ladies' Home Journal, November 1892

COOKBOOKS IN VIRGINIA

The most popular English cookbooks in colonial Virginia were Mrs. Eliza Smith's *The Compleat Housewife,* as well as those by Mrs. Hannah Glasse, Mrs. Sarah Harrison, Mrs. Elizabeth Raffald, and Mrs. Martha Bradley. Several Virginians also had Robert May's *The Accomplisht Cook.*

Mrs. Smith's book was very popular in Williamsburg and sold well at the *Gazette* office, as did Mrs. Sarah Harrison's *The House-keeper's pocket-book, and Compleat Family Cook.*

Since there was an abundance and variety of food in colonial Virginia, the housewife needed but a few things from England, such as spices, oranges, lemons, raisins, and prunes, packaged sweetmeats, European wines, English beer, West Indian rum. She resorted to her English cookbooks for her menus.

The main meal was served at two or three o'clock in the afternoon, and her cookbooks dictated two courses and how the table should be set. The basic plan of the menu varied according to the number of guests, but the number of dishes in each course still had to be on the table. The table diagrams were followed carefully.

Breakfast at 8 or 9 o'clock featured a variety of hot breads and cold sliced meats or a hashed dish with a choice of milk, coffee, chocolate, or tea. Occasionally, tea was served between dinner and supper and included tea accompanied by bread and butter, hot buns or crumpets or muffins, and cake.

CHILBLAINS

Put the hands and feet once a week into hot water in which two or three handfuls of common salt have been thrown. This is a certain preventive as well as a cure.

Godey's Lady's Book and Magazine, December 1860

CHESTNUTTING: *Diary of An Early American Housewife*

October 23, 1772—We are going nutting in the woods tomorrow since the wind and the rain today make this the proper time. As early as July, we watched for the long plume-like blossoms, to know if the fruit were likely to be abundant. We welcome the frosts because they would open the burrs, and later in the season, the showers of wind and rain are our helpers to beat off the nuts and lay them at our feet.

Cranberry-picking

CRANBERRIES

It is quite fitting that most of the cranberries which are made into sauce and eaten with turkey on Thanksgiving Day should come from New England, where the custom of serving cranberry sauce originated. The berry had existed in a wild state along New England shores long before the coming of the Pilgrims, who, because of the white blossom and stem which bore a fancied resemblance to the head and neck of a crane, called it the craneberry.

PUMPION PYE

(Author's note: Pumpion is early spelling of pumpkin.)

Take a pound of Pumpion, and slice it; a handful of Thyme, a little Rosemary, sweet Marjoram stripped off the stalks, chop them small; then take Cinnamon, Nutmeg, Pepper, and a few Cloves, all beaten; also ten Eggs, and beat them all together, with as much Sugar as you shall think Sufficient. Then fry them like a pancake, and being fried, let them stand till they are cold. Then fill your Pye after this manner: Take Apples sliced thin round ways, and lay a layer of the pancake, and another of the Apples, with Currants between the layers. Be sure you put in a good amount of sweet Butter before you close it. When the Pye is baked, take six yolks of Eggs, some White-wine or verjuice, and make a caudle thereof, but not too thick; cut up the lid and put it in, and stir them well together, and so serve it up.

The Gentlewoman's Companion, 1673, Hannah Woolley

A CERTAIN CURE FOR A COMMON COLD (Indian Recipes)

Boil a common sized turnip and put it into a sauce, and pour upon it half a cup of molasses, and let it stand fifteen minutes; then turn off the syrup, at the same time squeezing the turnip so as to express its fluid. The syrup to be drank warm on going to bed.

Our Own Book of Every Day Wants, 1888

'PRACTICAL HOUSEKEEPING'

THE TASTE OF FISH may be removed very effectively from steel knives and forks by rubbing them with fresh orange or lemon peel.
TO MAKE MEATS TENDER—A spoonful of vinegar put into the water in which meats or fowls are boiled makes them tender.

Practical Housekeeping, 1883

Southern recipes were sprinkled through most American cookbooks, especially those printed in and around Philadelphia, but few cookbooks came from the pens of Southern writers. *The Virginia Housewife* by Mrs. Mary Randolph, printed in

Washington, D.C., in 1824, and *The Carolina Housewife* (1847) by "A Lady of Charleston," were the most notable early examples of cookbooks that specialized in Southern foods.

The Colonial Williamsburg Foundation has in their Research Library a handwritten cookbook (c 1750). It contains medicinal recipes as well as food recipes. One of the recipes is:

> LEMON BISKETTS: Take nine Eggs, the peels of two Lemmons—grated, one pound of double refin'd sugar, reserving a fourth part to Strew upon them when the pans are fill'd. Beat all two hours without intermission. Then add to it seven ounces of flower, put it in just as oven is ready. Butter & fill your pans but not full. Bake them a quarter of an Hour in a Quick Oven. Lay fine paper at the bottom of the Pans—to make 'em rise lighter.

THE CORN-SHELLER

Here was something that needed no skill but elbow grease. Shelling corn took a lot of time and energy when there were numerous young animals to be fed, and a boy's arm could get mighty tired.

The aim of the sheller was to remove the kernels of corn from the cob, making the corn easier for the cow or calf or chickens to eat.

THE CORN SHOCK

Modern mechanical means have doomed the corn shock that stood in the fields after harvest, an unmistakable sign that summer was gone and fall had arrived for sure. The corn shocks often stood there well into the winter, until hauled to the barnyard to serve as fodder for the livestock. The passing of the corn shocks heralded the end of the corn-husking bees and contests.

RECEIPT TO STOP BLEEDING, EVEN THE LARGEST BLOOD VESSELS

Take of Brandy or Common Spirits 2 oz. Castile Soap 2 drachms Potash 1 dram scrape the soap fine & dissolve in it the Brandy then add the potash mix it well together & keep it in a close phial, when you apply to let it be warmed & dip pieces of lint in & the blood will immediately congeal it operates by coagulating the blood considerable within a few applications may be necessary when the wound is deep or a limb cut off.

Handwritten book of Isabella Ashfield, 1720's

DINNER AT MOUNT VERNON

Dinner was served in three courses and on two tablecloths. One cloth was removed between each course, and the fruit, nuts and wines were served on the bare table. In the center of the table was an elegant epergne, and handsome platters containing meats and fish were symmetrically about the table—with a suitable assortment of vegetables and "corner dishes" of sauces, relishes, and preserves located at other appropriate spots. The dinner customarily concluded with toasts around the table.

HABIT

As habit can reconcile us to what is even disagreeable in itself, how much more will it enforce and improve whatever is pleasing, amiable, and praiseworthy.

The Maine Farmer's Almanac, 1849, Daniel Robinson

Philadelphia, Pa.
October 12, 1853

Dr. J.C. Ayer

My Dear Sir:

I think it but right to inform you that I have seen a most remarkable cure of Consumption by your Pectoral in this place. A beautiful young lady, nineteen years of age, was reduced to the last stage of disease; her cough was most distressing, and the expectoration part blood, and part matter, mixed with large lumps like pieces of the lung. I used all the orthodox remedies without effect, and then had recourse to the Pectoral, which, to the indescribable joy of her family, has restored her to their arms perfectly well. It is not the custom for physicians to laud such preparation; but common justice demands this statement, and I shall always recommend the Cherry Pectoral in similar cases.

Yours respectfully,
JABEZ P. BURNET, M.D.

Ayer's American Almanac, 1861, Dr. J.C. Ayer & Co.

OMELETTE SOUP

Take half a pint of cream or milk, two ounces of flour, three eggs, and two ounces of melted butter, mix well together with cinnamon and salt; when well beaten, put a little butter or grease in the pan, and when it becomes hot and begins to smoke, put a large spoonful of the above mass into the pan, and turn it quickly, so that it runs all over the pan. When it looks brown on the lower side, and is dry on the outside, take it out and bake another in the same way, and continue to do so until the mixture is finished; when it is all baked, cut it into strips, lay the strips in the tureen, pour the bouillon over them, and serve with Parmesan cheese.

Carolina Housewife, 1847

COOKING PUMPKINS: *A Letter from Ruth*

Dear Hannah:

When the first pumpkins were ripe, Squanto showed us how to cook them, and most of us find the fruit an agreeable change from sweet puddings, parched corn, and fish.

This is the way Squanto cooked pumpkins. First he was careful to find one that was wholly ripe. In the top of the yellow globe he cut a small hole through which it was possible for him to take out the seeds, of which there are many. Then the whole pumpkin was put into the iron oven and baked until the pulp on the inside was soft, after which the shell could be broken open, and the meat of the fruit eaten with the sugar which we get from the trees.

Mistress Bradford invented the plan of mixing the baked pumpkin pulp with meal of the Indian corn, and made of the whole a queer looking bread, which some like exceeding well, but father says he is forced to shut his eyes while eating it.

Ruth

CRANBERRIES AND THEIR USES

Housekeepers should remember to cook cranberries in granite, agate-ware, or porcelain-lined dishes. They should not be allowed to stand in tin, iron or brass, the acid contained in them readily taking hold of these metals. In sweetening, it is best to use granulated sugar. There are a great variety of ways in which this fruit can be used.

CRANBERRY PIE: Line a pieplate with plain paste and fill it with uncooked cranberries; add half a cup of molasses and four table-spoonfuls of sugar, cover with an upper crust and bake thirty minutes in a hot oven.

Carrie May Ashton, *The Delineator*, November 1897

TO CHOOSE A TURKEY

If young it has a smooth black leg, with a short spur. The eyes full and bright, if fresh, and the feet supple and moist. If stale, the eyes will be sunk, and the feet dry.

The Good Housekeeper, 1839

APPLE MARMALADE

Take green fruit, sour, equal quantities of apples and sugar, cook the apples (a peck before they are cored) with a little water, and two lemons. When thoroughly cooked then sift, add sugar, boil fifteen minutes and can. This is delicious; much better than the ripe fruit, and it looks clearer, too. Common sour apples that are juicy, or crab apples, are the best for this. Try it.

Household, October 1884

APPLE CREAM

Five large apples, peeled and cored, and boiled until quite soft in a little water. Sweeten, and beat with them the whites of five eggs. Serve with cream poured around them.

The Ladies' World, October 1893

WEAVING: *Diary of An Early American Housewife*

October 28, 1772—I have been busy weaving some of the wool that we have ready. However, we are giving Daniel Worthington some of the wool to weave. He says that although he has much work from some of our neighbors, he will do ours first because we have been so kind to his family and gave them all the extra corn and apples that we did not need for our winter supply.

Early hand loom

WEAVING

If a stranger came up to the front door of a home in the fall, he was certain to be greeted with a heavy "thwack-thwack" from within, a regular sound which would be readily recognized as coming from weaving on a hand loom. These looms were found in every house of any considerable size, usually in the ell part of the house or in the attic or shed loft used as a weaving room.

Many towns, however, had professional weavers, and they often took this chore away from the housewife, who had so many others. These weavers took in yarn and thread to weave on their looms at their own homes at so much a yard. Occasionally they worked in one's home.

Cloth that came from the loom was not ready to use until it was fulled underfoot or in fulling stocks, washed well in water, scratched and dressed with teazels, and tented. If cloth was to be dyed, it was done at this period and then allowed to shrink and dry.

WHAT AND HOW WE EAT: *A Letter from Ruth*

Preparing the menu

Dear Hannah:

And now, perhaps, you ask what we have to eat when the table is spread? Well, first, there is a pudding of Indian corn, or Turkie wheat, and this we have in the morning, at noon, and at night, save when there may be a scarcity of corn. For meats, now that our people are acquainted with the paths through the woods, we have in season plenty of deer meat, or the flesh of bears and of wild fowl, such as turkeys, ducks, and pigeons. Of course there are lobsters in abundance, and only those less thrifty people who do not put by stores sufficient for the morrow, live on such food as that.

Every Saturday we have a feast of codfish, whether alone or if there be company. It is said by some that I am pampered because my father allows me to be seated at the table with himself and my mother when they eat, instead of being obliged to stand, as do other children in the village when their elders are at meals.

Of course, we have not chairs; but the short lengths of tree trunks which father has cut to serve as stools are most comfortable even though it be impossible to do other than sit upright on them or there is danger of losing the stool. If one is careless, one can tumble backward.

Ruth

PORK APPLE PIE

Make your crust in the usual manner, spread it over a large deep plate, cut some slices of fat pork very thin, also some slices of apple; place a layer of apples, and then of pork, with a very little allspice, and pepper and sugar, between—three or four layers of each, with crust over the top. Bake one hour.

The American Economical Housekeeper and Family Receipt Book, 1845

STRIPPING GOOSE FEATHERS:
Diary of An Early American Housewife

November 2, 1772—I have enough goose feathers, so I invited some of our neighbors, the Porters, the Tates, the Mores, and several of Priscilla's friends to join us in a feather-stripping party. I promised Priscilla that I would not strip geese unless I had killed them first. I do not like the thought of goose-stripping either. It is cruel.

GOOSE–STRIPPING

Goose-stripping was cruel work. Several times a year the feathers were stripped from live birds. A stocking was pulled over the bird's head to prevent its biting. The strippers had to wear old clothes and tie covers over their hair, since the down flew everywhere.

However, the more humane way to accumulate the feathers was by killing the geese first, in late summer or early fall. The geese were occasionally soaked to preserve them, but usually they were eaten as soon as they were slaughtered.

The housewife sorted the feathers carefully, separating the large feathers from the small ones. The small feathers were soft enough to be used as stuffing for feather beds. However, the large quills that had down on them were put into sacks and saved until a feather-stripping party was held some time later on in the year when it became colder. The down was then used as stuffing for soft cushions and quilts. The quills were used for pens.

Goose feather-stripping

All the men and women would sit at a long table in the center of the room, usually the kitchen. Open pillowcases were tacked to the edges of the table, and a man and a woman sat in front of each pillowcase. The woman would hold the basket for the discarded quills on her knees. Then each person would begin to strip down from the feathers as fast as possible. Each person held a feather by its tip with one hand and with the thumb and forefinger of the other hand stripped the soft down from the feather. Each couple raced to fill a pillowcase with down before it was time to stop work.

The young women stripped the feathers quickly, for their fingers were slender and nimble. Some of the men, however, had clumsy fingers that did not move fast. They told funny stories to make up for their slow work. Everyone laughed and talked so much that feather-stripping did not seem to be the hard, messy job it really was.

When the feathers and quills were cleared away, the workers usually ate a delicious supper of roast goose, venison, hot biscuits, and gingerbread. They drank gallons of cold sweet cider.

After the supper, the older folks usually went home, while the young people remained on to dance for many hours to the lively tunes of fiddlers. At last, the young people climbed into their sleighs and drove swiftly off into the night to the sound of sleigh bells and young laughter.

"Automatic" spit

GOOSE, TO ROAST

Chop a few sage leaves and two onions very fine, mix them with a good lump of butter, a teaspoonful of pepper and two of salt, put it in the goose, then spit it, lay it down and dust it with flour; when it is thoroughly hot, baste it with nice lard; if it be a large one, it will require an hour and half, before a good clear fire; when it is enough, dredge and baste it, pull out the spit, and pour in a little boiling water.

Virginia Housewife, 1824

MAKING SPOONS OR DISHES: *A Letter from Ruth*

Clam-shell spoons

Dear Hannah:

I wish you might see how greatly I added to our store of spoons during the first year we were here in Plymouth. Sarah and I gathered from the shore clam shells that had been washed clean and white by the sea, and Squanto cut many smooth sticks, with a cleft in one end so that they might be pushed firmly on the shell, thus making a most beautiful spoon.

Sarah says that they are most to her liking, because it is not necessary to spend very much time each week polishing them, as we are forced to do with the pewter spoons.

We can use the large, flat clam shells to skim milk.

After the pumpkins had ripened, and when the gourds in the Indian village were hardened, we added to our store of bowls and cups until the kitchen was much the same as littered with them, and all formed of the pumpkin and gourd shells.

Out of the gourd shells we made what were really the most serviceable dippers, and even bottles, while in the pumpkin shell dishes we kept much of our supply of Indian corn.

Father gave me two of the most beautiful turkey wings, to be used as brushes, but they are so fine that mother has them hung on the wall as ornaments, and we sweep the hearth with smaller and less perfect wings from the birds or turkeys father also brought home.

This no doubt seems to you in Scrooby as a queer way to keep house.

Ruth

Dancing the Roger de Coverly

SOCIAL LIFE ON A VIRGINIA PLANTATION

Philip Fithian, a tutor for the Carter family, kept a Journal, and in one of the entries he describes a private ball that was given by Richard Lee, to which he had been invited:

". . . Next I was directed to the Dining Room to see young Mr. Lee; He introduced me to his Father—With them I conversed til Dinner, which came in at half after four. The Ladies dined first, when some Good Order was preserved; when they rose, each nimblest Fellow dined first—the Dinner was as elegant as could be well expected when so great an Assembly were to be kept for so long a time.—For Drink, there were several sorts of Wine, good Lemon Punch, Toddy, Cyder, Porter &c.—About Seven of the Ladies & Gentlemen began to dance in the Ball-room—first Minuets one Round; Second Giggs; third Reels; And last of all Country-Dances; tho' they struck several Marches occasionally—The music was a French-Horn and two Violins—The Ladies were Dressed Gay, and splendid, & when dancing, their Skirts & Brocades rustled and trailed behind them!— But all did not join in the Dance for there were parties in Rooms made up, some at Cards; some drinking for Pleasure. . . ."

Journal of Philip Vickers Fithian

A CHEAP AND QUICK PUDDING

Beat up four large eggs, add a pint of milk and a little salt, and stir in four large spoonfuls of flour, a little nutmeg and sugar to your taste. Beat it well and pour it into buttered teacups, filling them rather more than half full. They will bake in a stove or Dutch oven in fifteen minutes.

Confederate Receipt Book, 1863

CREOLE SOUP

¼ cup rice; ½ cup cut onion; 2 tablespoons bacon drippings; 2 cups tomatoes; 2 teaspoons salt; 1 teaspoon sugar; ⅛ teaspoon paprika; 1 tablespoon cut parsley.

Wash rice, add 3 cups boiling water and boil 30 minutes. Cook onions in pan with drippings until tender, but not brown. Add tomatoes and boil 10 minutes; rub through strainer into boiled rice and water; add seasoning and sprinkle with parsley. Add a little chopped green pepper if desired.

Royal Cook Book, Royal Baking Powder Co

MARRIAGE

Newlyweds, whatever their social status or the form of their wedding, began housekeeping at once; a honeymoon trip was extremely rare. Where there was money enough, the couple moved into a house built or bought for them; more commonly, they shared the home of one set of parents until they accumulated enough cash for a house of their own.

Most wives accepted their status of subordination to their husbands and with it the almost continuous pregnancies that aged them rapidly.

However, no marriage could be guaranteed as perfectly harmonious; especially with marriage at so early an age, incompatibility could develop, and often did.

One oddity of the times was that estrangement was announced in public, in the form of notices like this:

Preparing a trousseau

"Salem County, December 18, 1775

"I, Sarah Smith, School-mistress, the wife of William Smith, take this method to inform the public not to trust or credit the said Smith on my account, for I shall never pay any of his contractions; my living shall go no more after that rate as it did last March. . . I will not trust it that false man. I nine years have been his wife, tho' he for a widower doth pass, when he meets a suitable lass; for his wicked doings I never more can him abide, nor he never more shall lie by my side.

Sarah Smith"

MAKING CANDLES: *A Letter from Ruth*

Dear Hannah:

Squanto has shown us how we may get, at only the price of so much labor, that which looks like tallow, and of which mother has made well-shaped candles.

You must know that in this country there grows a bush which some call the tallow shrub; others claim it should be called the candleberry tree, while still others insist it is the bayberry bush.

This plant bears berries somewhat red, and speckled with white, as if you had thrown powdered clam shells on them.

I gathered near to twelve quarts last week, and mother put them in a large pot with water, which she stands over the fire, for as yet we cannot boast of an iron backbar to the fireplace, on which a heavy kettle may be hung with safety.

After these berries have been cooked a certain time, that which looks like fat is stewed out of them, and floats on the top of the water.

Mother skims it off into one of the four earthen vessels we brought from Scrooby, and when cold, it looks very much like tallow, save that it is of a greenish color. After being made into candles and burned, it gives off an odor which to some is unpleasant; but I think it very sweet to the nostrils.

I suppose you are wondering how it is we get the wicks for the candles, save at the expense and trouble of bringing them from England. Well, you must know that there is a plant which grows here plentifully, called milkweed. It has a silken down like unto silver in color, and we gather it in the late summer.

It is spun coarsely into wicks, and some of the more careful housewives dip them into saltpetre to insure better burning. Do you remember that poem of Master Tusser's which we learned in Scrooby?

> Wife, make thine own candle,
> Spare penny to handle.
> Provide for thy tallow ere the frost cometh in,
> And make thine own candle ere winter begin.

Making candles

When candle-making time comes, I wish there were others in this household besides me, for the work is hard and disagreeable, to say nothing of being very greasy, and I would gladly share it with sisters or brothers.

Mother's candle-rods are small willow shoots, and because of not having kitchen furniture in plenty, she hangs the half-dipped wicks across that famous wooden tub which we brought with us.

It is my task to hang six or eight of the milkweed wicks on the rod, taking good care that they shall be straight, which is not easy to accomplish, for silvery and soft though the down is when first gathered, it twists harshly, and of course, as everyone knows, there can be no bends or kinks in a properly made candle.

Mother dips perhaps eight of these wicks at a time into a pot of bayberry wax, and after they have been so treated six or eight times, they are of sufficient size, for our vegetable tallow sticks in greater mass than does that which comes from an animal.

A famous candle-maker is my mother, and I have know her to make as many as one hundred and fifty in a single day.

The candle box which was given to us is of great convenience, for since it has on the inside a *hollow for each candle, there is little danger that any will be broken, and, besides, we may put therein the half-burned candles, for we cannot afford to waste even the tiniest scraps of tallow.*

Ruth

WASHINGTON'S BREAKFAST

During his Southern tour in 1791, President George Washington drove up in his handsome white coach to the home of Colonel John Allen. President Washington was on his way to New Bern, North Carolina. The visit was unexpected, and when he asked whether he could have some breakfast, Mrs. Allen summoned all the help she could get and in little over an hour had a breakfast prepared which consisted of a young pig, a turkey, country ham, fried chicken, sausage, waffles, batter cakes, various styles of eggs, and hot soda biscuits.

The President sat down at the table, looked at all the food, and asked whether it would be possible to have only one hardboiled egg and a cup of coffee with a little rum in it.

BRISKET OF BEEF, BAKED

Bone a brisket of beef and make holes in it with a sharp knife about an inch apart; fill them alternately with fat bacon, parsley, and oysters, all chopped small and seasoned with pounded cloves and nutmeg, pepper, and salt; dredge it well with flour, lay it in a pan with a pint of red wine and a large spoonful of lemon pickle; bake it three hours; take the fat from the gravy and strain it. Serve it up garnished with green pickles.

Southern Cook Book, Gary & Dudley Hardware Co.

HOG KILLING: *Diary of An Early American Housewife*

*November 14, 1772—*There will be a hog killing on our farm tomorrow. Everything is ready for it.

HOG KILLING

Cold weather in early winter was the favorite time for hog killing, and the event became an occasion for cooperation and jollity, especially with small farmers who had no hired help.

No matter how small the farm, it always had a few pigs. They were easy to feed and maintain and provided the mainstay of the winter's provisions.

Outside, long before the first light of a crackling cold dawn, a huge iron kettle was filled with water and a roaring fire built under it that lighted up the farmstead. The water was boiling by sunrise.

The men took a sharp knife to the pigpen, and after the hog was hit over the head with an ax to stun it, its throat was cut. Some people were careful to catch the blood for blood puddings. Many a gentle wife sat in the kitchen with her hands over her ears until the slaughter was over and the carcasses had been hauled to the side of the fire.

The hog was then hoisted up and dipped into the great kettle of scalding water. Scalding was necessary to loosen the bristles which had to be scraped off. The bristles were saved for brushes. If the farmer did not own a hog-sized kettle, a barrel could be made to serve. Water in a barrel was heated by throwing hot stones into it.

The animal was then hung head down from the crotch of a tree, disemboweled, and halved. It was next taken into the kitchen where the women, usually helped by neighbors, waded into the business of processing it. The small intestines, emptied and scraped clean, could be used for stuffing sausages, or they could be eaten as "chitterlings." Not everyone liked chitterlings.

After the hog was cut up, the fat portions were tried into lard, and everybody chewed on the "craklin's" that floated to the top of the lard kettle. The back meat was chopped up for sausage, seasoned, and stuffed into skins (intestines) for smoking. Some of the sausage meat was kept out to be eaten fresh, and this was traditionally shared with all the neighbors.

Hams, shoulders, and bacon flanks went into a barrel of brine, "strong enough to float an egg," for corning, before they were smoked. Heads and feet were cooked at once, and the meat from them was mixed with vinegar and spices and made into head cheese and "souse." The livers were cooked, too, and chopped fine for "pudding" that might be stirred into cornmeal mush and cooked in pans as "scrapple." The last of the job was done by candlelight, and the final "redding up" of the kitchen was likely to be left for the next morning.

Often there would be a barter system among neighbors. They slaughtered by turn, exchanged with each other, and kept tallies of who owed what to whom. It reduced the number of animals any one man had to maintain.

Where the winters were cold enough, choice pieces could be frozen and packed with snow.

The housewives made a social event out of making the sausages, and smoking and salting the meat.

Making sausages

CORN AND BEANS

Corn and beans have long been intimately associated as articles of food. Boston baked beans and Boston brown bread are as inseparable now as they were in the early days; and in many families the baked Indian pudding, another form of serving this healthyful grain, is still considered the only pudding suitable to accompany a dinner of baked beans. All three were baked at the same time in the capacious brick oven, even in its own special shaped pot or pan, and subjected to the uniformly moderate heat quite impossible to secure in the modern range; who can say that each dish was not the better for such close companionship during the long hours between the finishing of Saturday's baking and the Sunday morning meal?

Bean porridge, another colonial dish, was not considered complete unless the meaty portions and leguminous liquid were held together by thickening with the starchy corn meal, then made still richer by the addition of hulled corn and eaten with brown bread. No wonder the men of those days could fell the trees and chop wood from sun to sun, through the long, cold winter, on a diet so rich in muscle-making and force-giving compounds.

In the succotash of Pilgrim fame, the meat might be simply salt pork or corned beef, or when one could afford it chickens would accompany the beef, and vegetables were added or not as the Pilgrim housewife preferred, but the hulled corn and stewed beans were indispensable, were what gave character to the dish, and doubtless were often the only ingredients of this nourishing food.

Corn and beans are among our most delicious and nourishing summer vegetables; they are wholesome when prepared properly, and may take the place of much of the heavy meat too often served freely as in winter.

Mary J. Lincoln's Boston Cook Book, 1883

WAYS OF COOKING INDIAN CORN: *A Letter from Ruth*

Dear Hannah:

I must tell you of a way to cook this Indian corn which Squanto showed father, and now we have it in all the houses when we are so fortunate as to have a supply of the wheat in our possession.

It is poured into the hot ashes of the fireplace, and allowed to remain there until every single wheat kernel has been roasted brown. Then it is sifted out of the ashes, beaten into a powder like meal, and mixed with snow in the winter, or water in the summer. Three spoonfuls a day is enough for a man who is on the march, or at work, so father says, and we children are given only two thirds as much.

Mother says it is especially of value because little labor is needed to prepare it; but neither Sarah nor I take kindly to the powder.

The Indians also steep the corn in hot water twelve hours before pounding it into a kind of coarse meal, when they make it into a pudding much as you would in Scrooby; but mother likes not the taste after it has been cooked before being pounded, thinking much of the fine flavor has been taken from it.

Sometimes we make a sweet pudding by mixing it with molasses and boiling it in a bag. It will keep thus for many days, and I once heard Captain Standish say that there were as many sweet puddings made in Plymouth every day as there were housewives.

Next fall we shall have bread made of barley and Indian corn meal, so father says, and I am hoping most fervently that he may not be mistaken, for both Sarah and I are heartily tired of nookick, and of sweet pudding, which is not very sweet because we need to guard carefully our small store of molasses.

We girls often promise ourselves a great treat when a vessel comes out from England bringing butter, for we have had none that could be eaten since the first two weeks of the voyage in the MAYFLOWER.

Ruth

AUTUMN LEAVES

An exquisite transparency may be made by arranging pressed ferns, grasses, and autumn leaves on a pane of window glass, laying another pane of the same size over it, and binding the edges with ribbon, leaving the group imprisoned between. Use gum tragacanth in putting on the binding. It is well to secure a narrow strip of paper under the ribbon. The binding should be gummed all around the edge of the first pane and dried before the leaves, ferns, etc., are arranged; then it can be neatly folded over the second pane without difficulty.

To form the loop for hanging the transparency, paste a binding of galloon along the edge, leaving a two-inch loop free in the center, afterward to be pulled through a little slit in the final binding. These transparencies may either be hung before a window or, if preferred, secured against a pane in the sash.

Household, October 1887

THE POTATO HARVEST

One of the latest crops to be gathered is the store of potatoes which forms such an important part of the farmer's provision for himself and the rest of the world.

Latterly the poor potato has received more than its due share of condemnation. True, some household or some individuals are rather intemperate in the use of this vegetable, but that is its misfortune rather than its fault. We should pity its overworked condition and try to induce people to allow it to rest while they experiment with other vegetables for a while. It is unfair to condemn even a vegetable unheard, and the potato has much in its favor when well grown and properly cooked.

The potato harvest may well be celebrated by a potato roast on these cool autumn evenings. This is an appropriate festival to combine with the Halloween orgies.

The room should be lighted with candles stuck in potatoes. An open fire is indispensable where the potatoes can be roasted in the ashes. Chestnuts and apples may be cooked over the same fire. The hot potatoes should be served on little wooden plates and eaten from their shells with cream and salt. Other suitable refreshments would be Saratoga chips or potato salad accompanied by toasted herring.

Fortunes or gifts may be distributed in cases made of potatoes well washed, cut in halves, and hollowed out and allowed to dry a little; then the folded paper or article is placed inside, the two halves placed together again and tied with a ribbon to hold them fast.

Where there is room a potato race would be in order. For a quieter entertainment let each one tell a story or give a quotation of which the potato is the central figure, like this from Gerard: "Likewise a foode, as also a meete for pleasure, being either rosted in the embers, or boiled and eaten with oile and vinegar, or dressed in anie other way by the hand of some cunning in cookerie."

American Kitchen Magazine, October 1892

MINCE MEAT

Four pounds solid meat without fat or bone, boil till tender, chop very fine, 1½ lbs suet chopped very fine.

To four bowls of chopped meat take one bowl of suet; to these five bowls add twelve or fourteen bowls of apples, chopped; then add eight lbs raisins, washed, chopped and stoned; four lbs currants, four tablespoons cloves, six tablespoons allspice, four lbs "C" sugar. Pack in jars, moisten with peach juice from pickled peaches. Add brandy to taste.

Home Queen Cook Book, 1905

MOCK MINCE MEAT

Take 1 cup sugar, 1 cup molasses, 1 cup raisins, 1 cup currants, 1 cup vinegar, 1 cup water, 1 grated nutmeg, 1 teaspoon cloves, 1 tablespoon cinnamon, butter the size of an egg, 1 cup powdered crackers. Heat on the stove before putting in tins. This will make six pies.

Home Queen Cook Book, 1905

CREOLE APPLES

Southern fried apples are thus prepared: Cut the apples into thick slices or into eighths. Roll each piece in beaten egg, to which a couple of spoonfuls of milk or water has been added, and then in crumbs, and lightly dredge them with flour. Fry them in plenty of butter until they are tender and a nice brown. Then arrange them on a hot platter. Pour into the frying pan a little milk and stir until it is boiling; then pour it over the apples, and they are ready to serve.

Housekeeper's Dept, *The Delineator*, October 1896

BONED TURKEY

With a sharp knife slit the skin down the back, and raising one side at a time with the fingers, separate the flesh from the bones with knife, until the wings and legs are reached. These unjoint from the body, and cutting through to the bone, turn back the flesh and remove from the bones. When bones are removed, the flesh may be re-shaped by stuffing. Some leave the legs and wings, as they are the most difficult to remove. Stuff with force-meat, made of cold lamb or veal and a little pork, chopped fine and seasoned with salt, pepper, sage, or savory, and the juice of one lemon; sew into shape, turn ends of wings under and press the legs close to the back, and tie all firmly so that the upper surface may be plump and smooth for the carver. Lard with two or three rows on the top, and bake thoroughly done, basting often with salt and water, and a little butter. This is a difficult dish to attempt. Carve across in slices and serve with tomato sauce.

Practical Housekeeping, 1881

KITCHEN OR OTHERWISE

. . . When your kitchen work is done we hope to rest and have a bit of change if only for a short time, and there is, in the very association of the kitchen, a weary workday feeling. . .In summer we may flee to the porch, the door-yard, under the shade tree, even to the barn, but let every working woman flee her kitchen if she would enjoy a respite from its cares. . . . Perhaps some women can rest as contentedly in their kitchens as elsewhere, and their tastes may incline them to prefer their work-room to any other; but for others this would be no rest, and actual burdens only made heavier because of self-imposed restrictions.

. . . When the country was new, necessity compelled living in narrow quarters, as it did spinning and weaving at home and weaving home-spun. As things advance, these matters change, yet now many, with unused rooms at their command, still cling to the old kitchen ways. It may be no concern of ours, only we would plead for the young folks, that they have a voice in the matter, and with mothers-in-law that they condemn not the new daughter who may enter their homes to just their own narrow ways of living.

Although the kitchen may not be the place where we would choose to pass all, or ever a great part of our time, yet kitchen work cannot be ignored, neither will it be despised if we sufficiently take into consideration the really important place which it holds in the economy of every dwelling.

The kitchen may be called the heart of the household, for out of it, literally, are the issues of material and physical life, and as the line has not yet been fully determined which divides the material and physical from the mental and spiritual life—one holds sway over the other continually—we may assume that the latter depends more or less upon the kitchen, or rather upon the cook in the kitchen, and that the human heart is affected for good or ill, as our bodies are well nourished with sufficient and wholesome food or otherwise.

The Household, October 1879

A SHAKER THANKSGIVING

The following glimpse into Shaker life is taken from a firsthand account of a Thanksgiving meal in a Shaker village in 1905:

The feasting really began with breakfast for, in addition to the regular fare, there were boiled rice with maple syrup and canned peaches or cherries. At ten o'clock everyone went to church except the cooks, whose presence in the kitchen was an absolute necessity; there was much to be done. During the service, the elder brother read the President's and then the Governor's Thanksgiving proclamation.

The deacons and trustees, whose responsibility was the community's property and money interests, gave an accounting of the year's temporal blessings. Hymns were sung.

Dinner was held at noon; here chicken substituted for the traditional turkey. These chickens had been selected and fattened for weeks before. So important was it that they should be cooked exactly right, if an inexperienced cook was on duty, a more skillful one was appointed for the day.

The menu was fricasseed chicken with cream gravy, boiled potatoes, baked hubbard squash, mashed turnips, ripe tomato pickle, mince and apple pies, homemade cheese, bread and butter, milk and tea. It was simple, hearty fare, but good.

PUMPKIN PIE?

New York chefs have been telling the newspaper reporters of that city that it is no longer necessary to have the genuine, old-fashioned yellow vegetable in order to make pumpkin pies that will delight the taste of the most experienced epicure. These knights of the stove and pan say that with a few yellow potatoes and a squash or two they can, by the judicious use of a few spices, build a pumpkin pie that can't be told from the genuine article—like mom used to make. Pumpkin pie is the favorite dessert in the winter's months, and perhaps the scarcity of the vegetable in the country's metropolis has led the professional cooks of that city to invent a substitute that passes muster with those busy New Yorkers, whose palates are naturally affected by the continual smoking of good, bad, and indifferent cigars, but the average country epicure is "from Missouri" and must "be shown" before he will believe that any substitute has been found for the succulent vegetable that furnishes the principal ingredient of the pumpkin pie that melts in the mouth and leaves a taste that lingers long, even after the after-dinner cigar or pipe has been smoked. There's only one pumpkin pie worthy of the name and fame—and that pie is not made from potatoes and squashes.

These are busy days in the average country and village kitchen, for winter weather makes sharp appetites and suitable dishes must be prepared to go with the back-bones, spare-ribs, and other evidences of "hog-killing" days that are found upon the table.

Woman's Farm Journal, November 1900

FOR THANKSGIVING

An eight-year-old lad was asked to write out what he considered a good dinner bill of fare and here it is:

FURST CORSE
Mince Pie

SEKOND CORSE
Pumpkin Pie and Terkey

THIRD CORSE
Lemon Pie, Terkey, Cranberries

FOURTH CORSE
Custard Pie, Apple Pie, Mince Pie,
Chocolate Cake, Ice Cream and
Plum Pudding

DESERT
Pie

American Kitchen Magazine, November 1896

THANKSGIVING IN EARLY AMERICA

We all know that Thanksgiving began in New England and was a celebration to give thanks for being alive after the first year of disease and famine. The first Thanksgiving was a festival of several days' length, during which time the Pilgrims and their Indian guests feasted in the open air on the meat, wild fowl, and deer that had been barbecued for the occasion.

The Puritans were opposed to the observance of Christmas, which they regarded as a Catholic custom, and during the colonial period, Christmas was, therefore, not a New England holiday except in Rhode Island. For the orthodox Puritan, Thanksgiving Day, or rather week, took the place of Christmas. While the practice of setting aside a day for thanksgiving did not originate with the Puritans, the New Englanders took up the custom at an early date and gave it a large place in their recreational life. Before the end of the seventeenth century the Thanksgiving season had become a regular annual holiday in Connecticut and Massachusetts. It lasted about a week and was the most important series of holidays that the Puritans had. It was not an especially religious celebration but a time of festivity, like the English yuletide. It is thought that Thursday was chosen as Thanksgiving Day because of its popularity as lecture day.

THANKSGIVING DAY, 1779

The following account of a Thanksgiving dinner in 1779 is given in a letter of Juliana Smith's, copied by her into her diary—a praiseworthy practice not uncommon when letters were written with care and might easily be lost in transmission. Juliana Smith was the daughter of the Reverand Cotton Mather Smith of Sharon, Connecticut.

This letter was addressed to its writer's "Dear Cousin Betsey." Who the latter may have been is not known, but it is assumed that she was the daughter of Reverand Smith's elder brother Dan.

After the usual number of apologies for delay in writing, Juliana proceeds:

"When Thanksgiving Day was approaching our dear Grandmother Smith, who is sometimes a little desponding of Spirit as you well know, did her best to persuade us that it would be for the better to make it a Day of Fasting & Prayer in view of the Wickedness *of* our Friends & the Vileness of our Enemies. *I am sure that you can hear Grandmother say that and see her shake her cap border. But indeed there was some occasion for her remarks, for our resistance to an* unjust Authority *has cost our beautiful Coast Towns very dear the last year & all of us have had much to suffer. But my dear Father brought her to a more proper frame of Mind, so that by the time the Day came she was ready to enjoy it almost as well as Grandmother Worthington did, & she, you will remember, always sees the bright side. In the meanwhile we had all of us been working hard to get all things in readiness to do honour to the Day.*

"This year it was Uncle Simeon's turn to have the dinner at his house, but of course we all helped them as they help us when it is our turn, & there is always enough for us all to do. All the baking of pies & cakes was done at our house & we had the big oven heated & filled twice each day for three days before it was all done. & everything was GOOD, *though we did have to do without some things that ought to be used. Neither Love nor Money could buy Raisins, but our good red cherries dried without the pits did almost as well & happily Uncle*

Simeon still had some spices in store. The tables were set in the Dining Hall and even that big room had no space to spare when we were all seated. The Servants had enough ado to get around the Tables & serve us all without over-setting things. There were our two Grandmothers side by side. They are always handsome old Ladies, but now, many thought, they were handsomer than ever, & happy they were to look around upon so many of their descendents. Uncle & Aunt Simeon presided at one Table, & Father & Mother at the other. Besides us five boys & girls there were two of the Gales & three Elmers, besides James Browne & Ephraim Cowles. We had them at our table because they could be best supervised there. Most of the students had gone to their own homes for the week, but Mr. Skiff & Mr. ———[name illegible] were too far away from their homes. They sat at Uncle Simeon's table & so did Uncle Paul & his family, five of them in all, & Cousins Phin & Poll. Then there were six of the Livingston family next door. They had never seen a Thanksgiving Dinner before, having been used to keep Christmas Day instead, as is the wont in New York Province. Then there were four Old Ladies who have no longer Homes or Children of their own & so came to us. They were invited by my Mother, but Uncle and Aunt Simeon wished it so.

"Of course we could have no Roast Beef. None of us have tasted Beef this three years back as it all must go to the Army, & too little they get, poor fellows. But Nayquittymaw's

Preparing the Thanksgiving dinner

Hunters were able to get us a fine red Deer, so that we had a good haunch of Venisson on each Table. These were balanced by huge Chines of Roast Pork at the other ends of the Tables. Then there was on one a big Roast Turkey & on the other a Goose, & two big Pigeon Pasties. Then there was an abundance of good Vegetables of all the old Sorts & one which I do not believe you have yet seen. Uncle Simeon had imported the Seede from England just before the War began & only this Year was there enough for Table use. It is called Sellery & you eat it without cooking. It is very good served with meats. Next year Uncle Simeon says he will be able to raise enough to give us all some. It has to be taken up, roots & all, & buried in earth in the cellar through the winter & only pulling up some when you want it to use.

"Our Mince Pies were good although we had to use dried Cherries as I told you, & the meat was shoulder of Venisson, instead of Beef. The Pumpkin Pies, Apple Tarts & big Indian Puddings lacked for nothing save Appetite by the time we had got round to them.

"Of course, we had no Wine. Uncle Simeon has still a cask or two, but it must all be saved for the sick, & indeed, for those who are well, good Cider is a sufficient Substitute. There was no Plumb Pudding, but a boiled Suet Pudding, stirred thick with dried Plumbs & Cherries, was called by the old Name & answered the purpose. All the other spice had been used in the Mince Pies, so for this Pudding we used a jar of West India preserved Ginger which chanced to be left of the last shipment which Uncle Simeon had from there. We chopped the Ginger small and stirred it through with the Plumbs & Cherries. It was extraordinary good. The Day was bitter cold & when we got home from Meeting, which Father did not keep over long by reason of the cold, we were glad eno' of the fire in Uncle's Dining Hall, but by the time the dinner was one half over those of us who were on the fire side of one Table were forced to get up & carry our plates with us around to the far side of the other Table, while those who had sat there were as glad to bring their plates around the fire side to get warm. All but the Old Ladies who had a screen put behind their chairs.

"Uncle Simeon was in his best mood, and you know how good that is! He kept both Tables in a roar of laughter with his droll stories of the days when he was studying medicine in Edinborough, & afterwards he & Father & Uncle Paul joined in singing Hymns & Ballads. You know how fine their voices go together. Then we all sang a Hymn & afterwards my dear Father led us in prayer, remembering all Absent Friends before the Throne of Grace, & much I wished that my dear Betsey was here as one of us, as she has been of yore.

"We did not rise from the Table until it was quite dark, & then when the dishes had been cleared away we all got round the fire as close as we could, & cracked nuts, & sang songs & told stories. At least some told & others listened. You know nobody can exceed the two Grandmothers at telling tales of all the things they have seen themselves, & repeating those of the early years in New England, & even some in the Old England, which they heard in their youth from their Elders. My Father says it is a goodly custom to hand down all worthy deeds & traditions from Father to Son, as the Israelites were commanded to do about the

Passover & as the Indians here have always done, because the Word that is spoken is remembered longer than the one that is written. . . . Brother Jack, who did not reach here until late on Wednesday though he had left College very early on Monday Morning & rose diligently considering the snow, brought an orange to each of the Grand-Mothers, but, Alas! they were frozen in his saddle bags. We soaked the frost out in cold water, but I guess they as n't as good as they should have been."

THANKSGIVING SEVENTY YEARS AGO
by Mrs. Henry Ward Beecher

Are the holidays of the present time as conducive to real enjoyment and happiness as the free-and-easy home celebrations of seventy or eighty years ago?

We do not believe they are. There may be more refinement—no, that is not the word, but style—now, but is there half the true, genuine pleasure and happiness for the young?

We look back three-quarters of a century, to a large, old-fashioned home in New England,—white, with green blinds, of course,—situated on one of the beautiful hills in Worcester County, Mass., where ten "merry lads and lassies" dwelt.

By the middle of November how we counted the day,—for Thanksgiving was close by,—and grandpa and grandma would spend the week there, for who could think of taking a troop of ten children to their pretty, quiet home; and certainly all must go, if any, for the family must not be divided on Thanksgiving Day!

So the dear old people would come to their son-in-law, "the doctor's" house, where there were many quiet places in which they could be undisturbed if the young, joyous, frolicsome children became tiresome.

We can hardly tell of the Thanksgiving entertainment with-out recalling the busy week spent in preparing for it, quite as full of pleasant memories as the day in prospect.

"The boys" took charge of slaughtering the turkeys, chickens and ducks, and picking and dressing them in an outbuilding,—not so remote as to prevent those engaged in the house from hearing the merry laughter over the work, and often responding, but without interrupting active labors in the house.

There was the meat to be cooked ready to be chopped for mince-pies, and the next day, apples and pumpkins to be made ready, and raisins to be picked over and stoned.

In the evening, the brothers helped to chop the meat, pare and chop the apples for the mince-pies, and while all old enough were at work, the grandparents told the stories of those earlier days, when all were compelled to fight the Indians, or seek protection from them in the forts, risking the loss and destruction of the little homes they had worked so hard to secure; or recounting their adventures connected with the Revolutionary war.

While listening to all these stories,—at that time of comparative recent date, —labor was pleasure, and the work progressed rapidly.

The morning before Thanksgiving Day, pies, bread and cake were baked in the two large brick ovens, after which one was re-heated to receive the bread-trough filled with brown-bread dough, and the plum and Indian suet pudding, dark with huckleberries. These were to remain until taken out hot for Thanksgiving dinner.

Meanwhile the poultry was made ready to be cooked on Thanksgiving Day.

For so large a family, breakfast must necessarily be bountiful, but nothing extra was prepared for that meal.

The dinner was to be all that abundant materials and the best skill could make it, and, therefore, the sensible parents would not venture to allow their large troop of growing children any extra indulgence in the way of food.

On Thanksgiving morning, the doctor, if not called off by patients, took the grandparents and the younger members of the family to church, leaving the workers free from interruption.

It is said "many hands make light work." However that may be, we know that while under the gentle mother's supervision everything must be done methodically and "on time," yet there was never a jollier time than the hours spent in preparing Thanksgiving dinner, as we remember it, after we were old enough to lend a helping hand.

The brothers had charge of the two ovens, supplying fuel, and, when heated, clearing out the coals, ready to be filled with the chickens, ducks, and, of course, chicken-pie.

The turkeys in the large roaster, which no modern invention has ever equalled, were being roasted, not baked, before the great kitchen fire.

All is ready. The long table is spread, and hark! the carriage has turned up the lane, and the hungry occupants will soon be here.

The younger children rush in with merry voices, and then stand back surprised to see the tables set, not in the dining-room, but stretched through the long, wide hall, loaded with "costly piles of food." In a few minutes all are seated. Turkeys, ducks, chickens, baked, and always a huge chicken-pie, all varieties of vegetables, cranberry sauce, mince, pumpkin, apple and custard pies, plum pudding, Indian huckleberry suet pudding, tea, coffee, and the richest of cream, —all appeared in their appropriate order.

Rising from the table, when all were abundantly satisfied, they adjourned to the parlor for a little ceremony that was never omitted on Thanksgiving, and never repeated on any other day.

In the centre of the room stood a table on which was a very large bowl of milk punch, surrounded by tiny wine-glasses.

After telling us how much we had to be thankful for, what a blessing it was that we had enjoyed this day with no interruption or mishap, our father filled the little glasses from the punch-bowl, and with a smile and a kiss gave one to each of the children, and then all scattered to find such enjoyment as they chose till supper-time.

Supper! What could any one do with supper after sitting two hours and more at such a dinner, and eating to repletion?

Nevertheless, the table was spread temptingly, but not heartily complimented.

What little appetite there was left from dinner was reserved, certainly by the children, for a later entertainment in the evening, when all adjourned to the kitchen.

On the long table in the centre of the room was, first, a large glass bowl of lemonade,—and remember, in those early days, that was a luxury,—an abundance of such fruit as was in season, and a good supply of nuts and pop-corn. Now all were ready for fun. On the large stone hearth some cracked nuts, others popped corn over the large bed of coals, some of which was ground in a hand-mill, and served, in saucers, with rich cream to those who preferred, while the lemonade stood ready for all who wished.

While preparing and partaking of this repast, grandparents and parents entertained us all with a succession of stories. Then followed evening games in which the younger and, sometimes, the older members of the family took part.

This is a simple account of the Thanksgivings we remember, many, many years ago, a tame description of what used to seem to us—and does, even now—

more full of real pleasure and happiness than any other week could furnish in the whole year.

Household, November 1891

THE ROAST TURKEY

A gentleman in one of the eastern towns of Massachusetts, had a servant in his employ, who gave him not a little trouble on account of the complaints he made on the subject of his victuals. As is usual in many families, whatever remained from the table of the dining-room was placed upon that in the kitchen—the inmates of the latter fared in all respects as well as those of the former, with the exception of their being served last. The gentleman of whom we speak, took special pains that there should be no lack of provisions for the supply of all in his house, and was therefore at a loss to understand the grounds of the complaint thus made by his servant.

One day as he was passing through the kitchen, an opportunity presented itself for making some inquiries on the subject. While the other servants were partaking of their dinner with a keen relish, Sam, the disaffected servant, was tasting of it as reluctantly as if poison had been mixed with his food.

'How is it, Sam,' said the gentleman, 'that you are dissatisfied with your living—you fare the same as I do, and yet are not contented?'

'I know it,' said Sam, who was fresh from the country, 'but then I guess you are a little more fonder of corned beef than I be, to make a meal of it so often!'

'Corned-beef!' said the gentleman, 'I am indeed very partial to that dish, and am sorry that it is not equally agreeable to your taste—but since you are fastidious, tell me what dish of all others you would prefer, and you shall be entertained with it.'

'Why roast turkey, to be sure:' quoth Sam, 'I guess I aint seen nothing of that sort this many a day!'

'And you think, Sam, you would be contented to fare on roast turkey every day?'

'I guess, meister, if you'd only try me, you'd think so—nothing I relishes so hugely as roast turkey!'

'Well, then,' said the gentleman, 'to-morrow you shall be gratified—a turkey shall be roasted for your special benefit—no one but yourself shall partake of it, and you shall eat of no other meat till the turkey is gone.'

'By gumption!' exclaimed Sam, 'I agree to that willingly.'

The next morning the gentleman went into the market and purchased the largest and fattest turkey he could find, and sent it home with directions to be roasted and placed upon a separate table for Sam. In this he was strictly obeyed—the turkey was stuffed and roasted in the best style, and when Sam made his appearance at dinner, he found it smoking on the table which had been set for his sole occupation.

'By gauly now! if that aint curous though!' said Sam, drawing up a chair to the table, at the same time smacking his lips and feasting his eyes upon the scene before him. Forthwith he attacked the turkey in his own fashion, cutting a slice here and a slice there, just as inclination led him, without the slow and tedious operation of carving it, and having finished his dinner, he stretched himself out with the self-complacent air of an alderman. The next day the turkey was again served up as before, upon which, and upon which, alone, Sam made his dinner with apparent satisfaction. The third day, when the gobbler, shaved of his pinions and his exterior, was placed upon the table, Sam was not quite as prompt in commencing operations. Casting a wishful glance at his fellows, who were regaling themselves with a variety of dishes, Sam offered to exchange with them a portion of his turkey for a slice of beef, but to this proposition, having received instructions how to act in such an event, they all declined acceding, so that Sam was forced to make out his meal upon the cold carcass of the turkey.

The fourth day and the fifth came and departed, and found Sam still at work upon his turkey, more than two thirds of which was now consumed. He was by this time heartily sick of his bargain—pride prevented him from making complaint, while hunger compelled him to eat of what had become an object of disgust and loathing. At the end of a week's time, the turkey was reduced to a mere skeleton, and Sam was thanking his stars that he should soon see no more of it, when his master entered the kitchen and found him at his last meal.

'Well Sam,' said he, 'I see you've about finished the first turkey—it is high time for me to look out for another.'

'What, another!' echoed Sam, 'another turkey! you don't think a man can live on nothing but roast turkey, do you?'

'Certainly, I think you can—you cannot find fault with roast turkey—it is a dish of your own choosing.'

'I knows it—I knows it,' said Sam, 'but who would have thought of turkey to-day, and turkey to-morrow, and turkey next day, and turkey everyday—why,

I'd as lief feed on corned beef at that rate, and a little liefser!'

'But, Sam, you are neither satisfied with living as I do, nor with living as you prefer yourself—neither with corned beef nor with roast turkey—what shall I do in such a case?'

'Oh! anything! I'll feed on roast cats—roast dogs—anything but roast turkey —I can't do that—don't make me eat another.'

'Well, then,' said the gentleman, 'if you think you can content yourself to fare as I do—to take pot luck when I take pot luck, and roast turkey when I do, and if you can do so without complaining, I consent that to-morrow you return to your old way of living.'

'Oh, yes, I consent to anything,' said Sam, 'anything but roast turkey.'

New Jersey Almanac, 1832

TWAS THE WEEK BEFORE THANKSGIVING

Especially associated with childhood on the old farm was the keeping of the annual Thanksgiving. It was one of the days we reckoned by, the dividing line between summer and winter, as well as the days of reunions and festivities. The season's work, as far as the land was concerned, was expected to be done before Thanksgiving; and indoors, house-cleaning with its vexations must be well out of the way.

The winter supply of apple-sauce must have been made ere this. The apples from the Mt. Warner orchard had been laid up, and a generous quantity of the juice had been boiled down to the consistency of thin molasses, with which to sweeten the sauce, for our forefathers were economical.

The old cider-mill, which had been all the season screeching its protest against the sacrilegious use of one of Nature's best gifts by turning it into brandy, had uttered its last groan, and stood with naked jaws and bending sweep, a ghastly spectacle, until another season should compel a renewal of its doleful cries. The apple-paring, with its array of tubs and baskets and knives and jolly faces before the bright kitchen fire, was completed, with the Hallowe'en games of counting the apple seeds, and throwing the paring over the head to see its transformation into the initials of some fair maiden.

The great day for the conversion of the apples into sauce had lately come and gone, for it must be delayed as long as possible, that it may not ferment and spoil. The stout crane that swung over the huge fireplace was loaded with one or more brass kettles filled with apples, sweet and sour in proper proportion, the former being put at .the bottom because they required more time to cook. Sprinkled through the mass were a few quinces, if they were to be had, to give flavor, while over the whole was poured the pungent apple molasses which supplied the sweetening. The great danger was that the sauce should burn; and to prevent this, some housewives had clean straw prepared and laid at the bottom of the kettles, lest the apples should come in too near contact with the fire. It was an all-day process, but when completed an article was produced which was always in order for the table, and which, if slightly frozen, was enjoyed with a keener relish than the ice-cream of the restaurants of to-day.

Monday was devoted, of course, to the weekly washing, and nothing must interfere with that.

Tuesday was the great day for the making of pies, of which there were from thirty to fifty baked in the great oven that crackled and roared right merrily in anticipation of the rich medley that was being made ready for its capacious maw. Two kinds of apple pies, two of pumpkin, rice, and cranberry made out the standard list, to which additions were sometimes made. Then in our younger days we children each had a patty of his own. These were made in tins of various shapes, of which we had our choice, as well of the material of which our respective pies should be composed. The provident among us would put these aside until the good things were not quite so abundant.

Was not that a breath equal to the 'spicy breezes of Ceylon' that greeted us as the mouth of the oven was taken down, and the savor of its rich compounds penetrated every crevice of the old kitchen, like sacrificial incense? Then, as the pies were taken out and landed on the brick hearth, and a number of pairs of eyes were watching the proceedings with the keenest interest, it would not be strange if pies and eyes sometimes got mixed up. I remember once quite a sensation was produced in the little crowd because brother T. lost his balance, and, for want of a chair to break his fall, sat down on one of the smoking hot pies!

After cooling and sorting, the precious delicacies were put away into the large closets in the front entry or hall, which the foot of the small boy was not permitted to profane.

Wednesday was devoted to chicken pies and raised cake. The making of the latter was a critical operation. If I mistake not, it was begun on Monday. I believe the conditions must be quite exact to have the yeast perform its work perfectly in the rich conglomerated mass. In due time the cake is finished. The chicken pies are kept in the oven, so as to have them still hot for supper. The two turkeys have been made ready for the spit, the kitchen cleared of every vestige of the great carnival that has reigned for the last two days, and there is a profound pause of an hour or two before the scene opens.

The happy meetings, the loaded tables, the hilarity and good cheer that prevailed, checked but not subdued in after years as one and another of the seats are made vacant by their departure to the better land,—these are things to be imagined, but cannot be described. Warner, in his 'Being a Boy,' says that the hilarity of the day is interfered with by going to meeting and wearing Sunday clothes; but our parents managed that wisely by dividing the day, the first half of it being kept religiously, but the afternoon being given up to festivity,—by no means, however, common week-day work. This was wise, I say, because it would be almost cruel to allow a lot of young people to indulge themselves to the very extent of prudence, to say the least, in eating, and then sit down to reading good books. This distinction between relaxation and toil for pelf is, I think, too often forgotten nowadays, founded as it is on both religion and philosophy. I remember well the sad look mother gave my brother and myself after our having spent the afternoon in making a hen-house, a very 'cute operation, we thought, but which found no favor in her eyes, as contrary to the traditions of the forefathers.

But the day after Thanksgiving, it must be admitted, had its peculiar pleasures. I doubt if there was any other of the holidays of the year when we boys felt so strongly the sense of freedom, and it was all the sweeter because it was the last we should have before we were set to our winter tasks. Skating was pretty sure to be one of the sports, if the weather had been cold enough to make the ice strong; and indoors there remained for our keen appetite the broken bits of pie and cake, to say nothing of the remnants of the turkey and fowl of the day before, and which were enjoyed with a keener relish, if possible, than at first.

I forgot in its more appropriate place to speak of the roasting of the turkey. This was done in a tin oven with an iron rod running through it, and also through the meat that was to be cooked. This was the spit. The meat was fastened to the spit with skewers, so that, by means of a small crank at the end, it could be made to revolve in order to cook evenly. The oven was in shape something like a half cylinder, with the open side to face the fire. But there was a still more primitive way of roasting a turkey, and one which was resorted to sometimes when our family was the largest. Room was made at one end of the fireplace, and the turkey was suspended by the legs from the ceiling, where was a contrivance to keep the string turning, and of course with it the turkey. On the hearth was a dish to catch the drippings, and with them the meat was occasionally basted. The thing is accomplished much more easily now, but at an expense, I imagine, in the quality of the work.

It is interesting to observe the universality of some of the customs that were in vogue fifty and one hundred years ago. In looking over the Centennial of the Churches of Connecticut, I came across the remark that the festive board, so crowded with good things on Thursday, gradually took on a plainer and less profuse array of dishes, until it ended off on Saturday evening with a simple bowl of hasty pudding and milk. This was in Revolutionary times; but fifty years later, when I was a boy, the same practices prevailed; in fact, hasty pudding and milk was the standing dish for Saturday evening, as boiled Indian pudding was for Sunday's dinner. I have been reminded since reading this item of a couplet my brother once repeated to me when we were boys:—

'For we know Northampton's rule to be
Fried hasty pudding 'long wi' tea.'

Expressive, if not elegant, and it shows that Northampton, bating the slight innovation of the tea, was true to New England tradition.

The Christmas holidays, as they are now observed, were not known in the country towns then. New Year's presents were often made, and the 'Happy New Year' greeting was passed when neighbors met each other; but with most people we were too near the Puritan age to hear the 'Merry Christmas' so common to-day, without a shock as though it were a profanation.

New England Chronicle, November 1892

THE TURKEY'S LAMENT *by Susan Hubbard Martin*

I'm a melancholy turkey,—sad am I,
For a reign of awful terror draweth nigh.
    How I dread the smell of pie,
    And the cakes and tarts piled high,
    For I know that I must die
        Thanksgiving Day.

What avail my sparkling eyes, just like jet,
Or my slim and stately neck, proudly set?
    Though my glossy feathers shine,
    On my flesh will people dine,
    And pronounce me—luscious—fine,
        Thanksgiving Day.

How I wish I had been hatched some other bird,
Chicken, goose, duck or dove'd be preferred,—
    Any fowl, but what I am,
    In this land of "Uncle Sam,"
    For I'm slaughtered like a lamb
        Thanksgiving Day.

How I sympathize with Marie Antoinette,
How that dark and bloody ax haunts me yet,
    Soon on my neck, 'twill descend,
    Make of me a sudden end.
    Was a sadder verse e'er penned,
        Thanksgiving Day?

American Kitchen Magazine, November 1896

THE AMERICAN ECONOMICAL HOUSEKEEPER AND FAMILY RECEIPT BOOK *by Mrs. E. A. Howland*

This book was published in 1845 in Worcester, Mass., and sold for the magnificent sum of twenty-five cents. Although Thanksgiving was still celebrated only in those states where the governors issued proclamation, this book contained a Thanksgiving dinner menu. It was as follows, along with the recipes for various foods on the menu:

Roast Turkey, stuffed
A Pair of Chickens stuffed, and boiled with cabbage and a piece of lean pork.
A Chicken Pie
Potatoes; turnip sauce; squash; onions; gravy and gravy sauce; apple and cranberry sauce; oyster sauce; brown and white bread.
Plum and Plain Pudding, with sweet sauce.
Mince, Pumpkin, and Apple Pies
Cheese.

P.S. The chickens are to be prepared in the same manner as you would to roast them; fill the bodies and crops full of stuffing, and sew them up close; boil them an hour and a half, or two hours.

FOR TURNIP SAUCE.—Boil your turnips and mash them fine; add the same amount of mealy mashed potatoes; season with salt and pepper, moisten it with cream or butter.

SQUASH.—Boil it, peel it, and squeeze it dry in a colander; mash it fine, season it with salt, pepper, and butter.

ONIONS.—Boil them in milk and water, season them with salt, pepper, and butter.

GRAVY SAUCE.—Boil the neck, wings, gizzard, liver and heart of the fowls, till they are tender; put in a boiled onion, chop it all fine, then add two or three pounded crackers, a piece of butter, and a little flour thickening; season it with pepper and salt.

CRANBERRY SAUCE.—Wash and stew your cranberries in water; add almost their weight in clean sugar, just before you take them from the fire.

OYSTER SAUCE.—Put your oysters into a stewpan, add a little milk and water, and let them boil; season with a little pepper and butter, and salt, if necessary.

BROWN BREAD.—Put the Indian meal in your bread-pan, sprinkle a little salt among it, and wet it thoroughly with scalding water. When it is cool, put in your rye; add two gills of lively yeast, and mix it with water as stiff as you can knead it. Let it stand an hour and a half, in a cool place in summer, on the hearth in winter. It should be put into a very hot oven, and baked three or four hours.

PLUM PUDDING BOILED.—Three quarts of flour, a little salt, twelve eggs, two pounds of raisins, one pound of beef suet chopped fine, one quart of milk; put into a strong cloth floured; boil three hours. Eat with sauce.

PLAIN PUDDING.—Boil half a pint of milk with a bit of cinnamon, four eggs with the whites well beaten, the rind of a lemon grated, half a pound of suet chopped fine, as much bread as will do. Pour your milk on the bread and suet, keep mixing it till cold, then put in the lemon-peel, eggs, a little sugar, and some nutmeg grated fine. It may be either baked or boiled.

COMMON MINCE PIE.—Boil a piece of lean fresh beef very tender; when cold, chop it very fine; then take three times the quantity of apples, pared and cored, and chopped fine; mix the meat with it, and add raisins, allspice, salt, sugar, cinnamon, and molasses, to suit the taste; incorporate the articles well together, and it will improve by standing overnight, and if the weather is cool; a very little ginger improves the flavor. Small pieces of butter sliced over the mince before laying on the top crust will make them keep longer. A tea-cup of grape sirup will give them a good flavor.

PUMPKIN PIE.—Take out the seeds and pare the pumpkin; stew, and strain it through a coarse sieve. Take two quarts of scalded milk and eight eggs, and stir your pumpkin into it; sweeten it with sugar or molasses. Salt it, and season with ginger, cinnamon, or grated lemon-peel to your taste. Bake with a bottom crust. Crackers, pounded fine, are a good substitute for eggs. Less eggs will do.

APPLE PIE.—Peel the apples, slice them thin, pour a little molasses and sprinkle some sugar over them; grate on some lemon-peel, or nutmeg. If you wish to make them richer, put a little butter on the top.

CHICKEN PIE.—Cut up your chicken, parboil it, season it in the pot, take up the meat, put in a flour thickening, and scald the gravy; make the crust of sour milk made sweet with saleratus, put in a piece of butter or lard the size of an egg; cream is preferable to sour milk, if you have it. Take a large tin pan, line it with the crust, put in your meat, and pour in the gravy from the pot; make it nearly full, cover it with crust, and leave a vent; bake it in a moderate oven two hours, or two and a half.

STUFFING.—Take dry pieces of bread or crackers, chop them fine, put in a small piece of butter or a little cream, with sage, pepper, and salt, one egg, and a small quantity of flour, moistened with milk.

ROAST TURKEY.—Let the turkey be picked clean, and washed and wiped dry, inside and out. Have your stuffing prepared, fill the crop and then the body full up, sew it up, put on a spit, and roast it, before a moderate fire, three hours. If more convenient, it is equally good when baked.

DR. CHASE'S THANKSGIVING DINNER

Prior to 1900, the people who wrote cookbooks also included home recipes for the cure of various illnesses for man and beast as well as other little hints for home and farm. At the same time, those who wrote home remedy books included recipes for cooking as well as hints for home and farm.

One of the most popular books was written by Dr. Alvin Chase and was called *Dr. Chase's Receipt Book.* As a young man, Dr. Chase traveled, and it was not until the age of thirty-eight that he decided to study medicine. In 1868 he decided to write a book which not only covered the field of medicine but every field of endeavor possible. He wrote about brewing, farming, cooking, etc.

Here is Dr. Chase on the subject of Thanksgiving Dinner:

THANKSGIVING DINNER, WITH SUITABLE RECIPES, BILL OF FARE, HOW TO SET THE TABLE, ETC.—And now I don't think I can do better than to close the department of dishes for the table than in giving a bill of fare, with suitable recipes for a Thanksgiving dinner, which was sent to the Detroit *Post and Tribune* with the writer's plan for setting the table, etc., which will certainly be found of great assistance to new beginners and very handy to refer to by every one upon such occasion or when quite a number of visitors are to be dined upon any occasion. If the writer's name was given I have it not at this writing; but knowing the directions to be reliable, I will let her speak for herself. She says:

Thanksgiving is almost here, and how shall we celebrate the day? I for one believe in the old-fashioned Thanksgiving dinner. The following bill of fare may be of use to some of your readers:

Oyster Soup, Celery, Pepper Sauce, Roast Turkey, with Currant Jelly, Baked Potatoes, Mashed Turnips, Roast Pig, Carrots with Cream, Boston Baked Beans, Chopped Cabbage, Pumpkin Pie, Plum Pudding, Apples, Nuts, Cheese, Tea and Coffee

For the table I prefer a white cloth with fancy border, and napkins to match. A dash of color livens up the table in the bleak November, when flowers cannot be had in profusion. Casters in the center, of course, flanked by tall celery glasses. At each end, glass fruit dishes filled with apples and nuts. A bottle of pepper sauce near the casters, and a mold of jelly by the platter of turkey, and small side dishes of chopped cabbage garnished with rings of cold boiled eggs. The purple cabbage makes the handsomest-looking dishes. Serve the soup from tureens to soup dishes, handing around to the guests. After this comes the *pièce de résistance*, "Thanksgiving turkey." A piece of dark meat with a spoonful of gravy, and one of white turkey with a bit of jelly and a baked potato. I should prefer a spoonful of mashed turnip should be served on each plate, leaving the other vegetables to be passed afterward with the roast pig. After this the salad, and then the plates should be taken away and the dessert served. Then come the apples and nuts, the tea and coffee, well seasoned with grandpa's old-time stories, grandma's quaint ways and kind words and merry repartee from all.

THANKSGIVING MENU
American Kitchen Magazine, November 1896

Cream of Chestnuts, Croutons, Fricassee of Oysters, Olives, Salted Peanuts, Roast Turkey, Giblet Stuffing, Cranberry Sauce, Mashed Potatoes, Diced Turnips, New Cider, Apollinaris, Lemon Milk Sherbet; Roast Duck, Brussels Sprouts, Plum Jelly, Apple and Celery Salad, Cheese, Water Thin Wafers, Plum Pudding, Hard Sauce, Squash Pie, Mince Pie, Fruit, Nuts, Confectionery, Coffee.

Thanksgiving Dinner as given at Grandmother P.'s from 1830 *to* 1850.

Boiled Turkey, Roast Turkey, Chicken Pie, Potato Balls, Turnips, Squash, Onions, Cranberry Sauce, Celery, Plum Pudding, Mince Pie, Pumpkin Pie.

Thin gingerbread and crackers were passed late in the afternoon and between eight and nine o'clock; after the little folks were put to bed, the older members of the family had a supper of chicken salad and cold roast duck.

THANKSGIVING DINNER I

Oyster stew, celery, oyster crackers, roast stuffed turkey, brown gravy, cranberry moulds, oak hill sweet potatoes, turnips and carrots in white sauce, boiled onions, chicken pie, mince pie, squash patties, fruit pudding, brandy sauce, assorted nuts and raisins, coffee.

What to Have for Dinner, Fannie Farmer, 1905

THANKSGIVING DINNER II

Oyster soup, celery, roast turkey with cranberry sauce, mashed potatoes, baked sweet potatoes, mashed turnips, roast pig, carrots with cream, Boston baked beans, minced cabbage, pumpkin pie, plum pudding, fruit, nuts, cheese, tea and coffee.

Queen of the Household, 1906

CANDLE-DIPPING PARTY:
Diary of An Early American Housewife

December 10, 1772—Dorcas heard of the candle-dipping parties that are held in New York and she asked whether she could have one. Her father agreed to it since he saw no harm in having something different for a winter's evening entertainment. All we had to do was to be certain that there were enough aprons with long sleeves to protect the clothing of each of Dorcas' guests who was to participate in the candle-dipping. She invited eight couples.

CANDLE-DIPPING PARTY

In early New York, candle-dipping was an amusement that combined work and play. Candles were the main source of illumination in the homes and were too expensive to import from England so that they were made at home from tallow or bayberries.

The guests were invited to come early, about six o'clock in the evening, and as each guest arrived, he or she was given a huge apron with long sleeves to cover the clothing from the melted tallow. The candle-dipping was held in the immense kitchen which usually had heavy ceiling beams, darkened and polished by years of smoke, while bunches of dried herbs, ears of corn for popping, and dried apples hung from the rafters. The huge fireplace took up a large portion of one side of the room. In preparation for the candle-dipping, huge brass kettles were over the blaze on long-armed cranes and contained tallow which was kept liquid so that it could be easily poured. As a result, the room was very warm, but then it was usually midwinter and there was snow on the ground and frost in the air. The warmth of the kitchen was appreciated when one entered from outdoors.

Down the center, the longest way of the room, were set two long ladders lying side by side, supported at either end by a block of wood about the height of a chair seat. Under each ladder, at intervals of a foot or so apart, stood a row of big three-footed iron pots and one of footless brass kettles like those over the fire. On the floor between the pots and kettles were placed dripping pans and other vessels, both to protect the floor from grease and to prevent waste of tallow. On either side of each ladder was a row of chairs placed as closely together as possible. On these chairs were seated the candle-dippers, couple by couple.

The servants helped to set up the tallow kettles. Before the couples were seated, the two young people lifted the brass kettles full of melted tallow from the fire and poured their contents to the depth of two or three inches more than a long candle's length upon the water with which similar vessels on the floor were already half-filled.

As soon as the young folks were seated, each guest was handed the candle rods, four or five to each person. From each rod was suspended the wicks of twisted cotton which had been previously prepared, and the candle-dipping began.

Ordinarily, two pairs of industrious hands, with six kettles between them, could easily have completed as many in half the time as it took that night. There would be much laughter, and a festive air prevailed. By eight o'clock the candles were all finished and a supper was served which was finished off with cookies and hot cider.

If dancing was permitted in that particular household, there might be dancing for another hour or so and then all the guests would leave in the sleighs and one could hear the bells sound lower and lower as the guests went farther and farther from the house. It was an evening enjoyed by young and old alike.

CHRISTMAS IN EARLY AMERICA

There was Christmas in the South from the beginning. America's first recorded Yuletide ceremony took place on Virginia's soil. While Puritan New England shunned the ceremonial Christmas, the Southerners nurtured it and kept it ever before them. From the earliest days, Christmas in Virginia has been a period of jollity.

Captain John Smith and his followers had the Dominion's first real Christmas feast, a gift of the Indians. Calling on one of Powhatan's sons, they enjoyed richer fare than they had known for a long time. It was said that they were "never more merrie, nor fedde on more plentie of good oysters, fish, flesh, wild foule and good bread; nor never had better fires in England than in the warm smokie houses."

Christmas soon became a convenient and appropriate season for the gathering of friends, and one ceremony invited another. At an early date the holidays became a favorite time for weddings. Virginia also marked Christmas with a special ceremony of gunpowder.

A Virginia guest often brought his musket with him when he went to pay a call, and he joined his host in shooting, while the women put their hands over their ears and the children jumped up and down in delight. When a neighbor caught the echo, he took out his own firing piece and answered, and his neighbor did the same. In time an official proclamation cautioned against the overuse of gunpowder at entertainments.

Christmas was the season for punch bowls and balls. The people of Virginia also took greenery to their churches, transforming them in appearance. Christmas was also a succession of observances that went on without a letup from December 15 to January 6. Christmas itself was not December 25, but January 5, according to the old church calendar; it was not until about 1750 that the date was changed to the present one.

Christmas in the colonial period was not a day of great gift-giving. For the children there were a few toys, none of them elaborate; for the adults, a good wish, a kiss, or a handshake. It was not until the 1800's that the Virginians took part in the custom of exchanging gifts.

CHRISTMAS SEASON

Now Christmas comes, 'tis fit that we
Should feast and sing, and merry be:
Keep open house, let fidlers play,
A fig for cold, sing care away;
And may they who thereat repine,
On brown bread and on small beer dine.

Virginia Almanack, 1766

CHRISTMAS IN THE SOUTH—ANTE-BELLUM PERIOD

For several weeks after hog killing, the women of the house worked over boxes and bowls with the help of the cook and her helpers and any of the children who could be pressed into service. Nuts had to be cracked and picked over, raisins seeded, orange peel cut, currants washed. Candied citron was converted along with other delicacies into mincemeat, fruit cakes, and puddings.

Everyone worked in the kitchen to combine ingredients, tasting, thinning, thickening, pouring in the brandy and other spirits, then thrusting the baking tins into the ovens and carefully watching so that they could be removed at the proper moment of readiness. Again the fruit cakes were doused with brandy, cooled, and put into well-covered boxes to "set" and "ripen" during the days that remained before Christmas.

Meanwhile, more cakes were being made, such as layer cakes, wafer-like cakes, thick cakes, citron cakes. As they were baked, they were placed into the storeroom to be kept under lock and key along with the pies made of various fruits and custards.

From England the custom of the old Yule log had been introduced into the Southern states and it was an essential part of the holiday. Slaves were sent out to cut down the finest tree in the woods and it was brought back to the house to be placed into the largest fireplace.

As long as the Yule log glowed, the servants were traditionally freed from work. Even if the wood burned for more than a week, the master usually kept his promise. This resulted in the servants developing all sorts of schemes to prolong the burning of the log. Usually they wetted down the log so that it should burn more slowly, but it was the holiday season and although the master knew what had been done, he said nothing about it.

In the last days before Christmas arrived, hunters rode out to bring back any game within range, such as wild duck, partridges, and wild geese. From nearby waters, oysters were brought to the kitchen, while out in the poultry house the turkeys grew plumper and plumper.

With Christmas in sight, the women of the household sent the young men and boys out to the woods to bring back a plentiful supply of evergreens with which to decorate the house. Of course, mistletoe was always found and placed in hidden corners to be taken advantage of when an attractive young lady was under it.

Meanwhile, carriages filled with relatives and friends arrived at the plantation to spend the holiday. Christmas Eve was the time for toasts and the hanging of stockings before the mantel, while Christmas morning was the time for gift-giving to children and servants.

Christmas day heard fireworks crackling at the crack of dawn outside the house. After a hearty breakfast of ham and eggs, various breads, oysters, fish, fruit, and cheese, the boys went out to join in setting off the fireworks, while the men usually went off on a hunt.

The women of the house now turned their attention to the preparation of the dinner, which was served about three in the afternoon. Some of the family might attend church services before the meal. The dinner lasted anywhere from two to three hours, with second and third helpings the usual thing. There then followed a period of relaxation before there were songs and dancing by all.

Supper was light but supper there was. Then the plantation people attended the Christmas dance given for the servants. This lasted until midnight for the guests, although the servants might dance away until dawn.

Some guests, if they lived nearby, might go home, but usually all the guests remained for several days or a week. With the departure of the last guest, the house returned to normal, but there were enough memories to last at least another year for master and servant alike.

CHRISTMAS IN PHILADELPHIA, 1875

John Lewis was an Englishman who became a permanent resident of New York and who wrote letters to his brothers back home on many aspects of American life.

In 1875 he spent the Christmas holidays with his son in Philadelphia, where he enjoyed both the city and the holidays very much. One of the things that most impressed him there was the Christmas tree:

". . . There all the people seem to resolve themselves into Children for the occasion. I may say that the usual arrangement in this country is to have two parlours—be it a large or small house—opening to each other by sliding doors, the first being for state occasion. As large & fine a tree as could be accommodated being procured and set up, it is covered with every conceivable shape into which coloured & gilt paper & card can be cut, and little pictures, glass balls, chains, garlands, etc., anything to make a gay and imposing display. This being finished it is placed

mostly in the sliding door way, which allows it to be seen 2 ways. All the light possible is thrown upon it, often by reflectors, the lattice blinds being thrown open & it is thus open to inspection by passersby—which, as houses in Phila are only a little above the street, is an easy matter. Where the taste & industry of the owner prompts it, other attractions are added as fancy dictates—at one place I visited, an old doctor's, there was a very handsome river steamboat, perfect, 3 feet long with about 50 passengers (these last small pictures cut out) all of white, colour & gilt card; also a beautiful fire hose carriage. When the show commences people go round with or without their children to see them & frequently knock at the door to be admitted to a closer inspection which is readily granted. I heard of one house where 75 were admitted in about 2 hours. Riding through the better class streets on the cars, the effect is novel & very fine as every 2nd or 3rd may be exhibitors. I believe some keep it up 2 or 3 weeks."

CHRISTMAS DINNER I

Cream of onion soup, fried smelts, sauce tartare, potato balls, roast loin of pork, roast apples, carrots, hominy croquettes, celery salad, mince pie, deep apple pie, cheese, nuts, fruit, coffee.

American Kitchen Magazine, December 1896

CHRISTMAS DINNER II

Clam and tomato consommé, browned soup rings, olives, salted pecans, fillets of sole, mushroom sauce, roast goose, giblet gravy, frozen apples, riced potatoes, glazed silver skins, pimento timbales, chiffonade salad, English plum pudding, sherry sauce, coffee ice cream, almond cakes, bonbons, crackers, cheese, coffee.

What to Have for Dinner, Fannie Farmer, 1905

CHRISTMAS DINNER III

Clam or oyster soup, celery, baked fish with Hollandaise sauce, roast turkey, oyster dressing, celery or oyster sauce, roast duck, onion sauce, baked potatoes, sweet potatoes, baked squash, mashed turnips, canned corn, stewed tomatoes, Graham bread, rolls, salmon or other salad, plum pudding, peach pie, fruit, nuts, coffee, tea or chocolate.

Queen of the Household, 1906

MENUS FOR AUTUMN EATING

OCTOBER

MONDAY. *Breakfast*—Graham gems, broiled mutton chop, baked eggs, croquettes of cold vegetables. *Dinner*—Soup, roast beef with potatoes, carrots, plain boiled rice; baked custard, grapes. *Supper*—Cold beef sliced, bread, rice fritters with sugar.

TUESDAY. *Breakfast*—Hash, fried okra, fried fish, biscuit. *Dinner*—Boiled mutton with soup, celery, slaw, sliced pine-apples, cake. *Supper*—Sliced mutton, cottage cheese, bread, cake, grape jam.

WEDNESDAY. *Breakfast*—Brown bread, corn batter cakes, croquettes of mutton and vegetables. *Dinner*—Beef *a la mode*, mashed potatoes and turnips, succotash; apples, grapes, pie. *Supper*—Sliced beef, bread, cake, baked pears.

THURSDAY. *Breakfast*—Toast, croquettes of cold beef and vegetables. *Dinner*—Soup, fried or smothered chickens, mashed potatoes, Lima beans, pickles; bird's nest pudding, cake. *Supper*—Canned corned beef, sliced, rolls, cake, jam.

FRIDAY. *Breakfast*—Mutton chops, fried potato cakes, muffins. *Dinner*—Baked or boiled fish, boiled potatoes, corn, delicate cabbage; peach meringue, cake. *Supper*—Bologna sausage, toasted muffins, honey, cheese, cake.

SATURDAY. *Breakfast*—Plain bread, veal cutlets, cracked wheat. *Dinner*—Boiled beef with vegetables; cocoanut pudding. *Supper*—Soused beef, light biscuit, fried apples, cake.

SUNDAY. *Breakfast*—Vegetable hash, fried oysters, stewed tomatoes. *Dinner*—Broiled pheasant or chicken, sweet potatoes, tomatoes; peach meringue pie, plum jelly, cake. *Supper*—Cold beef sliced, rusk, baked apples.

NOVEMBER

MONDAY. *Breakfast*—Poached eggs on toast, broiled pork, potato cakes. *Dinner*—Roast beef, sweet potatoes, boiled turnips, chicken salad; economical pudding. *Supper*—Rolls, oatmeal mush, cold roast beef, cranberry tarts, cake.

TUESDAY. *Breakfast*—Graham bread, beef croquettes, potatoes. *Dinner*—Spiced beef tongue, baked potatoes, macaroni with cheese; grapes, pie. *Supper*—Toasted graham bread, cold tongue, baked pears, cake.

WEDNESDAY. *Breakfast*—Griddle cakes, broiled mutton chops, potatoes. *Dinner*—Soup, oyster pie, baked sweet potatoes, diced turnips, celery; apple pie with whipped cream. *Supper*—Cold rolls, chipped beef, custard cakes, marmalade.

THURSDAY. *Breakfast*—Waffles, broiled ham, fried sweet potatoes. *Dinner*—Brown stew, baked potatoes, plain rice, slaw; pumpkin pie. *Supper*—Cold sliced beef, short cake, jam.

FRIDAY. *Breakfast*—Corn batter cakes, broiled sausage, chipped potatoes. *Dinner*—Roast pork, apple sauce, mashed potatoes, turnips, cabbage; prune whip, cake. *Supper*—Light biscuit, bologna sausage, baked quinces, Swiss cakes.

SATURDAY. *Breakfast*—Graham gems, veal cutlets, potatoes. *Dinner*—Chicken pot pie, vegetables; warm apple pie, cake. *Supper*—Toasted gems, dried beef, baked apples, cake.

SUNDAY. *Breakfast*—Cream toast, broiled oysters with pork, fried raw potatoes. *Dinner*—Oyster soup, roast goose, baked potatoes, boiled onions, cranberry sauce, celery; peach pie. *Supper*—Cold biscuit, onions, sliced goose, grapes, cakes.

DECEMBER

MONDAY. *Breakfast*—Graham bread, griddle cakes, breakfast stew, fried potatoes. *Dinner*—Soup, boiled corned beef with turnips, potatoes and cabbage; baked apple dumplings with sauce. *Supper*—Biscuit, cold beef, canned cherries, cake.

TUESDAY. *Breakfast*—Buttered toast, fried apples, cold turkey broiled. *Dinner*—Roast turkey, cranberry sauce, potatoes, canned corn; canned fruit and cream. *Supper*—Cold turkey, mush and milk, buns, jam.

WEDNESDAY. *Breakfast*—Corn muffins, breaded veal cutlets, Saratoga potatoes. *Dinner* —Stewed oysters, roast mutton with potatoes, tomatoes, celery; pine-apple ice-cream, jelly, cake. *Supper*—Toasted muffins, cold mutton sliced, apple croutes.

THURSDAY. *Breakfast*—Hot rolls, scrambled eggs, breakfast stew. *Dinner*—Roast quail or fowl, baked potatoes, Lima beans, celery, pumpkin pie. *Supper*—Cold rolls, cold tongue sliced, baked apples, tea cakes.

FRIDAY. *Breakfast*—Buckwheat cakes, smoked sausage broiled, hominy croquettes. *Dinner*—Baked or boiled fish, mashed potatoes, squash, cabbage salad; hot peach pie with cream. *Supper*—Light biscuit, steamed oysters, canned fruit with cake.

SATURDAY. *Breakfast*—Buckwheat cakes, rabbit stew, potato cakes. *Dinner*—Chicken fricassee, baked potatoes, baked turnips; cottage pudding with sauce. *Supper*—French rolls, Welsh rarebit, cake, jam.

SUNDAY. *Breakfast*—Muffins, broiled spare-ribs, fried potatoes. *Dinner*—Soup, roast turkey garnished with fried oysters, mashed potatoes, turnips; cranberry sauce, celery, pudding. *Supper*—Biscuit sandwiches, cold turkey, jelly and cake.